SHAME ON THEM

A DCI Josh Mills Crime Novel
Book 1

A M MCKAY

Shame On Them – A M McKay

Copyright © 2024 A M McKay

The right of A M McKay identified as the author of this work, has been asserted in accordance with the Copyright Designs and Patents Act 1988.

All rights reserved. No part of this work may be reproduced in any material form (including photocopying or storing by any electronic means and whether or not transiently or incidentally to some other use of this publication) without write permission of the copyright holder except in accordance with the provisions of the Copyright, Designs and Patents Act 1988.

Applications for the copyright holder's permission to reproduce any part of this publication should be addressed to the publishers.

Contents

1. Chapter 1 — 1
2. Chapter 2 — 7
3. Chapter 3 — 11
4. Chapter 4 — 17
5. Chapter 5 — 22
6. Chapter 6 — 24
7. Chapter 7 — 31
8. Chapter 8 — 41
9. Chapter 9 — 44
10. Chapter 10 — 48
11. Chapter 11 — 59
12. Chapter 12 — 63
13. Chapter 13 — 66
14. Chapter 14 — 70
15. Chapter 15 — 80
16. Chapter 16 — 89
17. Chapter 17 — 93
18. Chapter 18 — 99

19.	Chapter 19	105
20.	Chapter 20	108
21.	Chapter 21	111
22.	Chapter 22	116
23.	Chapter 23	126
24.	Chapter 24	129
25.	Chapter 25	135
26.	Chapter 26	140
27.	Chapter 27	145
28.	Chapter 28	148
29.	Chapter 29	154
30.	Chapter 30	158
31.	Chapter 31	162
32.	Chapter 32	166
33.	Chapter 33	171
34.	Chapter 34	173
35.	Chapter 35	184
36.	Chapter 36	198
37.	Chapter 37	202
38.	Chapter 38	208
39.	Chapter 39	213
40.	Chapter 40	215
41.	Chapter 41	219
42.	Chapter 42	223

43. Chapter 43	228
44. Chapter 44	231
45. Chapter 45	234
46. Chapter 46	241
47. Chapter 47	247
48. Chapter 48	252
49. Chapter 49	256
Afterword	260

1

It was a welcome break for Dan Walsh and his group of friends. Having recently split up from his girlfriend of eight years, he was still heartbroken but didn't dare admit it in front of the lads, especially Jack Tomlinson, the groom-to-be and Dan's supposedly best friend.

Julia had been his everything. They had planned to marry and Dan had never been happier. It was Julia who had set him on the straight and narrow, following a short stint of being arrested for drunk and disorderly on several occasions when he had struggled to cope after the death of his sister.

But a one-night stand between Julia and her personal trainer had shattered his heart into tiny pieces. As much as he loved her, Dan wasn't prepared to commit to a marriage based on unfaithfulness and deceit.

Jack, on the other hand, seemed to have it all figured out.

He was the kind of guy who always managed to bag the nicest women, with his charming smile and confident demeanour.

Dan couldn't help but feel a twinge of jealousy every time he saw his best friend, knowing that he himself couldn't seem to hold down a relationship.

Dan was good-looking and successful in his own right, but there was something about Jack's effortless charisma that made him stand out in a crowd. And what made it worse, is that Dan knew Jack was seeing other women behind his fiancés back.

How could he? A beautiful woman on his arm that he was about to marry, and he was already cheating on her.

Despite his reservations about Jack, Dan was determined to be there for his friend on his stag weekend. He knew that Jack could be arrogant and a know-it-all at times, but he was still the closest thing Dan had to a best friend. They had been through a lot together over the years, and Dan felt like he owed it to Jack to celebrate this milestone with him, even if it meant putting up with his occasionally grating personality.

Being the only child left in the family, Dan's parents doted on him. Sunday lunches were a regular occurrence at his parents' house, and his mum looked forward to every weekend and an endearing hug from her son.

On the face of it, Dan appeared to be a coper, someone who was determined to always make things work no matter what life handed him.

But his mind crumbled constantly with negative thoughts, and no one knew about the trials and tribulations he was experiencing at work and in his head.

Having left school with outstanding qualifications, Dan had an entrepreneurial spirit but wanted the security of a salary, so a consulting career it was.

He had worked diligently at Catalyst Consultants in Manchester for ten years. The firm promised tailored strategies and actionable plans to help businesses expand and maximise profits, but lately, Dan had been struggling to deliver.

The firm had lost a couple of key people who took profitable clients with them. The setbacks were mounting, and the weight of it all pressed down on him heavily, especially after having to report unwelcome news to the board earlier in the week. The ordinarily good-looking, charming man with dark hair and tempting eyes had been drinking through his stress and internal torment. Fortunately, this weekend, he had a reprieve in the form of Jack's stag do.

An early start to the weekend and a couple of days away, was supposed to provide some respite from the pressures of work and his first proper break after splitting up with Julia.

It was a weekend that he was both looking forward to but also feeling apprehensive about. He didn't want the lads, especially Jack, to raise the subject of his ex and taunt him for not being good enough for her.

Heaven forbid if they did take the piss; he didn't know what he would say in retaliation. He hoped this weekend he could drown his sorrows, then forget about her and move on.

"Oi, watch where you're going!" The man at the bar almost had his pint knocked out of his hands as Dan Walsh stumbled through the Thursday night crowd at the Dog & Grain on Kirkby Lonsdale's main street.

The disgruntled punter held the drink in front of him to try and calm the beer down and stop the amber liquid from sloshing over the top of his glass, any more than it already had.

"Sorry, mate, sorry." Dan pushed his way through, feeling light-headed and woozy. He needed air. Fast. He dived for the men's toilet and pushed the door open.

"You alright?" Another punter looked at him with disdain and moved out of the way quickly as Dan just made it into a cubicle.

As he leaned over the toilet bowl, coughing up bile and half-digested food, he doubled over, the last remnants of phlegm and Prawn Biryani falling from his mouth.

"Dan! Dan! You alright, mate?"

Dan remained quiet. The last thing he wanted was a conversation with his mate, Rick, about the disadvantages of drinking too much. Rick had been on his soapbox about alcohol ever since he quit drinking twelve months ago, and he took every opportunity to gloat about giving up.

"Dan? Dan? Are you here?" Rick tried to push the door open to the locked cubicle but gave up. "You know where I am if you need me," Rick shouted on his way out. Shaking his head, he made his way back to the bar.

"Where is he then?" Jack shouted across to Rick, who shrugged his shoulders and held his hands out in confusion.

Jack and the rest of Dan's friends jeered and laughed in his absence. Dan could hear their mocking tones from the gents, and it only made him feel worse.

He knew that Jack was probably leading the charge, always ready with a cutting remark or a snide comment. It was the way Jack operated, using his wit and charm to keep everyone in line, even if it meant putting others down.

"Can't handle it, that's his problem!" Jack said, his voice carrying over the din of the pub.

"You do realise that the more you take the piss out of him, the more he'll drink just to fit in with you all?" Rick retorted, his tone tinged with concern.

"Oh, get off your pedestal, Rick. Not everyone can be like you, Mr I'm twelve months sober," Jack replied, trying his best to hide his jealousy.

As tensions simmered among the group, a tall man watched with keen interest, his eyes flickering with intrigue as he observed the dynamics unfolding before him.

He switched his phone to screen saver, checked the inside pocket of his coat, and watched.

Should he interfere and bring calm amongst the group? Or continue his evening out with his beloved wife?

"Right! You lot leave now!" Amos Crutchley, the landlord, had had enough.

Initially amenable to the men having a few quiet drinks in his pub, it was now late, and he was getting tired. He didn't have the strength or patience to deal with any trouble.

"Aw, come on, mate, just one more?" Jack and his friends protested, but Amos stood firm.

"I said, no. Drink up and leave."

"What about Dan? Where is he? We can't leave without him?" Jack said.

"Leave him, he'll be alright. He's still in the loos throwing up probably," Rick said, sighing.

"Come on then lads, let's go," Jack said, giving the landlord a look of distaste.

At the couple's table, the man stood ready to intervene.

His wife rolled her eyes. "Can't help yourself, can you? Can we not just come out for one evening without you feeling like you're on call all the time?"

He sat down again after he noticed the crowd dispersing and, hopefully, moving on.

As the group begrudgingly finished their drinks and headed for the door, Dan, feeling confused and drunk, found his way out to the back of the pub.

He stumbled into the courtyard, and leaned against the wall, trying to steady himself. His mind reeling with the events of the evening.

He couldn't help but feel a sense of resentment towards Jack and the others. They were supposed to be his friends, but all they seemed to do was mock him and make him feel small. He knew that he shouldn't let it get to him, that he should be stronger than that, but it was hard when he was already feeling so low.

As he stood there in the darkness, trying to gather his thoughts, he couldn't shake the feeling that something was about to happen. Something that would change everything, forever.

He just hoped that he would be ready for it when it did.

2

The cold night air hit Dan's flushed face as he stumbled out the back door of the Dog & Grain, his mind swimming in a haze of alcohol and regret. Confusion crashed over him like a wave as he struggled to make sense of his surroundings.

The unfamiliar pub yard spun before his eyes, shadows dancing and distorted in his alcohol-addled vision.

He definitely hadn't entered the pub this way earlier in the evening. Panic began to rise in his chest as he realised how disoriented he truly was.

Dan brought his hand up to his forehead, screwing his eyes shut in a desperate attempt to spark a memory, but his mind remained frustratingly blank.

The heavy rear exit door slammed shut behind him with a resounding bang. The thick metal fire escape bar, adorned with a tatty bright green emergency sticker, rattled ominously. The sound reverberated around the courtyard, making Dan jump and his heart race even faster.

An eerie stillness settled over the yard, broken only by the distant muffled sounds of revelry from inside the pub. It would have been pitch black save for the glimmer of moonlight in the starry sky, casting long, menacing shadows across the unfamiliar terrain.

The rhythmic cawing of crows punctuated the silence, accompanied by the occasional haunting hoot of an owl.

The sinister cacophony transported Dan back to the night he and Julia had watched Alfred Hitchcock's "The Birds."

The film had been terrifying enough when they were snuggled safely under a blanket with the lights on.

Now, alone in this alien environment, his fear ratcheted up to new heights, causing his heart to pound painfully against his ribs.

With trembling hands, Dan fumbled for his phone, desperate for the comforting glow of its screen. His new mobile - the latest model bought on a whim to soothe the pain of his breakup - refused to cooperate. As he struggled with the unfamiliar keypad, the device slipped from his sweaty grip and clattered to the ground.

Cursing under his breath, he dropped to his knees, hands blindly groping across the rough concrete.

'Shit, what was that?' he muttered as his fingers brushed against various detritus. The ground was a minefield of cigarette butts, shards of broken glass, and clumps of slimy moss.

The acrid smell of stale beer and rotting garbage assaulted his nostrils, nearly making him gag. A sharp edge caught his skin, and he hissed in pain. Bringing his hand to his face, he noticed a trickle of blood oozing from his finger.

'Uh, that's gross,' Dan said to himself, instinctively sucking on the wound. The taste that met his tongue was far from the metallic tang of blood, and he spat violently, fighting back another wave of nausea.

After what felt like an eternity of searching, his fingers finally closed around his phone. *'Great,'* he grumbled, noting the spider web of cracks across its once-pristine screen. Seven hundred pounds down the drain. With a deep sigh, he shoved the useless device into his back pocket and struggled to his feet.

Leaning heavily against the rough brick wall for support, Dan squinted into the darkness, searching for any gap in the metal fence that enclosed the courtyard.

His eyes darted nervously between the looming shapes of industrial-sized red bins, their contents spilling out onto the ground around them. The wall's coarse texture scraped against his palms as he inched his way forward, each step uncertain on the uneven ground.

His footsteps echoed hollowly in the yard, the sounds from the pub growing fainter with each passing moment. The silence pressed in on him, broken only by the erratic pounding of his heart.

With shaking hands, Dan fumbled for a cigarette - a habit he'd revived from his teenage years in a misguided attempt to cope with the loss of Julia, the love of his life.

The momentary flare of his lighter cast dancing shadows across the courtyard, and he took a deep drag, willing the nicotine to calm his frayed nerves.

As the smoke filled his lungs, the jeering voices of his mates echoed in his mind. *'Man up, Dan! No wonder she left you.'* The cruel words stung, but they also ignited a spark of defiance in his chest. He'd show them. He'd prove he wasn't the pathetic, broken man they thought he was.

Gritting his teeth, Dan took another determined step forward, resolving to catch up with his friends and salvage what was left of the night.

But before he could take another step, a menacing shadow detached itself from the darkness. Dan's heart leaped into his throat as he squinted through the gloom, trying to make out the figure.

There was something maddeningly familiar about the silhouette, but in his panicked state, he couldn't place it. He managed a weak smile, hoping the stranger would simply step aside and let him pass.

In that moment of hesitation, a glint of metal caught the moonlight. Before Dan could react, a searing pain tore through his abdomen. He gasped, stumbling backward, his cigarette falling forgotten from trembling fingers.

Warm, sticky blood blossomed through the shirt he'd bought to impress his friends, staining the designer fabric.

He tried to scream, but fear and agony choked the sound in his throat. His mouth gaped wordlessly, silently pleading for help that would never come.

The hooded figure loomed over him, face hidden in shadow. Only their eyes were visible, glinting with a cold, malicious intent that chilled Dan to his core.

With brutal efficiency, the attacker struck again and again, the knife plunging into Dan's chest with a sickening squelch that seemed to echo in the still night air.

The world spun wildly as Dan crumpled to the ground. His lifeblood pooled beneath him, mingling with the detritus of the yard - cigarette butts, broken glass, and weeds. These mundane objects became the silent witnesses to his final moments, indifferent to the tragedy unfolding before them.

As the cold embrace of death enveloped him, Dan's thoughts turned to all he would leave behind. Unfinished business, unfulfilled dreams, and the bittersweet taste of a revenge he would never see.

His vision dimmed, the world narrowing to a pinpoint of light. In that last flicker of consciousness, Dan's gaze locked onto his killer's shadowy form. He had no chance against this merciless enemy.

With a final, shuddering breath, Dan slipped away, his heart heavy with the regret of never again kissing the woman he loved.

3

DCI Josh Mills clicked the lid of his plastic sandwich box in place, grabbed a packet of crisps and a banana from the kitchen worktop, and put them in his leather work bag.

He picked his phone up, did a quick scroll through his messages, and after deciding there was nothing worth seeing, he slipped it in his back trouser pocket.

Crouching down to stroke the cat and giving her a tickle under the chin, he shouted up to his wife and Daisy, his ten year old Jack Russell. "See you both tonight, hopefully it won't be a late one." He waited for a moment to hear the sweet nothings from his wife being spoken from the bedroom.

Caroline mumbled something from under the duvet that was inaudible.

He smiled to himself then stepped outside and locked the door behind him.

Josh and Caroline had not long settled into their new home in Casterton, which lay on the outskirts of Kirkby Lonsdale. They had bought a double fronted, low ceilinged cottage which sat next to the church. It had been redeveloped by a local builder and after they spotted it for sale, their decision was made after stepping through the door on their first viewing.

The two bedrooms, both with en-suites, and decorated with a modern take on a country lifestyle, had views from the rear of the rolling fields beyond.

From the front, you could see down the slight incline towards the village. It was secluded, yet part of village life if they wanted to socialise.

This was the change of lifestyle they had decided upon following the death of their young son, Archie, who was just three years old. They lived in Kendal at the time, and they struggled with their loss and felt they needed to get away.

The tragedy had tested their relationship to its limits. There were days when Josh couldn't bear to look at Caroline, her grief-stricken face a constant reminder of their loss. And there were nights when she would wake up screaming, reaching out for a child who was no longer there.

But through it all, they had clung to each other, finding strength in their shared pain. They had attended counselling sessions together, learned to communicate their grief, and slowly, painfully, began to rebuild their lives.

This move to the countryside was as much about healing their relationship as it was about escaping painful memories.

A serial child killer, The Midnight Hunter, so nicknamed by Josh and his team, had been found guilty of the death of three young children, but not Archie - insufficient evidence.

Following another short stint at IVF, Josh and Caroline gave up on the hope of having any more children and moved away from the family home they had lovingly built. There were memories they would rather forget and erase from their minds but would be stapled to them forever.

Josh walked to the back of the house towards the rear driveway, near the old stone outbuilding that was now his gym, and unlocked his new car. He looked up to the blue-grey sky that was threatening rain once again and took a deep breath in. No matter what the weather, he would never get fed up with the fresh, Cumbrian air, and the countryside smells that were married to it.

The black Cupra bleeped twice. He opened the door, then sat down and fastened his seat belt. He put the car into gear, and it rolled smoothly off the drive.

DCI Josh Mills wasn't expecting a busy day today. He had been asked to investigate the death of Tommy Malham, who had gone missing but was found dead a short time later. The results of the postmortem were inconclusive, but it was thought the death could have been the result of foul play.

Haunting memories of The Midnight Hunter flashed in his mind, and he prayed that the small child had not been another victim of the ruthless, emotionless killer who was now firmly behind bars for the rest of his life.

As he drove, Josh's mind wandered to the cold case. The details he'd reviewed yesterday swirled in his thoughts. A child's body, found in woodland, estimated to have been there for about six hours before discovery.

Josh had tried his hardest to bring a conclusion to the case and closure for Tommy's parents, but there was very little evidence to go off.

A missing toddler, no leads, and a bash to the back of the lad's head. He couldn't help but draw some parallels to Archie's case.

The pain of not knowing, the endless questions that haunted him and Caroline.

What if Tommy was connected to The Midnight Hunter?

What if solving it could bring some form of justice, not just for Tommy, but for Archie too?

The weight of responsibility settled heavily on his shoulders. He knew he had to approach this case objectively, but the personal connection of Tommy being the same age as Archie when he died, made it difficult to maintain a professional distance.

He drove to work with one elbow resting on the edge of his door. With his left hand on the steering wheel, and the other rubbing his bottom lip, he was lost in thought.

Josh didn't notice the car pull out from the side street. With his limbic nervous system kicking in within a split second, he slammed his foot on the brake. "What the?" He lifted his hands up in the air to silently question the other driver.

The female driver behind the wheel of the '02 reg Red Ford KA stuck two fingers up at him, mouthed what Josh assumed were some expletives, then put her foot down and skidded off. The squeal of the tyres made the locals stop and shake their heads. They had had enough of young drivers not taking care on their precious roads.

Josh felt a surge of irritation rise within him. His heart was pounding from the near-miss, and the driver's reckless behaviour only fuelled his anger.

He briefly considered pursuing the car, his police instincts kicking in. But as he watched the KA speed away, he took a deep breath, reminding himself of the more pressing matters at hand.

Still, he couldn't help but mutter under his breath, *'Bloody idiot. Could've killed someone.'* He made a mental note of the licence plate, just in case.

Josh decided it wasn't worth his time or effort to go after her, he was too occupied with the cold case and circling thoughts of The Midnight Hunter.

The black Cupra had given Fiona a fright. Her fight and flight response kicked in, her cortisol and adrenaline levels were always on high alert. So, when she saw the car almost crash into her, she envisioned the driver getting out and kidnapping her.

The swearing and harsh mutterings were learned behaviour to always keep the fear within her at all times.

She decided she must speak to the counsellor about that.

As her heartbeat slowed to a steady pace again, she checked the mobile on her dashboard, which directed her to her destination.

As Josh continued his drive to work, he fleetingly thought about his weekend with Caroline. Maybe they would take a walk in the hills - if he was afforded a full weekend off work with no serious crimes to battle with.

Then he remembered. It was his Nana's hundredth birthday next week. A special trip to the seaside town of Prestatyn, where Linda was in a care home, would be his number one priority.

The thought of his dear old Nana, who he used to spend summer holidays with, brought a radiant smile to his face. Memories of playing in the back garden with Jet, the black lab, and his young cousins gave him a warm, fuzzy feeling.

How he longed to be a child again, without the stresses and strains of work, and the emotional hangover from traumatic events in his adult life.

How he craved to be back at her cottage right now in the sleepy village of Ffynnongroyw, where the only piece of drama would be the village gossip.

DCI Mills pulled into the car park of Cumbria Constabulary in Kendal. A 1970's block building, it wasn't the prettiest of buildings that Josh had imagined working in when he joined the police force back in 1999.

Still, he had worked his way through the ranks, and it was like a second home.

He got out of his car and grabbed his bag, looking up at the old paint weathered metal framed windows.

He smiled as he considered he would probably be there until retirement, but he could do worse.

He had a good, strong team behind him and, his track record for solving the most serious of crimes was often spoken about by his superior, Chief Inspector, Helen Musgrove.

Josh had a good relationship with her. It wasn't a relationship like the ones you read about in the thriller books, where egotistical battles between Chief and Detective raged on until one of them eventually moved on. This was a friendship built on trust, loyalty, and faith. Something that had transitioned into their working relationship.

Josh walked toward the main entrance then looked back twice. After a second thought he realised he had parked next to the Red Ford KA that had pulled out in front of him not twenty minutes earlier.

4

Doris awoke at 6.30am, the same time she woke up every Saturday and Sunday. *'I'm getting too old for this,'* she muttered to herself as she rolled out of bed.

Her husband, Billy, was snoring gently. She smiled fondly at him and wished she could stay under the duvet. But there were bills that needed paying and food to be put on the table.

Despite being retired, their pension wasn't quite enough to cover their debts and keep the household bills paid to avoid the bailiffs knocking at their door.

As she sat on the edge of the bed, memories of her younger years flooded back. Doris had once dreamed of becoming a teacher, inspiring young minds and making a difference. But life had other plans.

She married Billy young, had their first child before she could finish her education, and found herself trapped in a cycle of low-paying jobs and increasing responsibilities.

'Oh, my old bones,' she groaned, feeling every one of her 68 years. She slipped her feet into her £2.99 pink fleece slippers from the bargain shop in the town, and shuffled her way to the bathroom that looked like something out of the '80's.

She turned on the taps at the avocado green sink, put the plug on its chain into the plug hole, and watched it fill with water. The day-old soap dregs from the side of the sink sat shimmering on top of the water.

Sighing heavily, she took the slippery bar of Imperial Leather from its opaque glass holder, rubbed it in her hands, then smothered her face with the creamy suds. The soap stung her eyes but she didn't care anymore, she was used to it. Rubbing her face dry on the cheap, floral towel, she then dipped her finger in the thick, white cream in the deep blue tub and dabbed it on her face.

She slipped into her flowery skirt that hung heavily over her large, elderly hips, and decided on a powder-blue long sleeve top.

Glancing quickly at her husband and realising there was no sign of movement, apart from a gentle rise and fall of his chest under the duvet, she silently swore under her breath. *'Wish I could stay in bed, why is it me who is the one still working? He's the man, he should be doing it, useless he is.'*

The bitterness in her thoughts surprised her. She and Billy had once been so in love, full of hopes and dreams for their future together. But years of financial struggle, the stress of raising four children, and Billy's gradual withdrawal into himself had taken their toll.

She longed for the good old days when they would laugh together, make plans, and dream of travelling the world. Now, their conversations were mostly about bills and doctor's appointments.

She shook her head then went to make a hasty breakfast of toast and weak tea. As she ate, she allowed herself a moment of fantasy. What if she had finished school and had done her exams? What if she and Billy hadn't had any children?

Maybe they'd be retired comfortably by now, planning trips to exotic locations instead of scraping by from week to week.

Doris stepped out of their modest two-bedroom council house, which was located in a U-shape building with other properties. As she walked away from her home towards the large Victorian terraced houses near Booths, the lines of worry and shadows of lost dreams on her face were prevalent for all to see.

Doris looked up to the sky and noticed the clouds had disappeared for now. The streets were still deserted at this early hour, the only sounds coming from the occasional bark of a dog and the blackbirds' morning song.

Doris had worked hard all her life; she didn't think she would ever stop working even though she dreamt about an easy life. What would she do with all that time? Spend it with the grandchildren maybe?

When the grandchildren went home, what was left to keep her mind occupied and her fingers nimble? Billy wasn't exactly entertaining. She had to drag conversation out of him, make him listen, repeat herself at least twice over, and be the one to suggest they do something different for a change.

When they married, they were happy and in love. Four children followed, then eight grandchildren and, whilst Doris still loved him dearly, somewhere along the way Billy had lost his zest for life.

As she made her way to work, Doris couldn't shake the feeling of unease that gnawed at her insides.

The Dog & Grain, the pub where she worked as a cleaner, had stood in the town for years. It was never the scene of late-night brawls or drunken altercations, but there was still always plenty for her to clean.

As she walked through the churchyard and under the Leylandii framing the lychgate, the cry of a crow made her jump. *'Stupid thing,'* she mumbled, feeling angry that the large ugly bird had broken her from her thoughts, not that they were good ones. She shuddered slightly and walked on.

Arriving at the pub, Doris sighed and shook her head. Why couldn't the smokers dispose of their cigarettes in the metal box with holes in the top, provided just outside the front door?

She unlocked the door, stepped inside, then pulled the second, stained glass door towards her and walked towards the bar. She turned her head to the side in an effort to rid her nose of the stench of stale booze and a late night, she would never get used to it.

Still, it paid the bills and that's all that mattered, or so she thought.

Doris hung her coat on the hook in the space behind the bar, where staff gathered to scroll on the phones and grab a quick glug of coke when they weren't busy. Then she started her routine of clearing up.

Doris pulled out the grey plastic bin out from under the bar, removed the overflowing bin bag, and tied it at the top with a double knot.

She made her way to the back of the pub, walking on the blue emblemed carpet that had become a landmark in Kirkby Lonsdale. Patterned with pints of beer, trees, oranges, and fields, the carpet had landed itself a five star review on Tripadvisor and had been called *'quirky.' 'I could think of another name for it,'* she had muttered to herself when she read the review at the time it was published.

She walked past the cosy dining alcoves on the right-hand side and smiled as she remembered why so many people loved the pub, the food, and its staff.

Opening the rear exit door and holding it open with a small bar stool, she walked through the courtyard, looked around, and promised herself she would give it a sweep and a tidy before she left.

The outside of the pub wasn't in her job description, but she couldn't stand the mess.

She shook her head at the lingering smell and the cigarette ends, which she presumed belonged to the staff, and walked over to one of the red industrial waste bins and pushed back the black lid with effort. It was getting too heavy for her. Maybe she would ask for the lid to be left open next time, but then the rats would get in.

She dropped the bin bag a little by her side, then gripping it tightly, she lifted her arms and swung the bag in the air. She heaved it over the rim of the bin. Linda walked to the side so she could grab the lid and close it again, but something made her retreat in shock.

Her heart lurched in her chest. There, lying motionless in the large bin, was a body soaked in dried up blood, twisted and entangled with the remnants of the pub from the previous week.

The full bin bag had partially covered the feet from what she could tell.

She wanted to run but her legs wouldn't carry her, and something made her pause and stare. She brought her hand to her mouth knowing that she would never be the same again.

5

Why did it have to be her that found him?

She didn't have long left of her worrisome life with the weight of the world on her shoulders. All she ever wanted was to retire to one of those posh flats in Lytham St Annes by the sea, and sit on the balcony and play cards with Billy. Or, if her dreams would allow, be whisked away by a younger model who would lavish her with gifts and gourmet food on his yacht.

But no. Not Doris. She was destined to live out her days with the bloodied body firmly on her mind for the rest of her life, living with a man who had no desire for life left in him. It felt ironic.

Poor Doris, it could only happen to her. Her life had been a series of disappointments and unfulfilled dreams, and now this. She thought of her children, all grown and moved away, rarely calling or visiting. She thought of Billy, once her rock and now a silent presence in their shared life.

She thought of all the years of scrimping and saving, of putting others' needs before her own, of dreaming small dreams because big ones seemed impossible.

Dan Walsh's face was ashen, his clothes torn and bloodied. His legs were twisted, his arms clutched to his chest. Doris knew there was no point in phoning for an ambulance. Even with her limited knowledge from the dramas on the television, the man was very much dead.

As the horror of the situation washed over her, Doris felt a profound sadness. Not just for the poor soul in the bin, but for herself, for the life she had lived, and the one she would never have.

With trembling hands, she reached for her phone to call the police, wondering how this gruesome discovery would change the quiet desperation of her everyday existence.

6

Tall and impeccably dressed, Josh Mills cut a striking figure, exuding an air of confidence and authority, and one that any woman would love to be married to.

With his dark hair, charming looks, and physically fit frame, Detective Chief Inspector Mills floated past the notice boards on the walls of the station, and gave an encouraging smile to officers who were about to head out for the day.

As he walked through the bustling corridors of the station, heads turned to watch him pass. Josh was known for his success record in solving crimes, his sharp mind, and unwavering determination earning him the respect of his colleagues and the admiration of the public.

Many of the team were jealous and wondered if they would ever be as highly respected as him.

But today, there was a weight on his shoulders that no amount of accolades could lift.

The cold case had stirred up memories he had long tried to bury. Josh tried to link it to The Midnight Hunter, who had been behind bars for the past decade. The same killer who he wanted to blame for his son's death.

Tommy's body had been found ten years ago but, just like Archie's, the case had never been solved. After a firm word from up above, Josh had been tasked with doing a bit more digging.

Apparently, there was a small budget to look at old files and this one took priority.

Josh's thoughts drifted to his wife, the only person who truly understood the depths of his pain. They had been there for each other, offering unwavering support and love in the face of unimaginable loss. And yet, even their deep, understanding love for each other couldn't fill the void left by the absence of their son.

His wife's voice echoed in his mind, urging him to move on, to forget about the past and focus on the present. But how could he forget, when every waking moment was consumed by thoughts of their lost child?

Just then, a voice broke through his thoughts, pulling him back to the present. He looked up, irritated by the unexpected interruption making him lose the train of thought that was picking up momentum in his mind.

A look of incredulity crossed his face as he recognised the woman who had burst into the room.

The slim figure with dark hair, and deep brown eyes, seemed to glide across the floor. Whilst appearing to ooze with confidence, Josh noticed that she carried a shadow that could turn out to be darker than the one he bore.

The doors to the department were left swinging backward and forwards, and didn't settle to a standstill until the newcomer took her jacket off and flung it over the coat stand.

She then turned around to face everybody and realised she had initiated a silence and stillness in the office as if time had stopped.

"Morning, everyone. I'm Fiona, I'm looking for someone called Josh Mills, can anyone direct me to him?"

PC Stewart Whippet, an unfortunate surname if ever you heard one, looked over in Josh's direction. He eagerly awaited the interaction between his credible, likeable boss, and this woman who had burst in unannounced. His mouth parted a little in awe at how confident she appeared and seemingly without a care in the world.

Josh Mills closed his eyes for a moment and shook his head. He swore this was the woman who stuck two fingers up at him. What the hell was she doing here? He watched her walk over to his desk and for once in his life, remained speechless.

Fiona Mitchell let out a breath as she got closer to her new boss. She stood in front of him with her arms folded. "Oh, it's you."

"Who are you? I didn't think I'd be crossing your path again. I could have had you arrested," Josh said.

PC Whippet cringed inside and watched the interaction like a tennis match.

"What for? I didn't do anything wrong. I just mis-judged your driving speed, it wasn't intentional, and no harm was done. Besides, I was in a rush to get here and start on time."

"The way you sped off I would have expected you to have arrived sooner."

"Needed fuel, Sir. I'm sorry if I'm late, but I didn't do anything wrong for you to arrest me."

"Do you mean apart from swearing at a police officer?"

"Yeah, but I didn't know that at the time, did I?"

"Suppose not," Josh mumbled.

The rest of the team in the office remained silent and enjoyed the show. They had a feeling they would like this new addition, whoever she might be.

"Anyway, I'm Detective Sergeant, Fiona Mitchell, pleased to meet you," she said, chewing gum at the same time.

"Right, I'd forgotten you were coming," Josh said, with annoyance in his voice. It was unlike him to forget such an appointment. A knock-on effect he presumed from having The Night Watcher on his mind. "Find yourself a desk, in fact, you can sit opposite me."

"Fancy keeping an eye on me do you?" Fiona winked at the handsome detective and regretted it instantly when she saw his gold wedding band. "Right, well, tell me what I can help with and I'll make a start," she said, hastily, changing the subject in an attempt to hide her embarrassment.

"Tell me why you're here again?"

"Transfer, Sir, needed a change of location. Wanted to leave some things behind and move on." Fiona swivelled in her chair and looked around the department.

"Sounds like most of the police force. We all have internal battles and life events we want to escape from, but sometimes you just have to get on with it. And please, call me Josh, can't stand the *'Sir'* thing."

Fiona felt a lump in her throat. She had heard good things about DCI Josh Mills and was looking forward to a new start and new team. Others had told her before she moved that he was supportive and empathetic, but so far her experience of him was anything but.

"Is one of those for me?" Josh said, looking at the two take-away cups of steaming hot liquid.

Fiona followed his gaze and looked down. "Er yeah, I thought I'd make a good first impression. But it feels like I've stepped into the wrong building."

Josh instantly felt guilty. He knew what it was like to leave stuff behind and realised he had been too harsh on her. It wasn't exactly the welcome into a new team he would have liked. "Look, I'm sorry, it's just this case I have, it's a bit, let's say, raw."

Fiona nodded once and spat her gum out into the round dustbin at the side of the desk. "No problem, we can always start again."

Josh sat back in his chair and drank the coffee before it went cold. "You chose right with this by the way, did someone tell you what my favourite coffee was?" Josh drank the double espresso with steamed milk. Cortados never stayed that hot for long.

"I might have made some enquiries," she said, grinning.

"Seems like we will get along well then." Josh turned his attention back to the file on his desk.

Fiona let out a silent breath of relief, thanking God that Josh was warming to her. She'd had enough of men's attitudes before she left her hometown. "Can I help with anything?" Fiona said, looking over at him.

"Remember The Midnight Hunter?"

Fiona's expression darkened. "Do I? It was the talk of the station. News of how well this team did travelled up to Scotland CID. They even made us sit for four hours in a room with no heating to go through *'the learns,'* and how we could implement your qualities in the next investigation."

Josh blew out air. "Wow, didn't realise we'd had that big an impact." His cheeks flushed pink a little. Josh leaned forward, his voice low. "What do you remember about the case?"

Fiona's brow furrowed as she recalled the details. "He targeted children, didn't he? Always at night. Left no traces, bodies found weeks later in wooded areas."

Josh nodded, a haunted look in his eyes. "Three confirmed victims. But I believe there may have been more."

"More?" Fiona's eyes widened. "How many?"

"At least two," Josh said, his voice barely above a whisper. "One's the cold case I'm working on now. The other..." He trailed off, unable to finish the sentence.

Fiona waited for a couple of moments for him to finish the sentence. She looked at her new partner and felt nervous for him. She leaned in, her voice gentle. "Josh, are you okay? What aren't you telling me? Of course, you don't have to tell me. I appreciate that we have only just met. Forgive me for asking."

He took a deep breath. "The other was my son, Archie."

Fiona's hand flew to her mouth. "Oh, Josh. I had no idea."

"You wouldn't have done. That is unless you watched it on the news."

Fiona rigorously shook her head. "I try to stay away from the news, all doom and gloom."

"You can say that again, although it is useful to find witnesses sometimes."

"True."

"Anyway, The Midnight Hunter. This case is important. Maybe we can finally get justice for Tommy's family."

"Tell me more," Fiona urged. "What makes you think these cases are connected?" she asked, sensitively.

Josh pulled out a file, spreading photos across the desk. "The Midnight Hunter always left a calling card. A small toy with each victim."

Fiona studied the photos, her stomach churning. "And the cold case?"

"A young boy, found in the woods ten years ago. With a small teddy bear next to the body."

"Christ," Fiona breathed. "No wonder this case is getting to you. We must solve this, Josh. For Tommy's parents and you, and for your son."

Josh nodded, grateful for her understanding. "That's why I need your help. Fresh eyes, fresh perspective. We might spot something we missed before."

Fiona raised her eyebrows and silently nodded. "Why is it back on your desk, anyway? The Midnight Hunter is tucked away firmly behind bars isn't he?"

"He is, but this one is unsolved." An emotional ball of heartache formed at the back of Josh's throat. He re-focused on Fiona in front of him and pushed his thoughts to one side. It wouldn't do to show emotion in front of his new partner.

"Are you okay?"

"Yes, good. Let's crack on, shall we? We need to make contact with the parents again, it will be hard, but there may be something we missed." Josh stood up to grab his coat but was interrupted by his phone. "Mills?" His eyes widened slightly whilst he looked at Fiona. "Will do, we're on our way."

"What's up? You looked shocked."

"I am." Josh said. "A body has been found outside the Dog and Grain, I was there last night. Let's go. A good start to your first day, hey."

"You're telling me." Fiona put her leather jacket on and followed Josh Mills out of the building. She sighed deeply, shook her head, and sincerely hoped this was a one off. "Any ideas whether it was suicide?"

"Stab wounds to the abdomen and chest don't sound like suicide to me."

Fiona ignored the sarcasm as they both sped towards the scene in Josh's car.

7

A chill ran down Josh's spine. He couldn't shake off the feeling that this wasn't just any ordinary crime scene at the Dog & Grain.

He looked around the courtyard wondering what the hell had happened, and why someone would choose to kill then dump their victim's body in a bin.

Final act of retribution maybe? Treating them like a piece of rubbish in retaliation to hurt, anger? Or a random murder on a Thursday night? Josh doubted the latter very much.

The crime scene was busy with flashing lights, bustling officers, SOCO, and an ambulance. *'Fat chance that will do any good now,'* he thought. It must have been sent when the emergency call was made, just to be sure the victim could definitely not be saved.

As Josh and his new partner crept around the yard in boot covers and protective suits, Josh caught sight of something that sent a shiver down his spine.

A small, familiar object lying on the ground caught his eye. It was a child's toy, abandoned and forgotten amidst the chaos.

Josh's heart tightened like it had a metal claw wrapped around it and squeezing it harder. He stooped to pick up the toy, a pang of sorrow piercing through him like a knife. He crouched for a while and held it in his hands and did all he could to fight back his emotions. His long dark lashes threatened to drip with tiny droplets of tears.

It was a small wooden truck, worn and weathered from years of play and enjoyment. But despite its humble appearance and basic mechanics, it held a weight of memories that threatened to overwhelm him. Memories of a time when his son's laughter had filled their home with warmth and light. Memories that now lay shattered and scattered like shards of glass, torn apart by the cruel hands of fate.

As Josh held the toy, he could almost hear Archie's excited voice, see his bright eyes shining with joy. He recalled Archie pushing a toy truck across their living room floor. Josh remembered scooping his son up, both laughing as they played together. Josh squeezed his eyes shut, willing the memories away. But they persisted, taunting him with what he'd lost.

With a heavy heart Josh looked up to make sure no one was looking and pocketed the toy, his fingers trembling with emotion and guilt for interfering with a crime scene.

Ever since the cold case file had landed on his desk a couple of days ago, he felt the presence of his son, but he hadn't told Caroline yet.

She had been coping well recently and he didn't want to burst her bubble. He knew she would carry the burden of grief and guilt until her final resting place. She should never have made the cup of tea, she should never have said *'I'll be back in a minute,'* she should never have assumed Archie would be safe.

Josh's beautiful wife blamed herself and was tormented with *'should haves,'* daily.

When Josh went to see the counsellor that work had provided for him, he was asked if he blamed her? It was unquestionable. How could he possibly blame his wife for something when she was simply doing the best she could?

They both adored Archie with all of their hearts, so to place blame on something so horrific on the woman he loved dearly was unpalatable.

The cold case and unforgivable details of Tommy found in Gelt woods, threatened to drag up something that he and his wife had both learned to live with and dealt with. He wasn't going to allow that to happen.

Fiona watched him silently across the courtyard, her eyes filled with compassion and understanding. She knew that there were demons lurking in Josh's past, shadows that threatened to engulf him in darkness. But she also saw strength and resilience in him, a determination to confront his demons head-on and make the world a better place to live in.

She thought of her own past and how terrible it was. At one time she didn't think she would meet anyone else with such horrific memories as herself.

Fiona's mind drifted to her own painful past. The screeching of tyres, the sickening crunch of metal, her sister's scream cut short... She shook her head, trying to dispel the images. But like Josh's memories of Archie, they clung stubbornly, refusing to be forgotten.

She remembered the aftermath - the hospital corridors, the beeping machines, the devastating news. "I'm sorry," the doctor had said, his face a mask of professional sympathy. "We did everything we could."

Fiona had collapsed then, her world shattering around her. The guilt had been overwhelming, suffocating.

She started to walk over to Josh when she thought she saw something out of the corner of her eye. Confused, and questioning her own sanity, she squinted into the trees behind the courtyard. Was that a figure that she saw or just her imagination?

She shook her head to get rid of the memories of the past. He wouldn't have followed her here, surely? Fiona didn't trust the bane of her life one bit, so anything was possible.

She re-focused on the job in hand. "Josh?" She said, walking over and dipping her head slightly to grasp his attention.

He looked at her hesitantly for a second, then remembered where he was and focused on her.

"SOCO is wanting a word I think." Fiona looked in the direction of Serena Blackwood, an experienced crime scene officer who had worked with DCI Mills for what felt like most of her career.

"Josh," she said, with a heavy smile and an exhausting sigh.

"Serena, what have you got?"

"I found this in his back pocket, the murderer obviously wasn't too concerned about prolonging our investigation into establishing who the victim was."

Josh slipped on his white forensic gloves before handling the wallet Serena was passing to him, as Fiona watched intently over his shoulder.

"He's been dead I would say for at least eight hours, and it looks like it was brutal. Here's hoping it was quick and he was out cold before the murderer continued his stabbing rampage. It looks vicious," she said, raising her eyebrows.

Josh looked around the courtyard at the back of the pub. "Why here? A tourist town on a Thursday night when holiday makers are supposed to be out enjoying themselves, I don't understand it."

"That's what we're here for, Josh, let's start unravelling this shall we?" Fiona stood with her hands on her hips.

Josh admired her positivity and drive for solving the horrid crime.

"I saw him in the pub last night but don't recognise him as a local," Josh said.

"Would you, though? Recognise him?" Serena responded.

"I've been policing the town for years, I know most people, but there is no familiarity with him." He rubbed his chin then glanced down to the victim's wallet and pulled out his driving licence. "Dan Walsh, 1 Deansgate, Manchester. Sounds pretty upmarket to me." He turned over the driving licence as if looking for more evidence then slipped it back into the wallet.

On the inside of the wallet beneath a plastic cover, he noticed a photograph of a woman with long dark hair, deep brown eyes, and flawless skin, her details clearly written on the back of the photo. "Fiona, take a picture of this will you, on your phone? We'll need to contact her. Looks like he might have been married, or at least have a partner."

Fiona looked at him. "Are you making assumptions?"

"What do you mean?" He said, furrowing his eyebrows together.

"Could be a sister, best friend, cousin ..." Fiona shrugged her shoulders and raised her eyebrows. Noticing Josh's confusion, she said, "just a suggestion, that's all."

Josh admired her level of detail and questioning; she was clearly following the ABC down to a tee. Assume nothing, Believe nothing, and Check everything. She was definitely checking alright. "Could be, I suppose, we'll find out soon enough when we make contact."

Josh put the wallet in the clear evidence bag that Serena was holding open ready.

Fiona walked off and continued to wander around the courtyard.

"Anything of interest so far in terms of evidence, Serena?" Josh asked.

"No, sorry, SOCO has the big red bin to sift through, God knows how long that will take. Then there is the fingertip search on the ground. I can't see anything obvious as yet, this may be a long one. I'll call you if anything is found. I want to get started on the postmortem as soon as possible, care to attend?"

Josh shook his head. "Give me a ring when it's over and you have your findings. I have something else I'm working on. Both of these cases are going to take up my time. I need to get moving."

Serena smiled at him, a thought of sorrow and regret behind her eyes at what they could have had if they hadn't had been so young and foolish at the time. "Okay, catch up later."

Josh looked at the athletic build of his former love and briefly wondered how life would have been if he hadn't been such an idiot.

Suddenly there was shouting from behind the cordon.

"Hey, hey you? What's happening?"

Fiona walked over to the burley looking man who looked red eyed and agitated. "Sir? How can I help?"

"I've just been called by one of your officers. This is my pub. What's going on here?"

"And your name is?" Fiona asked.

"Amos. Amos Crutchley, I'm the landlord here," he said, trying to look over Fiona's shoulder at the action in the courtyard behind her.

"Okay, give me a minute." Fiona walked away from the cordon and towards DCI Josh Mills who was observing Serena.

"Josh?"

"Yes, what's up?"

"Amos Crutchley, the landlord, he's here."

"Oh good, let's have a word with him."

"We also need to go and speak to the cleaner who found the body, she's pretty cut up apparently. Not long off retirement, poor thing. What a memory to take with you into the sunset," Fiona said.

"Mm, let's go and talk to her and we can take Amos with us." Josh followed Fiona out of the courtyard and around the front of the pub.

"Mr. Crutchley?" Josh said.

"Josh? How are you? What's happened? You were in the pub last night, can you tell me anything?"

"Come with us and we'll take you inside. Unfortunately, Doris, your cleaner found a body early this morning."

"A body? It's not someone I know is it?"

"I doubt it. Although he was in the pub last night. He was part of the group that you moved on about 10.45."

Amos ran his fingers through his hair. "Oh my God, that's terrible."

Josh, Fiona, and Amos Crutchley walked into the bar area.

"Doris! How are you, love? I'm so sorry you had to find that," Amos said, sitting down next to his long serving, loyal employee.

"Oh, Amos, I'm so glad you're here. It was terrible," Doris said, her hands visibly shaking.

Josh made a small interrupting cough. "Doris, is it?" Josh offered the cleaner his hand.

She rushed to take hold of his masculine hand to steady herself. "Doris Brown."

Josh gave her bony fingers a reassuring squeeze. "I know this must have been a shock for you, but could we ask you a few questions?" DCI Mills had a calm, reassuring approach when speaking to witnesses. He believed it separated the truthful ones from the liars.

Doris looked at him. "I left Billy at home, I'm not sure if he'll be up yet."

"Who is Billy?"

"Oh, my husband, if I'm not home soon he will get worried." Doris sat with her hands in her lap, stroking a tissue that was almost in shreds.

Josh knew it was the shock. Random thoughts coming out of nowhere were a common occurrence in people witnessing scenes that would haunt them for the rest of their lives.

"Don't worry about that, we won't be long and we can take you back."

"Oh no, don't you be wasting your time on me, I'll walk."

"Please, allow us, it's what we do," he said, giving her a reassuring smile.

Doris nodded. "Can Amos stay, please? I know him well, he's like a son to me."

"Yes, of course. Now if you'd like to tell me what happened?"

"It was just a normal morning, not one that I cherish, mind. I'm hoping to retire soon, I'm getting too old for this."

"You look like you have plenty of life in you yet if you don't mind me saying. My Nan is almost a hundred and one."

"A hundred and one? No thank you, I don't want to live to that age, I'll never make it."

Josh looked at the lines on her face and concluded she'd had a hard life of working long hours just to help keep things afloat at home. He thought of his Nan and how she had worked until the age of seventy, as a very valued and efficient cleaner, and even then she hadn't wanted to leave Pontins.

Fiona sat next to Josh taking notes. She desperately wanted to show she was capable by asking the right questions, but thought she would step back just for this one. She didn't want to seem over keen or interrupt Josh's line of questioning.

"Doris, can you talk us through what happened before you found him?"

Her stare was vacant, many times Josh had seen witnesses look to the left or the right, trying to recall the memories and timeline of events, but not this one.

"Doris," he said gently. "Do you think you could tell me what happened?"

She suddenly looked up as if Josh and Fiona were complete strangers and had interrupted her blank mind, where she felt safe from the bloodied memory of a dead body. She didn't want to remember, or recall, and she certainly didn't want to talk about it.

"Take your time," Fiona offered, woman to woman. It seemed to do the trick.

Josh didn't acknowledge his new partner, instead he remained focused solely on what Doris was about to say next and the behavioural intricacies.

"I came to work as normal, my first job is to empty the bin. I do that to try and reduce the stench from the night before. It always smells of stale alcohol in here, a bin full of sucked and decimated slices of lemons doesn't help." She curled her top lip and closed her eyes.

"What happened then? Can you recall?" Josh said expectantly.

"I took the bin bag to the back, opened the lid. I struggle with it, you know. It's quite high and I'm not as strong as I used to be. Those lids were not made for short people like me."

Josh gave another reassuring smile. "I think most people struggle with them to be honest, even tall people like me." He offered her a smile.

Doris relaxed a little, at least she wasn't the only one. "It was then that I saw him. When I walked to the side of the bin to heave it back in place, I saw him. Well, I ran back inside and dialled 999."

"Oh, Doris, you poor thing," Amos offered.

Josh smiled at the landlord, urging him to stay quiet for the moment. "You didn't touch anything apart from the bin, Doris?"

She looked at him hoping the questions would stop. "No, no I didn't. I just wanted to run away."

Josh looked at the old woman with concern across his face. He turned to Fiona. "Do you think we can get her checked over? Given her age and the shock she's had, we can't be too careful. Call ahead to the surgery, let them know what's happened and that we'll be there shortly," he whispered.

Fiona nodded her understanding, stood up, and walked away, making a quiet call into her mobile.

"I think that's all for now, I'd like you to see a doctor though. If there is anything else we can think of after that, then we'll be in touch." Josh smiled and looked at her, fondness growing across his face as he remembered how much she reminded him of his Nan in her younger years. Caring, thoughtful, and wouldn't wish harm on anybody.

"And Amos, I have to ask this I'm afraid. Where were you last night? Did you go anywhere after you locked up? I witnessed you moving the group of lads on who the victim was with."

Amos blew out some air. "Yeah, I went to The Fox. I finished at eleven, I'd had enough after I threw those lads out. Ed, the landlord can vouch for me. I was there until erm ..."

"After closing?" Josh said, raising his eyebrows.

"Erm, yeah. After closing."

"Well, don't worry about the after hours thing for now, we've got more important things to worry about."

Amos sighed. "This is awful, poor lad."

"Can you remember, Amos, how many of them left?"

"I think it was only four of them. Thought I'd look for the other one when I had a minute, but never got around to it."

"Yes, I thought only four left too. I'll look into that."

Suddenly, a figure burst through the double front doors to the pub. "Can someone help me? I can't find Dan. He's my best man!"

8

Josh looked at the dishevelled, red faced man who didn't look like he'd changed all night. "Who are you?"

"Jack, Jack Tomlinson. I've been wondering where my mate is, he didn't come with us after we moved on from here last night." Jack's eyes flitted from side to side, trying to get a look at what was happening in the bar area.

Josh Mills caught Amos Crutchley eyeing up the young man, he thought he saw a look of guilt in the landlord's eyes as he quickly averted his attention back to Doris.

"Jack, come and sit down please," Josh nodded to the seat across from him.

"What's going on? Tell me? I'm worried about Dan," Jack said, as he pulled the chair out from under the table and sat down.

"Jack, I'm afraid I have some terrible news."

"What is it?"

"A body has been found in the courtyard, and we're pretty certain it's your friend, Dan Walsh."

Jack rubbed his face. "What? Can't be. What do you mean, a body?"

"Like I said, a body has been found."

"Is he alright, like? Will he be okay? He's my best mate, he means everything to me, he's like a brother." Jack's eyes started to fill with tears.

"I'm so sorry, Jack, your friend is dead."

Jack blinked slowly, his bottom lip started trembling. "He can't be, he was with us last night. I know he was sick but he wasn't at death's door or anything."

"Jack, his death is suspicious. Can you tell me what happened last night? Where were you?" Josh asked.

"Erm ... erm, let me think," he said, running his hand through his hair. "We left here about half ten, that man there threw us out." Jack pointed to Amos who was looking sheepish.

Josh momentarily looked at Amos, already knowing what had happened because he witnessed the landlord telling the lads to leave. "Okay, and what happened then?" Again, Josh noticed Amos looking a little suspicious.

"Well, after a quick one at the brewery, we went onto The Fox."

"The Fox? What time was this?"

"It was erm ... it was late," Jack hesitated.

"And can anyone verify that and who you were with?"

Jack looked up. "Yeah, he can," he said, pointing to Amos. "He was there with us. One of the stag party knows the landlord of The Fox, so we erm, got a bit of a lock-in."

Josh sighed. What was it with people breaking the law? It meant more work for him and lock-ins at pubs normally meant trouble too. "Okay, don't worry about the lock-in for now." Josh looked at Amos Crutchley. "Is this true, Amos? You saw the men in The Fox?"

"Yeah," Amos sighed, his cheeks flushing pink. "I saw all four of them, they were there until at least 2am."

"I can't believe it, this is the worst possible news. I can't get married after this, we'll have to cancel everything. I thought Dan was going to follow us last night after we left here, I should have waited for him."

"Jack," Josh said, leaning forward and putting his hand on Jack's knee. "Listen to me. I understand your grief, but get married, okay? Do it for Dan, do it in his memory."

Jack nodded his head. "Yeah, maybe," he said, still in shock.

"Why don't you go back to your friends?"

"Er, yeah, yeah, okay," he said, standing up.

"Can you give me your details before leaving, just in case we need to talk to you again. I'll also need the names and numbers of the people you were with."

Jack nodded. "Okay," he sighed.

Josh took the details down and watched the devastated young man leave. His stag weekend would be remembered for all the wrong reasons.

9

Fiona walked back over to where Josh was sitting with Doris and Amos, and nodded confirmation that they should be heading to the doctors as soon as possible. She had heard a little of what had happened whilst waiting to speak to the doctor. "That was tough," she said to Josh.

Josh stood up in front of Fiona and whispered, "yeah, tell me about it. I don't think Jack's involved though, Amos has verified he saw Jack and his mates in The Fox until about 2am. May need to follow up on that, but I'm sure CCTV and Ed at The Fox will verify it too."

"This is a tough one to deal with, hey."

"Yeah. Anyway, let's get Doris sorted, shall we?"

Josh walked over to Doris and Amos. "Come on, Doris, let's get you seen to." He gently took her by the elbow making sure she didn't stumble. "Amos, you can go, there's nothing you can do here. Needless to say you will have to close up for at least the rest of the day and night, just whilst forensics finish up. I know it's not great for business, but there's not much we can do. They will be as quick as they can."

"Don't worry, I wouldn't have opened up anyway. Bad taste and all that." Amos looked towards the floor and shook his head several times as he left his pub.

Josh led Doris out to a waiting police car. Making sure she was fastened in the front seat, he spoke before he closed the car door. "We'll be right behind you and come into the surgery with you to make sure you get seen."

Still in shock, Doris simply looked at the handsome detective without saying a word before he got in his own car and closed the door. As he settled into the car, Josh felt the weight of the toy truck in his pocket.

"I noticed you pocketed a toy," Fiona said, looking sideways at Josh.

Josh nodded, his throat tight. "It reminded me of Archie. He never went anywhere without a toy truck."

Fiona hesitated, then spoke. "I know it's not the same, but... I understand how you're feeling. The way past trauma can suddenly resurface."

Josh looked at her curiously. "What do you mean?"

Fiona took a deep breath. "Earlier, when I thought I saw something at the back of the pub, it brought back memories. Bad ones." She paused, gathering her courage. "I had a stalker once. An ex who couldn't let go. It got pretty ugly."

Josh's expression softened with sympathy. "I'm sorry you went through that, Fiona. Is that part of why you transferred?"

She nodded. "Partly. I needed a fresh start. But also, I wanted to make a difference, you know? Stop other people from going through what I did."

Josh felt a newfound respect for his partner. "I understand that feeling all too well," he said. "Every case, every victim. I can't help but see Archie. It's what drives me."

They sat in companionable silence for a moment, each lost in their own thoughts.

"As soon as we have dropped Doris back and then notified Dan's next of kin, let's get back to the station as soon as possible, get the incident room set up and the investigation started. I don't want this murder to become a problem in the town or affect tourism. Otherwise, the landlords and business owners will have something to say about it."

"Yeah, I agree," Fiona said.

As Josh started the engine and pulled out of the parking lot, a sudden sense of unease washed over him. "I can't help but feel there's more to this case than meets the eye. The brutality of the murder, it's odd for a tourist town, don't you think? It's odd for any town, and rare, thankfully. But here, in Kirkby Lonsdale? It just doesn't make sense."

Fiona nodded, her brow furrowed in concentration. "I agree. And what I thought I saw in the trees, I know it might have been nothing, but my instincts are telling me otherwise."

Josh glanced at her, noting the tension in her posture. "We'll look into it. If there's even a chance someone was watching the crime scene, we need to know."

As they drove, the weight of their shared confessions hung in the air between them. Josh found himself grateful for Fiona's understanding, even as he worried about the implications of their conversation.

"You know," he said softly, "I've never really talked about Archie with anyone at work before. Not like this. It's unusual considering we only met a few hours ago."

Fiona offered a small smile. "Sometimes it's just the right time to share the burden. Perhaps he is on your mind more because of the cold case. And besides, we're partners now, right? That means having each other's backs, on and off the job."

Josh nodded, feeling a mix of emotions - gratitude, sorrow, and a renewed determination. "You're right. And Fiona... Thank you for trusting me with your story too."

They pulled up to the doctor's office, where Doris would be checked over. As Josh opened one of the rear passenger doors of the police car to help Doris out, he thanked PC Whippet.

"Let's get Doris settled," he said to Fiona.

As they walked Doris into the doctor's office, Josh's mind raced with possibilities. The toy truck in his pocket seemed to grow heavier with each step, a tangible reminder of the past colliding with the present. Whatever was unfolding here in Kirkby Lonsdale, he had a sinking feeling it was far from over.

10

DCI Josh Mills stood before the weathered oak door of Julia Burrows' home, with Detective Sergeant Fiona Mitchell at his side.

The cool Cumbrian air was thick with a slight breeze, which gave them both a shudder that was more than necessary. Fiona's deep brown eyes scanned the quiet street and she shifted from one foot to the other.

It had been months since she had had to notify next of kin. Her mood lowered considerably in readiness for helping to deliver the news.

"Ready?" Josh's voice was just loud enough to break the silence of the street without disturbing the stillness.

Fiona gave a faint nod, her past experiences shadowed her pale face.

Josh raised his hand, about to tap the polished brushed-brass knocker when the door abruptly swung open.

A woman stood in the doorway, her face flushed pink, and her hair ruffled as if she had just got out of bed. She glanced at the two strangers who had graced her with their presence.

"Ms Burrows?" Josh's question hung in the air, and he waited for an answer even though he recognised the woman from the photograph.

Julia's mouth opened slightly, then closed and she fidgeted with the ends of the tie of her pink silk dressing gown. "Yes," she finally managed, the word barely slipping past her lips.

"Detective Chief Inspector Josh Mills, Kendal CID," he introduced himself, the ID badge in his hand catching a flash of grey light from the cloudy day. "This is Detective Sergeant Fiona Mitchell. May we come in for a moment?"

Julia's breath halted and she nodded mutely. She stepped aside granting them entry into her cherished home and prayed she'd shut the kitchen door behind her.

"Come through," she said tentatively, directing them to the front living room that housed two, two-seater mocha fabric sofas with scatter cushions, a large TV on a media wall, and various materialistic replaceable objects, which looked like they were designed to make the place welcoming.

To Josh it felt nothing but cold and calculated.

"May we?" Josh said, looking at the sofa by the window.

"Yes, yes of course." Julia followed suit and sat on the other sofa opposite.

"Ms Burrows," Josh began, his voice cutting through the tense air. "Do you know Dan Walsh?"

Julia simply nodded, not a word passed her lips.

"What relation are you to him, if I may ask?"

"Erm, he's my ... he's my ex."

Josh caught a quick glance at Fiona and blinked slowly. He knew this would hurt her even though they were separated.

He'd seen the look of terrifying anticipation before on a loved one. He braced himself, this job never got easier. "I'm afraid we have some difficult news."

Julia knew that whatever the police were going to say next, it would shake her to the core. She placed her hands on the sofa by her knees as if to steady herself from falling face first onto the thick pile carpet.

She looked up and searched Josh's face for answers to her unspoken questions.

The colour drained from her face because she knew. "Dan?" Her voice quavered, barely above a whisper, each syllable trembling with the onset of dread. "What's happened to him?"

Fiona observed silently, as she watched the play of emotions across Julia's face.

"I'm very sorry to tell you that Mr. Walsh was found dead this morning," Josh said, the words dropping like stones into the quiet room. "We are currently treating it as suspicious, and we needed to inform you because we found your photo and details in his wallet as an 'ICE' contact, you were in his phone too," he said, referring to the 'In Case of Emergency' acronym brought in a few years previously.

A gasp escaped Julia's lips, her hands flying to cover her mouth as if to stifle the scream that wanted to leave her whole being.

Her body felt like it was contorting, and she couldn't breathe.

Tears formed and fell on to her dressing gown that spread like tie dye on a tee-shirt. "Dead? How? I'm not sure why he still has me in his wallet to be honest, have you told his parents?" All her questions came out at once, piling on top of each other.

"We will visit them and let them know. Were you still in touch with him?"

Julia shook her head rigorously. "We separated a couple of months ago but I don't think he ever got over it." Julia looked down towards the floor with regret, remembering what she had lost.

Their last encounter, fraught with tension and words they both regretted, made its way to the forefront of her delicate mind and she could still feel the sting of their parting.

Josh exchanged a glance with Fiona, both acutely aware of the delicate balance between compassion and inquisition.

"Ms. Burrows," Josh's voice cut through the haze of her memories, firm yet not unkind. "Can you tell us about your relationship with Mr. Walsh? How long had you known each other?"

"Just... just over eight years," she whispered attempting to keep the past at bay.

"Was your separation amicable?" Fiona inquired, her tone neutral. She understood the complexities of human relationships, how love could so easily entwine with darker threads, secrets and lies.

"Amicable?" A bitter laugh escaped Julia's throat. "Hardly. We fought—argued about everything towards the end. But I never wished him harm."

"Can you think of anyone who might have held a grudge against Mr. Walsh?" Josh probed gently.

"No one would hurt Dan, not that I know of anyway," Julia said, her fingers twisting a loose thread on her sleeve. "He was kind, thoughtful, generous, he loved me ..." she said, staring into space.

"So can I ask, why did you split up?" Fiona asked, sensing there was more to what appeared to be just a loss of love in a relationship that had run its course.

Julia sniffled, stood up, and walked to the corner of the room to get herself a tissue from the box sat on the sideboard.

"We understand this might be difficult, Ms. Burrows, but—"

"Please, please, call me Julia, I can't stand these formalities at a time like this."

Fiona nodded. "We understand this might be difficult, Julia, but anything you can tell us may help to catch Dan's killer. Was there someone else in the relationship perhaps?"

"No, not really. Well, not on Dan's part there wasn't. I had a personal trainer at the time, but something only happened briefly. Dan made too much of it and it started to grate on me that he had no trust in our relationship," Julia whispered, her eyes flicking to the side towards the kitchen.

Josh noticed the change in direction of her eyes and decided to pursue it further. "Was there anything more to the relationship with ... sorry, what was the name of your personal trainer?"

"He is called Mark Thompson."

"Is called? Does that mean you are still seeing him? Do you think he could have gotten jealous?"

"No, nothing like that, Mark wouldn't hurt a fly. He's not that kind of person."

"Is there anything else you would care to tell us, Julia?" Josh's voice was soft and caring.

"Once or twice, Dan mentioned disputes at work, some were heated during board meetings, but it didn't seem to bother him."

Josh leaned forward, his interest piqued. "Can you tell us more about these disputes? Any specific incidents that stand out?"

Julia furrowed her brow, trying to recall details. "Well, there was this one time, when Dan came home really agitated. Said he'd had a massive row with a colleague named Bill Smith. Apparently, Bill had been cutting corners on a big project, and Dan threatened to report him to the board."

"Did anything come of that?" Fiona asked, jotting notes.

"I'm not sure. Dan was pretty stressed about it for a while, though. He mentioned that Bill had connections higher up in the company and was worried it might backfire on him. I mean, Bill is one of the directors so pretty high up himself. But Dan was worried."

Josh nodded, encouraging her to continue. "Any other incidents?"

Julia bit her lip, thinking. "There was another situation with a woman named Sarah. I don't know her surname. She and Dan were competing for a promotion. Things got nasty from what I heard. Dan said she was spreading rumours about him, trying to sabotage his chances."

"How did that turn out?" Josh pressed.

"Dan got the promotion in the end, but he said the atmosphere at work was really tense afterward. Sarah apparently refused to speak to him except when absolutely necessary."

Fiona's pen flew across her notebook. "Anyone else?"

Julia hesitated. "There was one more thing. Dan mentioned overhearing something he shouldn't have. He didn't give me details, but he said it involved one of the directors, Marcus Blackwood. Something about financial irregularities. Dan was really on edge after that, kept saying he didn't know what to do with the information."

Josh and Fiona exchanged a significant look. "Did Dan ever mention feeling threatened because of this information?"

"He did say once that he felt like he was being watched. But I thought he was just being paranoid. You don't think...?" Julia's voice trailed off, her eyes widening with realisation.

Josh politely ignored the incomplete accusation.

"Do you have anything else you can tell us with regards to that? Where did he work? Do you have his boss' name?" Fiona still had her notebook in her hand, her pen trying to keep up with the information she was being given.

"It's called Crystal Consulting, in Manchester. Bill Smith is his boss, a bit of a jerk if you ask me. Privately educated and has got too far in that place without putting the effort in. A bit of a trouble causer," Julia tried not to let her anger show.

Josh raised his eyebrows slightly and looked at Fiona, directing her to make a note to follow up on.

"Can you tell us more about Bill Smith? Did he threaten Dan with the sack or anything?" Josh asked.

Julia sighed. "Bill Smith. He always seemed to be in the middle of everything. He'd play people off against each other. Dan said he thrived on the drama. There were times when Dan felt like his boss was deliberately stirring up trouble between him and his colleagues."

"Any specific examples?" Fiona prompted.

"Well, with the financial irregularities situation, Bill Smith knew about the corner-cutting but didn't do anything. And with this Sarah woman, Dan suspected that his boss had promised the promotion to both of them, just to see what would happen."

Josh nodded thoughtfully. "Anything else, Julia?"

Julia shook her head. "Not that I know of. Dan was really stressed though. He did say once that he didn't trust his boss as far as he could throw him."

Josh raised his eyebrows slightly and looked at Fiona, directing her to make a note to follow up on.

"And you don't have anything further to elaborate on with regards to Mark?"

"No, nothing."

Josh noticed her gripping the tissue in her hand then ripping it to shreds.

"I'm sorry, I should have offered you a drink, would you like a tea or a coffee, perhaps?" She stood up and headed towards the kitchen door.

"A coffee would be nice," Josh said, speaking for both himself and Fiona. "Then we must get going."

Julia stood up and walked to the kitchen.

Josh walked towards the back of the living room where a dining room table with four chairs sat in the middle of the floor. He bent slightly to look at the photographs on the oak sideboard.

There were no photos of Julia and Dan together, but he noticed amongst what he assumed were Julia's parents and siblings in one family photo, there was a thin strip of four photographs that had been taken in a booth.

Both Julia and the man with her had obviously been fooling around, tongues out at the camera and one which showed the man blowing a raspberry against Julia's face. They looked close romantically. Josh's train of thought was interrupted by hushed sounds from the kitchen. He stood up then looked at Fiona. He frowned and flicked his head towards the kitchen.

Julia walked through from the kitchen to the living room with a cafetière of coffee, some mugs, and a small jug of milk, she laid the tray on the coffee table. "Here we are, sorry it took so long."

Josh ignored her. "Is there someone in there with you? I could hear voices."

"Erm—no, I don't think so."

"You don't think so, or you know so?"

"I—"

Suddenly a figure appeared from the kitchen.

"I'm sorry, Julia, there is no point in lying. Mark Thompson, Julia's friend," he said, offering a handshake that Josh ignored.

"Why, Mark?" Julia said, looking incredulously at him.

"We might as well tell them the truth, they will only find out anyway."

Julia forgot about pouring the coffee and went to sit back down on the sofa again.

"And what is the truth?" Fiona enquired.

"Julia and I have been seeing each other. And I am the reason that she and Dan separated," he looked up at Julia and glanced at her, silently asking for forgiveness.

"Thank you for being honest, Mr. Thompson," Josh offered.

"Please, call me Mark."

Josh nodded once. "Can I ask where you were last night?"

"He was with me, we went to The Vines for a meal, you know, the one at the side of the local shop on the corner opposite the pub. We were the last ones in there until closing time."

"And what time was that?" Josh was curious. He had no idea of the time of death yet, but needed to know more about Mark and Julia's movements.

Josh made a mental note to check the time of death with Serena when he returned to the office.

He looked at Mark. "Is there any point in me asking whether what Julia has just said is true or not?"

"Yes, it's true. Then we came back here, had a couple of drinks, and went to bed to watch a film."

"What film did you watch? Anything decent?" Fiona enquired.

"Er, Saltburn, quite a shocker if you ask me. I wasn't expecting that ending, that's for sure. I told my mum and dad not to go near it," Mark said, letting out a laugh at the end of his sentence.

Three pairs of eyes were upon him instantly and he remembered why the police were there. "Sorry, that was insensitive of me."

"What channel did you watch it on?"

"I downloaded it on Amazon Prime, and had to pay for it too," he said, rolling his eyes and sighing. "I'm a bit broke to be honest, but it was worth it, wasn't it love?" he directed the question at Julia.

She gave him a nonchalant smile and it faded as quickly as it had appeared.

"Okay, well I'm sure we will be able to check that with Amazon if we have to. Is there anything else you think we should know about?"

Mark and Julia shook their heads.

"Thank you, both of you. That's all for now but we may need to speak with you again as the investigation progresses," Josh said.

"Of course," Julia replied, her voice barely above a murmur, her eyes distant. "Anything to help. I'll show you out."

Julia followed Josh and Fiona to the door and held on to it as they both stepped outside. Josh turned around. "Anything else you can tell us, or remember, please call us." Josh handed her a card and she placed it in the pocket of her dressing gown.

Josh and Fiona walked back to the car when they heard Julia's voice. They both turned around together in anticipation.

"I just... I hope you find who did this."

All they could do was offer a reassuring smile, no promises were made. They both knew better than to do that.

"What do you think?" Josh asked Fiona when they got back in the car.

"Don't know, there doesn't seem to be anything untoward with them, just two people who met but were scared of telling us straight off about the relationship for some reason."

"Maybe they thought suspicion would fall on Mark. Why do people assume when the police turn up and question them they think they will be found guilty of something?"

"Fear, I suppose. Not many like the police."

"True enough," Fiona confirmed.

"Right, let's get over to Arkholme and tell Dan's parents. I'm not looking forward to that one bit." Josh sighed deeply, started the car, and set off to deliver more distressing news.

11

Mrs. Walsh sat rigid in her seat, her fingers twisting and turning nervously as she stared off into the distance.

Her husband sat by her side with a comforting arm wrapped around her trembling shoulders. The air between them was thick with tension and hurt, their emotions palpable even without saying a word.

Mrs. Walsh's face was set in a tight frown, her eyes flashing with anger and betrayal. She couldn't bring herself to look at her husband, knowing that he would see the pain etched on her features. "I'll never forgive her," she hissed through gritted teeth, the bitterness echoing in her tone.

And as Dan's father held his wife close, he could feel the weight of her words crushing both of their hearts.

"Why do you say that, Mrs. Walsh?" Josh asked gently, trying to draw out more information.

Mrs. Walsh's head snapped up, her eyes blazing with a mixture of grief and fury. "Why? Why?! Because she was the death of him! That woman, that... that Julia," she spat the name like it was poison on her tongue. "She broke our Dan's heart, and now he's gone. Gone!"

Her husband tried to soothe her, "Margaret, please."

But Mrs. Walsh was beyond consolation. "No, Frank! They need to know. They need to understand what she did to our boy!" She turned back to Josh and Fiona, her voice rising with each word. "If they hadn't split up, then maybe he would still be alive. He wouldn't have been off drinking with his friends, he would have been away with Julia, somewhere romantic. Our Dan always treated her kindly, he loved her. Instead, she has probably been living out her romantic fantasies with that other man whilst my Dan is dead."

"Mrs. Walsh, we don't know the circumstances yet." Josh took a silent breath in and briefly raised his eyebrows, trying to maintain a professional demeanour in the face of such raw emotion.

But Mrs. Walsh was inconsolable, her words pouring out in a torrent of grief and anger. "Oh, don't we? I'll tell you what I know. I know that my son is dead, and that woman is to blame! She betrayed him with that despicable personal trainer. Who needs those modern gimmicks anyway? In our day, walks and swimming were sufficient for staying fit. It's just a passing trend."

She paused, her breath coming in short gasps as the reality of her loss hit her anew. "Oh, this is beyond terrible," Dan's mother wailed, her tears falling like a torrential downpour. "I have no family left now, none at all. What will become of us, Frank? It's just the two of us against the world. First Lisa, now Dan."

"Lisa?" Josh said.

"Yes, Lisa, our daughter. She was killed by a drunk driver a few years back. Such a beautiful woman, Dan was heartbroken over it."

Josh watched Frank Walsh rub his wife's shoulder, the poor man probably now resigning himself to spending the rest of his life with a jabbering wreck of a woman.

The raw, unbridled anguish on Margaret Walsh's face was enough to make anyone's heart ache. Josh's own eyes started to sting with memories of being told his Archie had died.

Battling against the tidal wave of emotions threatening to overwhelm him, he swallowed hard and forced himself to remain composed. But deep in his heart, he knew that the pain would never truly go away.

"Mrs. Walsh," Josh said softly, trying to redirect the conversation, "I understand you're in pain, but we need to focus on finding out what happened to Dan. Is there anything either of you can tell us that might help our investigation?"

Margaret looked up at Josh, her eyes wild with grief. "What else is there to tell? That woman destroyed our family! She took our Dan away from us long before... before this happened." Her voice broke on the last words, fresh tears spilling down her cheeks.

Frank cleared his throat, speaking for the first time. "I'm sorry, officers. Lisa's accident, it's just... it still feels like yesterday. We are still struggling to make sense of Lisa, now Dan."

Josh and Fiona both nodded, knowing full well the grief the couple were experiencing.

"Okay, well I think we will leave it there for the moment, I know this is really hard, so I thank you for your time and patience."

Margaret looked up at Josh, questions, pleading, and grief all evident in her eyes. "You'll find who did this, won't you? You'll make them pay for taking our boy? I won't ever see him or hug him on a Sunday now. It was our thing together, just the three of us. He would come round for a roast dinner and tell us all his news. He would tell us he loved us. We won't ever hear those words again." Margaret shook her head and blew her nose into a soggy tissue.

Frank simply nodded, his own eyes glistening with unshed tears.

"We'll see ourselves out." Josh indicated to Fiona and they left the comfortable 1980's four bedroom home that would now hold shattered memories.

Josh let out a breath. "That was tough, poor sods. They won't ever get over that. I was shocked when Frank told us about Lisa. I don't think there's a connection though. Sounds like Lisa's fatal car accident was a freak incident. Still, best just give it a once over when we get back to the station. I don't want any corners cut or stones left unturned with this one."

"Did you see his mum when she told us about how Dan would go round every Sunday for dinner? This weekend is going to be the worst she's ever lived when he doesn't walk through that door." Fiona gave some thought as to how they would both feel.

"I know. But we can't get caught up in the emotion. We must carry on and stay focussed, as tough as it is sometimes." Josh gripped the steering wheel, composing himself. "Let's head back to the station and start figuring this out," he said, trying to piece together the death of Dan Walsh in his mind.

12

Jess Chepstow's reflection smiled back at her as she stood in front of the full length mirror, taking in her appearance in their luxurious five star bedroom. She twirled gracefully from side to side, admiring her new outfit - a sleek black dress with delicate lace detailing and a pair of stiletto heels that elongated her legs perfectly. *'This should do it,'* she muttered confidently to herself, thoughts of her distant husband fuelling her determination.

As the soft glow of the chandelier illuminated her flawless features and the silkiness of her dress, Jess couldn't help but feel empowered and alluring. Her husband may have become disinterested, but she knew tonight would be different.

She had been looking forward to a short break in Kirkby Lonsdale for weeks. Jess had worked tirelessly, sacrificing her free time to find the perfect place to stay. She was determined to make this a special trip, and her high standards and perfectionist tendencies had led her to search endlessly for the best accommodation.

But as they arrived at the spotlessly clean and modern hotel, Jess couldn't shake the nagging feeling that she had gone overboard with her demands.

Would Alex be disappointed? Was it worth all the extra effort?

Things had been difficult between them for months. Alex was jealous, Jess told him not to be so stupid, even though she knew she had done wrong. But how could she get divorced so soon? Her marriage was worth a second try.

Despite the glowing five star reviews on Tripadvisor, Jess couldn't shake off the feeling of unease as she daydreamed about the perfect getaway at the romantic gastro pub with rooms. She desperately wanted to believe that it would live up to her Instagram-worthy expectations, but deep down, she knew that perfection was just an illusion.

As she excitedly told her husband Alex about their surprise break, she couldn't help but notice his lack of enthusiasm. Was he really looking forward to spending two whole days with her? Or was he just putting on a polite front? Jess couldn't decipher his emotions, as he was a man of few words and stoic expressions. But she chose to brush off her doubts and looked forward to reconnecting with him and having some much-needed time together with no distractions.

As she dressed in her new outfit for dinner, Jess couldn't help but wonder if this break would truly bring them closer or if it would only highlight the growing distance between them. Despite her hopes, she couldn't shake off the nagging feeling that something could go wrong and ruin what she envisaged, as a time to reconnect with Alex.

She carefully applied her favourite shade of red lipstick and checked herself in the mirror before grabbing her small clutch bag. As she opened it, the light caught the coral Ted Baker purse inside, its vibrant colour a welcome change from the drabness of day-to-day life.

Feeling determined to enjoy the night with Alex, Jess smoothed down her dress and headed towards the door of their hotel room.

She did one last scan of the room to make sure everything was in order.

She straightened the duvet on their bed and picked up a few items that Alex had carelessly left lying around. As she tidied up, she couldn't help but think how much she felt like a mother cleaning up after a teenager, rather than a young wife enjoying a romantic weekend away. But as long as everything was *'just so'* for when they returned later, it would all be worth it. This would be the night when she and Alex would start again. She'd made her decision and that was final.

Without warning, a loud and urgent knock shattered the peaceful silence. "Sorry, I'm here now," she said, without looking at who had knocked.

Panic reared its ugly head and her heart pounded. For a moment she froze not knowing what to do.

Her voice trembled with fear and suspicion. "Who the hell are you?" Her eyes darted around, searching for a way to escape from this unknown intruder.

Before she could even let out a scream, a cold hand covered her mouth and dragged her forcefully back into the room. Her limbs flailed and her heart raced as the intruder's overpowering arms pushed her.

She thrashed and kicked, desperately trying to break free from the overpowering grip, but her efforts were futile against his brute strength.

A sense of helpless terror washed over her as she was forced to give in, her body trembling with fear and adrenaline.

In a split second, her entire future hung in the balance, all because of one momentary lapse in judgement.

As tears streamed down her face, she finally realised the grave consequences of standing up for what she believed was right.

13

After waiting for over half an hour in the bar, Alex had checked his watch again and sighed in frustration. He had given Jess specific instructions to meet him in the bar in twenty minutes, but she was nowhere to be seen. He couldn't help feeling irritated by her disregard for his time and patience.

Small inconveniences and minor frustrations had never been a problem for them when they first crossed paths. It was love at first sight - sparks flew, chemistry crackled, and they both knew they were meant to be together. Within weeks, they had fallen deeply in love, their bond unbreakable.

Alex remembered those early days with a bittersweet ache. They'd stay up all night talking, laughing at inside jokes only they understood. Jess would surprise him with little gifts - a book by his favourite author, tickets to a concert he'd mentioned wanting to see.

She'd look at him with such warmth and adoration that it made his heart swell. They'd make plans for the future, dreaming of the life they'd build together.

But as the months passed and Jess received a senior promotion at work, something shifted within her. There was something ... or someone else on her mind, he could just tell.

The change was gradual at first, almost imperceptible. She'd come home later and later, too tired to engage in their usual banter. Their weekend adventures became less frequent as Jess prioritised networking events and client dinners.

Suddenly, she began nitpicking Alex's appearance and speech, criticising him for things that had never bothered her before. The way he dressed was now *'too casual'* for her corporate crowd.

His jokes, once a source of shared laughter, were now *'inappropriate'* around her colleagues.

Alex recalled with a pang the first time Jess had openly winced at his table manners during a dinner with her new work friends. The embarrassment and hurt he'd felt in that moment still stung. He'd tried to adapt, to fit into her new world, but it never seemed to be enough. He never seemed to be enough, and he doubted he ever would be.

The once harmonious relationship now faced its first challenge as tension brewed between them like a storm on the horizon. Communication broke down; where they once shared everything, now there were awkward silences and unspoken resentments.

Alex seethed with resentment as he watched Jess flaunt her newfound status among the elite in her Corporate Finance department. The woman who had once loved curling up on the couch with him in pyjamas now seemed obsessed with designer labels and exclusive events.

She had become a different person, chasing after money, perfect families, and unattainable perfection.

He remembered the night Jess had come home, gushing about a colleague's new sports car. The look in her eyes - a mixture of envy and determination - had made Alex's stomach churn. It was as if their modest but happy life was no longer enough for her.

Her actions showed that she no longer saw Alex as an equal, but rather as a small and unworthy partner. At social gatherings, she'd introduce him with a dismissive wave, quickly moving on to more *'important'* conversations. He'd catch her glancing at him with something like disappointment, as if he were a project she'd given up on.

The final straw had been last week's charity gala. Jess had insisted he attend, only to leave him standing alone for most of the evening while she schmoozed with executives and the other man. The guy who she said she had no feelings for and it was only because they had shared eight years of their life together that they were so close.

When Alex tried to join her conversation, she'd given him a look that clearly said, *'you don't belong here.'*

He refused to spend his life feeling inferior to her and the wealthy social circle she now craved. It was time for him to take a stand and demand the respect he deserved.

This weekend getaway was supposed to be a chance to reconnect, to remind Jess of the love they once shared. But her lateness, the text messages with *'him,'* and her disregard for his time and who he was, only reinforced the growing distance between them.

Alex left the bar and walked up the stairs, dragging his hand along the iron balustrade. The iron spindles meant you could look down into the reception area from each floor.

He felt himself get more angry and impatient with her lateness with every step that he climbed.

He reached their bedroom door and his eyebrows furrowed together in confusion about the bedroom door being slightly ajar. He immediately sensed something was wrong. He didn't know what, and he didn't know why his gut was kicking him that something was up.

With trembling hands, he pushed the door open, fearing what he might find. Peering through the small gap, he initially couldn't see Jess.

His heart raced with nerves and anticipation and panic surged through him.

As he pushed open the heavy wooden door, his heart raced with worry for his wife.

He couldn't quite believe what he was seeing in front of him. His wife was lying on the bed, dressed in the stunning black dress she had proudly shown him just last weekend after her solo shopping trip. The black delicate fabric now seemed dull and lifeless against the stark white sheets.

A deep red stain spread from under her neck, staining the soft Egyptian cotton linen. Her clutch bag lay discarded at the side of the bed, in stark contrast to the chaos around it. Panic set in as he struggled to comprehend what had happened and what to do next.

Jess's lifeless body lay before him, sending waves of shock and guilt crashing over Alex.

In a daze, he instinctively patted his pocket for his mobile phone, only to remember it was back at home. With trembling hands, he picked up the receiver from the phone on the desk in the bedroom and desperately called for the police, the weight of reality crushing down on him.

14

No sooner had Josh and Fiona left Margaret and Frank Walsh to their grief and sadness, Josh's mobile phone vibrated in the car phone holder.

Josh pressed the green button. "Josh Mills."

"Oh, hi, Sir. It's PC Whippet. I just rang in about a gentleman finding his wife dead in a hotel room. The control room patched me through to you. They said you needed to know given what you found at The Dog & Grain."

Josh ran his hand through his dark hair and sighed. He looked at Fiona, baffled by what he had just heard. "Dead you say? Is it suspicious do you think?"

"I would say so. Can we expect you here, Sir?"

"Yes. We were on our way back to the station, but we'll come to the scene straight away."

"Where is it?" Fiona asked in the absence of Josh missing the detail.

"The Kings Hotel, second floor."

Josh hung up. "What is going on in this town?" He started the car and headed towards Kirkby Lonsdale.

Fiona sat back and stared at the countryside passing by the window. She had been in the force for a little over ten years, making her way up through the ranks after displaying quick thinking, tenacity, and being part of a team that solved a couple of high profile cases in Scotland.

She hadn't been ready for a double murder investigation in a new team quite so quickly.

Josh and Fiona parked up in front of the hotel, a crowd was already milling outside. Tourists and locals alike wondered what would warrant the attendance of an ambulance, a Crime Scene Investigation van, and three police vehicles.

Josh ignored the stares, pulled on his protective gear, and followed the trail of police and bright yellow evidence markers to a hotel room on the top floor.

His colleagues nodded at him and Fiona as they walked into the bedroom. Silent shakes of heads and solemn smiles said it all.

As he observed the sight before him, Josh silently sighed. The heaviness in his chest sitting like a deadweight pulling him down.

Josh carefully sifted through Jess' handbag. He inspected each item with gloved hands and a keen eye, making sure nothing suspicious was hidden inside. After thorough examination, he found the usual contents of a woman's purse - a makeup bag, wallet, tissues, and crumpled receipts at the bottom. *'Where was her phone then?'* Mills said to himself. *'Everyone has a bloody phone these days, we are practically attached to them.'* "Erm, guys, have you found a mobile phone yet?" He asked the rest of the team.

Everyone shook their heads.

"Nothing here," Serena replied.

Josh furrowed his brow and leaned against the wall, crossing his arms over his chest. "Fiona, we need to find her phone immediately," he said. A thought occurred to him. "Who found the body?"

"Alex Chepstow, husband, has been married two years apparently." Fiona said.

"Where is he now?" He directed the question at Fiona.

"In the back of PC Whippet's car, Stewart grabbed me before I came upstairs and gave me a thirty second lowdown."

"Maybe the husband has the phone." He glanced around the room, checking in the closet and drawers. "Let's finish up here first before we talk to him," Josh suggested.

The forensics team was split in two, each member moving with a sense of urgency and focus. One group meticulously searched the room for any shred of evidence, their gloved hands dusting every surface for fingerprints that could be traced back to a suspect.

Meanwhile, the other team captured the gruesome scene in photographs, methodically examining Jess' lifeless body for any clues about her final moments. As they peeled back her dress to inspect her wounds, it was clear that her throat had been viciously slit.

Serena's voice cut through the sombre atmosphere, reminding them all not to jump to conclusions until hard scientific evidence could confirm the cause of death. "It's never as simple as it seems," she stated aloud, as if already anticipating Josh's question about the obvious injury.

The tension in the room amplified as they waited for answers, knowing that one wrong move or overlooked detail could mean justice denied for Jess.

Graham Barker, one of the forensic assistants who Mills had briefly met at the scene of Dan Walsh's murder, approached Josh and spoke in a hushed tone. "Sir?" he said, pointing under the bed with a gloved hand. "I've found something."

Mills followed Graham, knelt down, and looked under the bed. He saw a phone resting on the plush grey carpet. The edges of the device glinted in the dim light, beckoning for closer inspection.

Both men carefully manoeuvred themselves to get a better view. Graham snapped several photos of the phone's position before gently lifting it up and cradling it in his hands. He placed it in a clear forensics bag, making sure not to disturb any potential evidence. With steady hands, he marked the bag as evidence and sealed it shut.

Graham's eyes narrowed as he examined the phone more closely through the plastic. "This is potentially crucial evidence. There's visible spatter on the device, we'll need to run a presumptive test to determine if it's blood. We should prioritise this for trace evidence collection. There could be touch DNA from the perpetrator, especially if they handled the phone after the attack."

Turning to Mills, he passed the bag over to him. The weight of its contents was palpable, a stark reminder of the gravity of their investigation.

"I recommend we get this to the lab ASAP for full digital forensics," Graham added. "We'll need to create a forensic image of the device to preserve all data. Then we can run it through Cellebrite to extract call logs, text messages, location data, and any deleted information. Given the time-sensitive nature of digital evidence, every minute counts."

Josh looked down at the phone and noticed the six missed call notifications on the screen within the space of ten minutes from someone called James. "Interesting. Missed calls from a male when she's away with her husband?" he mused.

Graham nodded, his forensic mind already racing. "Those notifications could be crucial, we can correlate the timestamp of those calls with our estimated time of death. It could provide valuable timeline information or even point to a potential suspect."

"I'll take it first though and see if the husband has the security code. Could do with seeing if he knows who James is," Josh said.

"Absolutely, Sir," Graham responded, his fingers already writing in his notebook to flag the forensics as priority. "I'll put a rush on this at the lab."

"I'll bring it right back, promise to keep it in the bag," Josh said, winking. "Right, Fiona, let's go and see the husband now," he said with a frustrated sigh.

As Josh and Fiona prepared to leave, Graham called out, "Sir, one more thing. Given the presence of blood on the device, we should consider the possibility that it could have been used to hurt her, maybe a bash to the head to knock her out or daze her. I'll make sure we check for any microscopic tissue transfer or blood spatter patterns that might indicate its position during the crime."

Josh nodded appreciatively at Graham's thoroughness. "Good thinking. Keep me updated on any findings, no matter how small they might seem."

Josh and Fiona unzipped their forensic suits, climbed out of them, and took their gloves and masks off. They both discarded the clothing in a labelled bag outside of the hotel room, which had been placed there by SOCO.

Josh looked down at the phone, it was another notification. "Another message, Fiona."

Fiona raised her eyebrows as she followed Josh outside.

The two detectives opened the car doors and sat down. Josh sat in the front passenger seat beside PC Stewart Whippet, Fiona sat in the back with Alex.

Josh turned around to face the back seat. "Alex, I'm DCI Josh Mills and this is Detective Sergeant, Fiona Mitchell, we are both from Cumbria CID. We are here to establish what happened to Jess and ask you a few questions if that's ok? We are both incredibly sorry for your loss. It must have come as a deep shock to find your wife like that."

Alex looked at Josh Mills completely blank. "I can't believe it," he said, then looking down at his hands in his lap as if they held the answer to the tragedy.

Josh followed his gaze and noticed no blood anywhere on him. It was unlikely he was a suspect or the killer. *'Never say never,'* he thought.

"We are going to need to ask you a few questions, Alex, we know this is—," Josh didn't have a chance to finish his sentence.

Suddenly there was banging on the passenger window.

"Alex, Alex!" The woman's voice pierced through the thick glass of the police car like a desperate plea. With frantic fists, she pounded against the unyielding barrier, her desperation clear in each strike. Her face contorted in agony as she strained to be heard through the cold, unforgiving glass.

As Alex turned to face her, his expression was a mixture of surprise and hesitation. He knew that any words he spoke now could potentially make things worse.

His mind raced with conflicting thoughts, all vying for dominance in this tense moment.

Should he speak up or stay silent? Either option seemed to have its own set of consequences, leaving him paralysed with indecision.

Fiona stepped out of the car. "I'll get this," she said, directing her statement at Josh.

"Excuse me, who are you?" Fiona said, looking the woman up and down. She pulled out her notebook and pen.

"I'm Jenny, Alex's best friend. Oh my God. Is he ok? What's happened?" She kept looking over Fiona's shoulder to try and get a glimpse of her friend.

"If you can give me your full name, address and phone number, Jenny, and leave this to us please," impatience evident in her voice.

"I need to know, is he okay?" Tears started forming in the corner of her eyes.

"Jenny, please. Details. Alex is fine," she said sternly, wondering why the distraught woman hadn't asked about Jess.

"Jenny Faulkner," she replied abruptly, folding her arms across her chest.

"Finally, we're getting somewhere. And where do you live, Jenny?"

"Coniston, 39 Threadbare Street, Coniston."

"Coniston? That's a long way away, what brings you out here so late in the afternoon?"

Jenny looked at Fiona blankly.

"Never mind, we can deal with that in a minute. Phone number?" Fiona asked.

"Huh?" Jenny said, still trying to get a glimpse of Alex sat in the back of the police car.

"Phone number?" Fiona felt like she was trying to drag information out of the woman in front of her.

"07985 281764. Can I see Alex?"

"No, you can't."

"What's happened to him?"

"If you're his best friend, I'm sure he will tell you soon enough. Can you go, Jenny, we'll contact you later."

Jenny turned around to leave but opened her mouth before walking on. "If it's Jess, then I'm glad if she's dead, perhaps he'll come back to me now." She turned around and walked away without saying another word.

Fiona watched the woman walk away and then got back in the car.

"What was all that about?" Josh asked.

"I can't believe she was here, what was she doing here?" Alex rubbed his face in his hands. "I can't take this," he said.

"Alex, Alex, look at me," Fiona said. Just take some deep breaths, you're in shock."

Alex stared at Fiona and followed her directions.

"In ... out ..." Fiona said, breathing in and out for four seconds at a time.

Alex followed her lead meticulously and felt his shock dissipating.

"Better?" She asked.

"Yeah, thanks. I'm finding all of this overwhelming."

"Hardly surprising. Your wife has died. Can I just ask though, did you know Jenny was in the town?"

Alex looked confused. "No, no I did not. She lives about thirty five miles from here in Coniston. I was surprised when she knocked on the window, she hardly ever comes here. She has a full time job with the National Trust at the local Tourist Information Centre in Coniston. It's not far from the village where she lives."

"So you didn't know she was in Kirkby Lonsdale then?" Enquired Josh.

"Er, no. No, I didn't."

"Okay, Alex. I know this is very early in our investigation but do you have any idea of who would want to do this to Jess?" Josh said.

"No, definitely not."

"Alex, what did you and Jess do today? How did you spend your day up until you found her?"

"Well, we got up this morning, a bit later than usual because we went out for drinks last night. Then we strolled into the pub's restaurant at about 9.40am. We had a nice breakfast." The words come out in a disbelieving sense that Jess had now left his life. "Then we went back up to the room, put our coats on and went shopping. Jess likes the tourist shops full of knick knacks that eventually get sent to charity. Then we went to the cafe at the top of the high street. You know the one? It's just before the Italian on the left hand side, through a ginnel, and there is a courtyard too. Fully Baked I think it's called. We had lunch there yesterday. It wasn't great but I wanted to give it a second chance. People deserve a second chance, don't they? Jess is ... sorry, was, a bit harsher than me though. Then we decided to go straight to the brewery."

"And what time was this?"

"We went for lunch at one, then on to the brewery at about two thirty before Jess went back to the pub to sort some work calls out. I think that was about five o'clock. She didn't say it would take long. Then she was going to get changed and meet me in the bar before dinner. But when she didn't turn up, I—I naturally went to look for her. I was worried."

"Is there a reason Jess went to get changed and you didn't?" Fiona tried not to judge what Alex was wearing. If her boyfriend had decided to wear a scruffy tee shirt and jeans for dinner, she wouldn't have been impressed.

"Jess wanted to make some calls about work, she's never off that bloody phone. Always messaging someone and asking me not to disturb her. I thought I'd leave her to it. I suppose I just didn't think to change my tee shirt," he said, noticing Fiona looking at him. "Besides, I'd had a few beers so couldn't be bothered."

Fiona took a breath in. "And nothing has happened in the past few days or months that would make you think Jess was under some sort of threat, being followed, anyone with a grudge or anything like that?" asked Fiona.

"No, nothing."

"Thanks, Alex. Can I suggest you go home and we will contact you there when we need to speak to you again or have any more news. Oh and just one last thing, do you know the security code to Jess' phone?"

Josh asked. "There have been some missed calls from someone called James."

"You're joking, aren't you? Firstly, her phone is sacred, no one gets to look at it apart from her. There's no way she would ever have given me her security code. And as for him ... what a joke." Alex shook his head and got out of the car.

Fiona, Josh and Stewart watched the widower walk up the hill towards Booths.

"What do you think?" Fiona asked.

"No blood on him anywhere as far as I could tell, but that doesn't mean he's not guilty. Do you not think it's strange that his best friend was here?"

"I do, yes. Particularly as she lives in Coniston, I'll follow that up."

"Thanks. Right, Stewart, great job. We'll leave you here in case you're needed and see you back at the station."

"Okay, boss. No problem," Stewart said, watching Alex disappear up the road.

As Alex got in his car and started the engine, the weight and shock of what had happened bore down on him. He rested his head in his arms on the steering wheel and sobbed heavily at the thought of his wife never coming back.

15

After parking the car outside the police station, Josh and Fiona walked across the tarmac in silence. The weather had turned chilly and Fiona zipped up her jacket as her shoulders shivered a little.

She looked up and focussed on where she was heading and, as she approached the front doors to the station alongside her partner, she noticed a gentleman standing to the side of the doors, smoking a cigarette. A tidy beard, leather jacket, and tattoo on one side of his face emphasised his gangster looks along with his dark eyes.

He stood against the wall, one leg crossed over the other, taking long drags on his cigarette and stared at Fiona as she approached the station's main entrance.

As Fiona drew closer, she felt a chill that had nothing to do with the weather.

The man's eyes locked onto hers, and a flicker of recognition passed between them. Her steps faltered for a moment as memories she'd tried hard to bury came rushing back.

A circling scar around his left eye was hauntingly familiar somehow but there was a disconnect somewhere.

The man's lips curled into a knowing smirk as he flicked his cigarette away and pushed off from the wall. He moved with a predatory grace that set Fiona's nerves on edge. As he passed by, he brushed against her shoulder, the contact brief but deliberate.

"Long time no see, Fi," he murmured, his voice low enough that only she could hear.

Fiona's breath caught in her throat, but she kept her face neutral, refusing to give him the satisfaction of a reaction. She watched from the corner of her eye as he sauntered away, disappearing around the corner of the building.

Josh looked to the side at her. "Are you okay? Who was that? It looks like you've seen a ghost."

Fiona blinked, realising she'd been staring after the man. She forced a smile, hoping Josh wouldn't pursue it further. "Yeah, yeah, I'm fine." She wasn't going to reveal problems so early on in her transfer to a new team, a new office, and a new start. But inwardly, her mind was racing. How had they found her? And more importantly, what did they want?

Josh seemed satisfied with her answer for now, he would delve deeper later once they had made the worrying case of two murders a priority on the incident board.

Josh and Fiona burst through the doors of the station, their faces etched with confusion and disbelief. How could a peaceful tourist town in Cumbria, with no murders in over six years, suddenly be struck by two brutal killings within a matter of days?

Josh's mind raced as he discarded the notion of coincidence for once and drew his own conclusion that the murders could very well be connected. They just had to find the link before another victim was claimed.

"Right, let's get to it. We have a lot to do." Josh clapped his hands, gathering his team together.

Fiona followed closely behind. In her mind, she wanted to reach out and grab him and hang on for dear life as a way of protection. But she composed herself and got to work. Her mind whirred with faces from her past as she tried to picture who the man was, then without warning, it came to her.

Dexter Stone. Someone from her past who she thought was dead. She had killed him, hadn't she? But it couldn't be. The snake tattoo around the eye had gone. Then she realised the scar had replaced the ink from the tattoo.

Fiona shivered and shook her head trying to erase the shadow of her past from her thoughts. But her heart took over and raced with anticipation and nerves knowing what Dexter Stone was capable of.

Detective Chief Inspector Josh Mills stood in front of the board, black marker in one hand, post-it notes in another. A dim light cast above him as he mulled over the facts of the case.

Beside him, Fiona Mitchell stood at the side of the board, her fingers drumming on the metal frame.

Josh looked at her, raised his eyebrows, and she stopped.

"I'm trying to concentrate, Fiona," he said.

"Sorry, something on my mind. Where shall we start?"

"Alright, let's run through what we know so far," Josh began, his voice low and measured. "Dan Walsh was murdered outside the Dog & Grain pub, stabbed to death and then his body was dumped in the industrial-sized bin at the back of the pub." Josh placed Dan's photograph on the board at the top on the left hand side. "Aged 32, worked in Manchester. Fiona, make a note to follow up on his employer, Bill Smith, will you?" He turned around and looked at her.

"Yes, sure."

Josh continued. "Dan was recently separated from his girlfriend, Julia, apparently because of her fling with her PT. Incidentally, she was still his ICE contact and when Fiona and I called around to notify her, she was hiding the PT, Mark Thompson, in the kitchen. He gave himself up and said there was no point in lying about the relationship."

"Anything suspicious about these two, Sir?" Stewart asked, having made his way back to the station because he wasn't needed at the crime scene.

"I don't know, Stewart. I guess either of them could have a motive if Dan was getting in the way of them living happily ever after, but nothing so far tells me that Dan was being difficult with them. According to his mum he was just devastated."

Stewart gave an upside smile and folded his arms in front of his chest. "We can keep them in mind though, can't we?"

"Definitely," Fiona responded.

"Serena rang me before and said that Dan had been killed roughly between the hours of 10pm Thursday and 1am Friday. I know his mates left the pub around 10.45pm."

"Has that come from the landlord, Sir?" Stewart asked.

"No, I was in the pub with Caroline and I saw a bit of a fracas at the bar. I saw the landlord had had enough of them so he turfed them out. When I saw Dan, the victim, this morning, I remembered from last night that he hadn't left the pub with his mates when the landlord told them to leave.

"Do you not think someone would have seen something? Bar staff maybe throwing out rubbish or bottles? Someone sneaking out for a fag on their break?" Stewart asked.

"Doris, the cleaner, told us that everything which needs doing after they have closed the pub is left to her. I suppose towards the end of the night there is not much to do apart from lock up if you know you have a cleaner coming the next morning. Most staff will want to get home I would have thought. Mm, good point though, Stewart. Perhaps you could go and see the landlord, Amos Crutchley again, and ask him a couple of questions about what time the staff finished."

"Will do," Stewart said with a smile on his face, feeling honoured with the additional task.

"Fiona, do you want to continue for a minute?" Josh decided to let Fiona take over and test her summarising skills.

Fiona nodded, her gaze flicking to the board where the details of Dan's murder had begun to be displayed in stark black and white. "Doris, the cleaner, found the body. She's married to Billy," she added, her tone thoughtful. "We interviewed her at the time but I don't think she'll be able to offer us anything else that might be useful. She's close to retirement, poor sod. Fancy finding that when you turn up to work." Fiona shook her head.

Josh raised his eyebrows in agreement and looked over what was on the board.

"So to summarise, we need to speak to Dan's employer. Just out of interest, his parents are devastated and they blame Julia for running off with the PT. They didn't offer as such that she might have murdered Dan, just that indirectly she killed him."

"How come, Fiona?" Stewart asked.

"Mrs. Walsh said that if her son and Julia had still been together then he wouldn't have been on a lad's weekend away. So I don't think there is anything suspicious there, just something to bear in mind." Fiona looked at Stewart who nodded.

"He doted on Julia apparently and nothing would have got in the way of that." Josh leant back against a desk and folded his arms across his chest. "Sorry, Fiona, for interrupting. Just another thing, Stewart, whilst I remember, can you speak to Amazon and get the search and download history for anything Mark and Julia watched on Saturday please? Pay special attention to anything they watched on Saturday night. It might seem like a small detail, but it could give us insight into their movements and state of mind."

Stewart nodded, "On it, boss. I'll contact Amazon right away and push for expedited access to their records," he replied, jotting down a note on his pad before turning his attention back to the incident board.

Josh nodded at Fiona to continue summarising.

"Moving on to Jess Chepstow," Fiona continued, her gaze shifting to the section of the board dedicated to her murder. "She was found dead in the Kings Hotel. No forced entry, so did she know her attacker? Her husband was waiting for her down in the bar, so she could have answered the door thinking it was him chasing her up. Alex Chepstow tells us she was running late."

Fiona pressed her mouth into a thin line as she considered her own question. "Alex has been questioned outside the hotel," she said. "But we need to speak to him again. And why was Jenny in Kirkby Lonsdale on a Friday night? Just for everyone's information, Jenny Faulkner is Alex's best friend who lives in Coniston. She told me she was shopping for a present for her parents. The shops were closed by the time Jess was found, so why not go home sooner?"

"Any other connection with Jenny Faulkner?" PC Sam McKay, a recent addition to the team, was standing at the back. He had been absorbed in what Josh and Fiona had offered so far in terms of information.

"We were interviewing Alex in Stewart's car when she banged on the window. It was strange if you ask me that she was there. Jenny was very concerned about Alex but didn't mention Jess until later in the conversation. Said she was glad if Jess was dead."

"Sounds like there are some gaps in what she was saying," Sam said, trying to make a good impression.

"I agree, we need to question her again. Do you fancy doing that, Sam?" Josh said.

"Yes, boss, I'll do it."

"Great, let's brush up those skills shall we? Fresh out of training college and straight into a murder investigation. Nothing like the real thing."

"I agree, Sir," Sam said, making a note of what he had to do.

Josh sighed, the weight of the investigation pressing down on his shoulders. "She definitely has motivation for killing Jess, doesn't she, Fiona?"

"Yes, she does, she was quite blunt about the fact that she was glad if Jess was dead because maybe now ..." Fiona flicked through the pages of her notebook. "I quote, *'If it's Jess, then I'm glad she's dead, perhaps he'll come back to me now.'*"

"Odd thing to say, isn't it?"

"Very," Fiona replied to Stewart. "Alex was in the police car and if somehow she knew they were together at the weekend then perhaps...? I don't know, it's odd. Follow it up, will you, Sam?"

"Sure."

"I also want Alex's story corroborating about where he and Jess had been that day.

Josh then addressed Sam. "Sam, you're going to handle Jenny Faulkner. I want you to dig deep. Her presence in Kirkby Lonsdale doesn't add up, and that comment about Jess's death is raising red flags. Get her background, her relationship history with Alex, any potential conflicts with Jess. Leave no stone unturned."

Sam straightened up, eager to prove himself. "Understood, Sir. I'll start with a thorough background check and then prepare a comprehensive list of questions for the interview."

Turning to Fiona, Josh continued, "Fiona, first, get in touch with Dan's employer. We need to know about his work life, any recent changes or conflicts. Then, head over to that café where they had lunch and check out what the owner has to say. See if the staff remember anything about Jess and Alex's visits. Chase up any CCTV from the buses too, and see what time Jenny got to Kirkby Lonsdale."

Fiona nodded, pushing thoughts of the gangster-looking man to the back of her mind. "Got it. I'll start with calling Dan's employer, although I probably won't be able to see them until Monday morning, given it's the weekend and a two hour drive away. Should I bring anyone in for formal questioning if their stories don't match up?"

Josh considered for a moment. "Use your judgement. If something feels off, bring them in. Better safe than sorry at this stage."

He looked around at his team, feeling a surge of pride at their focus and determination. "Remember, people, we're not just dealing with one murder now, but two. The pressure's on to solve this quickly and prevent any more deaths. Keep me updated on any developments, no matter how small they might seem. We're only as strong as our communication."

The team nodded in unison, a sense of shared purpose filling the room.

"Alright," Josh said, his voice firm but encouraging, "let's get to work. We've got families waiting for answers, and a killer - or killers - to catch. Stay sharp, stay focused, and let's bring justice to Kirkby Lonsdale."

As the team dispersed to their assigned tasks, Josh couldn't help but notice Fiona's distracted glance towards the window. He made a mental note to check in with her later.

For now, though, he had his own task to face - the cold case file that had been weighing on his mind.

He sat down at his desk with a heavy heart and opened the file, steeling himself for what he might find within its pages.

16

Josh sat down at his desk, put his head in one hand, and opened the file. His fingers traced the front page. *'Cold case, Tommy Malham,'* it read on the label in neat black lettering. Just reading the name gave him tingles and cast guilt for not solving the case sooner.

As he stared at the label, Josh's mind wandered back to the day he'd been assigned the case. He'd been a detective for five years having been in the police for almost ten years previously, before he was promoted to CID as Detective Sergeant.

He was still eager to prove himself in front of the Assistant Chief Constable, even though he had a proven track record of solving the most difficult of crimes, including The Midnight Hunter.

He remembered the mix of excitement and trepidation he'd felt when his superior had handed him the file. "Mills," his boss had said, "This one is for you."

Josh had nodded, determined not to let anyone down.

The pages had now yellowed with age and were filled with handwritten notes, statements, criminal records, and information on The Midnight Hunter. It had been ten years since the body of young Tommy Malham had been found, hidden in the woods not far from his home.

His parents had been interviewed and probed over and over again at the time of the boy's death.

But despite the best efforts of the police, no conclusion had been brought. The postmortem showed a bash to the back of the head.

Accident? Maybe.

But why hide the body? The case was still unsolved, something that Josh Mills was longing to rectify to bring closure for the sake of Tommy's parents.

Josh could still remember the countless hours he'd spent in the incident room, surrounded by maps and timelines, trying to piece together the puzzle.

He'd been so sure he was on the verge of a breakthrough, working late into the night, fuelled by cheap coffee and determination.

His colleagues had started calling him "Tommy's Shadow," because of how obsessed he'd become with the case.

Josh scanned through the details of the case, his mind drifting back to that fateful day, the memories still fresh in his mind despite the passing years and involvement in other cases. He had been a young detective back then, eager to make a name for himself in the force.

The memory of seeing Tommy's body that day hit him like a physical blow. He'd been the first detective on the scene, arriving just as the forensics team was setting up.

A ruined building had loomed over them, a stark backdrop to the tragedy unfolding. Josh remembered the chill that had run down his spine as he'd approached the small, covered form on the ground. When the sheet had been pulled back, revealing Tommy's pale face, Josh had to turn away for a moment to compose himself. It had been another child victim and the impact was devastating.

There was only one similarity between his own son's death, Tommy's murder, and those attributed to The Midnight Hunter. The age of the victims. But something was niggling at Josh about it all and he didn't know what, yet.

All victims had been young, but unlike the victims of The Midnight Hunter whose injuries had been brutal, there was just one wound to the back of Tommy's head. No suffocation or knife wounds were visible and the pathologist at the time said he had died quickly. Unlike the long drawn out deaths of The Midnight Hunter's young victims.

Josh remembered the frustration he'd felt during the autopsy. He'd been hoping for some clear evidence, something concrete to point them in the right direction. Instead, the lack of physical injuries, just a bash to the back of the head, had left them with more questions than answers. He'd spent weeks afterward poring over medical texts, trying to understand what could have happened to Tommy.

With a heavy heart, Josh closed the folder, rubbed his eyes, and turned his thoughts to his own son. There was no suspicion at the time of Archie being murdered. It had been assumed that he had fallen into the pond whilst Caroline was making a cup of tea. She had only been gone a moment.

She did nothing but blame herself for her son's death and at one point, threatened to take her own life. It was made even harder by the fact that she had been consumed by the IVF treatment.

Josh's eyes stung with the pain and loss and he could only imagine what little Tommy's parents were going through.

He looked up and decided there was only one thing for it, as tough as it might be. He had to go and see Tommy's parents again.

He remembered the last time he'd spoken to them, just before the case had gone cold. The hope in their eyes had been unbearable, their trust in him absolute. "You'll find who did this, won't you?" Tommy's mother had asked, her voice trembling. Josh had promised he would, a promise that had haunted him for ten years.

He didn't expect them to be welcoming, but it had to be done if he had any chance of trying to resolve this case once and for all. He owed it to them, and to Tommy, to see this through to the end. He was determined to bring Tommy's killer to justice.

As Josh stood up, preparing to leave, he caught sight of his reflection in the window. The eager young detective he'd been when he first took on Tommy's case was long gone, replaced by a seasoned investigator with his own share of personal tragedies.

But the determination in his eyes was the same. This time, he silently vowed, he would solve the case. For Tommy, for his parents, and for the young detective he'd once been, who had never stopped searching for the truth.

17

Josh Mill's heart felt heavy and bruised. Having spent over twenty five years removing trouble from the streets, solving the darkest of crimes and the most brutal of murders, you would have thought he would be used to interviewing victim's loved ones.

When the cold case file had landed on his desk, he tried hard to dismiss his feelings, to pretend that this was *'just another unsolved murder,'* but no matter how much he tried to detach himself, he found himself sat outside Christine and Colin's house on Hallbankgate in Brampton.

The village school combined the nursery ages with infants. A place that little Tommy loved and where his friends created a mural for him when it was clear he was never going back. Tommys friends would now be at high school without a second thought to the three year old.

Josh Mills wiped the tears from his eyes, gathered himself and got out of his car. He knew he should have Fiona with him. He had asked her for a fresh pair of eyes, but it was important he did this now whilst it was fresh in his mind after reading the file again.

He held the brown manila folder firmly under his arm and braced himself for a cold reception as he rang the doorbell.

What he received was very different.

"Oh you poor soul, we wondered when you would call again. We were so sorry to hear about Archie." Christine Malham took Josh into her arms and wrapped them around his neck, standing on tip toes so she could embrace him even harder.

Josh felt like a long lost friend. He swallowed down the lump in his throat. "Mrs. Malham, I'm sorry to call on you."

"Nonsense, I won't hear of it. It's good to see you."

Josh had never heard such pleasantries from a victim's family before. He gave a sympathetic smile and followed Tommy's mum through the hall with its immaculate decoration and oatmeal carpet, into the equally perfect living room.

"Colin? Look who's here," Christine shouted through to the kitchen.

"Josh, how are you?" Colin said as he walked through the kitchen door to the living room. He wiped his damp hand on the tea towel then offered it to Josh giving a firm handshake. His long bony fingers grasping Josh's.

"I'm well Mr. Malham, thank you. And you?" The question seemed empty under the circumstances but meaningful nevertheless.

"Well, you know, time ticks on and you get used to living from one day to the next."

Seconds of silence followed whilst they all absorbed the enormity of the vacant space that Tommy had left behind, and a shared life experience of losing children who had barely stepped foot in the world. Both boys had equally left gaping holes in their parents' hearts.

"We were very sorry to hear of your little boy. Archie, wasn't it? We watched the news avidly and followed the story."

Josh Mills felt guilty. His son had been taken too soon and so had little Tommy. But Christine and Colin had never had closure on how he had died.

It was assumed Archie had died in the family garden pond, although Josh wasn't convinced. Still, it was some form of closure which is more than the Malham's had.

Looking at Tommy's parents, Josh couldn't help but think both Mr. and Mrs. Malham had aged significantly, looking well beyond their late forties, more of a retirement age.

"Yes, it's tragic and we feel your pain. I remember being away with work at the time and watching the news in my hotel room. I couldn't eat that evening, too many memories and a shared sorrow of two boys the same age."

Josh looked nonchalantly at Mr. Malham whilst a fleeting thought flew through his mind, too quick for him to make any sense of it.

"What can we do for you anyway? This isn't just a courtesy call after all these years is it? You must have news with a manila file under your arm with our son's name on it."

Josh sighed heavily and regretted not covering Tommy's name up. "I have been given Tommy's file to look at again."

"Cumbrian Police have an extra budget do they?" Colin held his tongue between his teeth and went schtum.

Christine looked at her husband with distaste. "Colin! Don't be so cruel, DCI Mills is just doing his job, aren't you?"

"I'm sorry, I know this is hard. To be honest I hesitated in coming over but I wouldn't be doing my job properly if I didn't speak to you again," Josh said.

"If you had all done your job properly at the time, we wouldn't even be having this conversation."

"I think you should go back to the kitchen and finish that quiche off, Colin. Leave this to me," Christine said, straight faced. The short, fair hairs above her top lip twitched ever so slightly.

"Please, Mrs. Malham, he doesn't have to, I fully understand how you both feel."

"She's right. It's no reflection on you, Josh. We might be making the most of life the way we can, but it doesn't stop me being angry. I can't give you any more information than you already have from me, Christine can deal with this." Colin stood up, still holding on to the sage green tea towel and gripping it a little too tightly. "I'll put the quiche in the oven and make some tea."

Josh smiled and sat back on the sofa, crossing his long legs, his shiny black brogues catching the reflection from the table lamp on the side board.

"Now, what can I do for you, Detective?"

"Please, call me Josh. Do you mind if I go over around the time Tommy went missing?" Josh took Christine's smile as permission. On the day he went missing, where were you?"

"Me and Colin were at home. It was such a beautiful day weather wise, I remember that. We had a new gas barbecue, Colin put it together and went to the local hardware store for a gas bottle. I stayed home with Tommy and we sat on a blanket in the garden. You could see the hills in the distance at the back of the house. I remember Sacha must have been in the woods to the left of the garden, Tommy kept calling her but there was no sign."

"Sacha?" Josh said, confirming who it was.

"Yes, Sacha, our black cat. She was only nine months old, Tommy adored her. Cuddled her, stroked her, pulled her tail, but she was so placid and patient with him. It's a wonder she didn't claw at him. Perhaps she knew what he was doing was affectionate rather than intentionally aggravating," Christine said, looking into the distance.

"And did Sacha come home?"

"Oh yes, lived for another nine years before dying in her sleep. We lost her just last year. I don't think she ever got over Tommy either. They had such a close bond."

"What else can you tell me?" Josh made the odd note in his book whilst listening intently. He knew the smallest of detail could unravel and resolve the death of little Tommy.

"Well, me and Tommy stayed in the garden until Colin came back from the shop. I heard Colin's car pull up on the gravel driveway," she said, looking over Josh's shoulder at the front window and beyond onto the drive as if it happened yesterday.

Josh looked at Mrs. Malham and nodded slightly.

"I left Tommy on the blanket. The garden is secure you see. A small stone garden wall runs along the back of the garden, a wooden fence to the left which fences off the woods, and tall hedging to the right bordering our neighbours. They were so shocked about our news, they helped with the search." Christine snivelled slightly, bringing the tissue to her nose.

"And remind me again of your neighbours. Do they have family? Did they have young children at the time?" Josh looked down at the notes in the file. He had all the information to hand, the questions were routine to confirm the information he already had. Any slight difference in detail could lead him down a different avenue of investigation.

"Mr. and Mrs. Davidson are such wonderful people, they are more like family than friends. They have two boys, they were thirteen and fifteen at the time Tommy went missing. It completely shook them up."

"Did they know Tommy well? Did they babysit? Look after him? Play with him?" Josh took a short pause after each question.

"Oh yes, and completely trustworthy too. They even raised money in the village to plant a tree and get a plaque engraved. You've probably seen them driving through. Me and Colin paid for a bench to be placed next to the tree. I sit there regularly and think about my little boy."

Josh's heart started to feel heavy, he and his wife had not done anything like the Davidsons and Malham's had done for Tommy. He made a mental note to speak to Caroline about it when he got home. "I know this is difficult, Mrs. Malham, but can I ask, were you suspicious of anyone in the local area who might have wanted to hurt Tommy?"

Christine brought her hand to her lips and her eyes began to water. Her voice shook as she spoke. "Oh no, how could I possibly think that? I know everyone in this village, have done my entire life. There's not one person around here that would harm him, not one I tell you. I would much rather believe that he got disoriented, lost in the woods, and died in the cold of the night than to think anyone would hurt my Tommy. Perhaps you had better close the file again."

"I know they are not nice questions, Mrs. Malham, but they are needed to find out what really happened."

"You don't know anything, Detective," Christine said sternly.

Josh noticed the warmth and pleasantries had disappeared without warning.

"Please, Mrs. Malham. Let's bring closure for you and Colin."

"We had closure, he's gone. I don't want to talk about it anymore, now please leave."

Josh stood up whilst Christine remained seated. He looked down at her then across at Colin who had been leaning against the kitchen door frame, listening to every word that was coming out of his wife's mouth.

18

The late afternoon sun cast long shadows across Hallbankgate, its golden light softening the edges of the quaint village houses. Sandra Davidson stood at her living room window, her thin fingers parting the lace curtains just enough to peer out onto the street. Her eyes, lined with the wrinkles of worry that had deepened over the past ten years, widened as she spotted a familiar figure striding down the Malham's driveway.

"Daniel," she called out, her voice barely above a whisper. "Daniel, come quick!"

The urgency in her tone brought her husband rushing from the kitchen, a dish towel still clutched in his hands. "What is it, love?" he asked, joining her at the window.

Sandra's trembling finger pointed towards the retreating figure. "It's that police officer, you know, the one who investigated Tommy's death. I'm sure of it. He's just left the Malhams."

Daniel squinted, his face paling as he recognised the tall, broad-shouldered silhouette of Detective Chief Inspector, Josh Mills. The man's purposeful stride and the tell-tale folder tucked under his arm sent a chill down Daniel's spine.

"Christ," he muttered, his knuckles whitening as he gripped the window sill. "What is he doing around here after all this time?"

Sandra turned to her husband, her eyes searching his face for reassurance she knew he couldn't provide. "You don't think... after all these years... they couldn't have found out, could they?"

Daniel ran a hand through his thinning hair, his mind racing. "I don't know, love. But we can't take any chances." He moved swiftly to the mobile phone in his back pocket, his fingers pressing the screen with a familiar number with practised ease.

"Who are you calling?" Sandra asked, though the answer was already forming in her mind.

"Robert," Daniel replied, his voice tight with tension. "We need to warn the boys."

As the phone rang, Sandra sank into her favourite armchair, her hands clasped tightly in her lap. The ticking of the grandfather clock in the corner seemed unnaturally loud, each second stretching out as they waited for their eldest son to answer.

Finally, after what felt like an eternity, a deep voice came through the receiver. "Dad? What's up?"

Daniel took a deep breath, steeling himself. "Son, listen carefully. That detective, the one who investigated Tommy's death, he's been to see the Malhams again."

There was a sharp intake of breath on the other end of the line. "What? Why?"

"We don't know," Daniel said, his eyes meeting Sandra's worried gaze across the room. "But you need to tell Harry. Both of you need to be prepared, just in case."

"Dad, it's been ten years," Robert's voice cracked slightly, a hint of the scared teenager he once was bleeding through. "Surely they can't..."

"We're not taking any chances," Daniel cut in, his tone leaving no room for argument. "Remember what we agreed. Understand?"

There was a moment of silence before Robert responded, his voice now steadier. "Yeah, Dad. I understand. I'll call Harry right away."

"Good lad," Daniel said, some of the tension leaving his shoulders. "Your mother and I will keep an eye on things here. We'll let you know if anything else happens."

After hanging up, Daniel turned to Sandra. Her face was ashen, her normally rosy cheeks drained of colour. "What are we going to do, Daniel?" she whispered, voicing the fear that had haunted them for a decade.

As the afternoon light began to fade, casting long shadows across their living room, Daniel and Sandra Davidson sat in contemplative silence. The weight of their shared secret seemed to press down on them more heavily than ever before.

Sandra broke the silence, her voice trembling slightly. "Daniel, I've been thinking. Maybe it's time we told the truth."

Daniel's head snapped up, his eyes widening in shock. "What? Sandra, you can't be serious."

"But I am," she insisted, wringing her hands in her lap. "It's been ten years. Our boys are grown men now. Maybe if we come forward, explain what happened, they would understand."

Daniel stood up abruptly, pacing the room. "Explain what, exactly? Do you have any idea what that would do to them? To us?"

Sandra's eyes filled with tears. "I know it would be hard, but living with this secret is killing us, Daniel. It's eating away at our family. Robert barely visits anymore, and Harry has become so distant."

"And you think destroying their lives will bring them closer?" Daniel's voice rose, his face flushing with anger. "They've built careers, relationships. All of that would be gone in an instant if the truth came out."

"But what about Tommy's family?" Sandra countered, her own voice rising to match her husband's. "Don't they deserve to know what really happened to their son?"

Daniel stopped pacing, turning to face his wife. "Of course they do. But at what cost? Our boys were just children themselves when it happened. It was an accident, Sandra. A terrible, tragic accident."

"An accident we've lied about," Sandra said softly. "How many more years can we keep this up? What if the police do find something? Wouldn't it be better if the truth came from us?"

Daniel sank back into his chair, running a hand over his face. "And what about the Malhams? Have you thought about what this would do to them?"

Sandra's brow furrowed. "What do you mean?"

"Think about it," Daniel said, leaning forward. "If we come forward now, after all this time, it won't just be our family that suffers. The entire village will be turned upside down. And the Malhams ... they've finally started to heal. Do you want to rip that wound open again?"

Sandra was quiet for a moment, considering her husband's words. "I just can't help but think about Tommy. About what his parents must go through every day, not knowing."

Daniel's expression softened. He moved to sit beside his wife, taking her hands in his. "I know, love. I think about it too. But we made a choice back then, to protect our boys. And as hard as it is, we have to stick to that decision."

"But at what cost, Daniel?" Sandra's voice was barely above a whisper. "Look at what it's done to us, to our family. The boys might be safe, but they're not happy. They're carrying this weight just like we are."

Daniel sighed heavily. "I know. But think about the alternative. If we tell the truth now, they'll lose everything. Their careers, their freedom. They could go to prison, Sandra. Is that what you want for our sons?"

Sandra shook her head, tears spilling down her cheeks. "Of course not. I just want our family back. I want to be able to look at our boys without seeing the guilt in their eyes. I want to be able to walk through the village without feeling like everyone can see right through us."

Daniel pulled his wife close, his own eyes misting over. "I know, love. I want that too. But the only way we can have any semblance of that life is by keeping this secret. We have to stay strong, for Robert and Harry."

Sandra nodded against her husband's chest, her voice muffled. "You're right. Of course, you're right. It's just that sometimes the weight of it all feels like too much to bear."

Daniel stroked her hair gently. "We bear it together, Sandra. That's how we've made it this far, and that's how we'll continue. We protect our family, no matter what."

As they sat there, holding each other, the sound of a car door slamming outside made them both jump. Sandra pulled away, wiping her eyes hastily. "Do you think it could be the detective again?"

Daniel moved to the window, peering out through the curtains. He let out a relieved sigh. "No, it's just Mrs. Higgins from down the road. Probably back from her shopping trip."

Sandra nodded, her shoulders sagging with relief. But the tension in the room remained palpable.

The brief argument had brought their long-buried fears and doubts to the surface, and neither of them could shake the feeling that their carefully constructed life was teetering on the edge of a precipice.

Daniel turned back to his wife, his expression grave. "We need to be more careful than ever now, Sandra. No more talk of telling the truth, even between us. The walls have ears, and we can't risk anyone overhearing."

Sandra nodded, her face set in determination despite the lingering doubt in her eyes. "You're right. We've protected them this long. We can't falter now."

As the evening wore on, Sandra and Daniel tried to go about their normal routine, but the weight of their earlier conversation hung heavy in the air. They moved around each other carefully, as if the slightest misstep might shatter the fragile peace they'd managed to maintain for so long.

19

Tension hung in the air.

Christine and Colin stood in their hallway, the echo of the closed front door still reverberating through the house. Detective Chief Inspector Josh Mill's visit had left them both shaken, though for very different reasons.

Christine's eyes flashed with anger as she rounded on her husband. "What were you thinking, acting like that with DCI Mills? It'll only raise suspicion!"

Colin's jaw clenched, his fists balling at his sides. "What was I supposed to do? Invite him to stay for dinner?"

"You were supposed to act normal," Christine hissed. "Like a grieving father, not a guilty man with something to hide!"

At her words, Colin's face darkened. He strode towards his wife, his fingers roughly grabbing her chin. "Listen to me," he growled, his face inches from hers. "They must never know. Ever. Do you understand?"

Christine's eyes widened, a mixture of fear and defiance in her gaze. She nodded slowly.

Colin released his grip and turned away.

Christine's hand unconsciously went to her throat, her mind racing. The weight of their shared secret pressed down on them both, a burden that had grown heavier with each passing year.

She watched her husband's rigid back as he walked to the window, knowing that the unexpected visit from DCI Mills had shaken him to his core.

"Colin," she said softly, approaching her husband. "We need to be careful. We can't have Mills suspecting anything."

Colin turned from the window, his face a mask of determination. "He doesn't suspect a thing. He can't. We've been careful for ten years, Christine. We haven't slipped up once."

Christine nodded, though doubt lingered in her eyes. "I'm going to get ready for bed, take my mind off things."

Colin followed his wife through to the bedroom in tense silence. As Christine brushed her hair, she caught Colin's reflection in the mirror, watching her with an unreadable expression.

"What?" she asked, her voice sharper than she intended.

Colin shook his head. "Nothing. I was just thinking about Tommy. About how old he'd be now."

Christine's brush clattered to the dresser. "Don't," she whispered. "Please, Colin. I can't."

He crossed the room, placing his hands on her shoulders. "I'm sorry. I didn't mean to upset you. It's just seeing Mills today, it brought it all back."

Christine nodded, leaning back against her husband. "I know. For me too." She paused, hesitating before voicing the thought that had been nagging at her all evening. "Colin, do you ever think about—"

Colin's hands tightened on her shoulders. "Stop!" he said firmly. "The less we say the better."

Christine nodded, though the doubt lingered in her eyes. As they climbed into bed, she couldn't help but wonder how long they could continue living with the weight of the past.

20

As night fell over Hallbankgate, four individuals in two separate houses grappled with the weight of their secrets. In the Davidson home, Sandra busied herself in the kitchen, preparing a meal neither she nor Daniel had any appetite for. The familiar routine of chopping vegetables and stirring pots provided a welcome distraction from the turmoil in her mind.

Daniel sat in his study, pretending to work on some paperwork but was unable to focus. His thoughts kept drifting to his sons – to Robert, now 25, working as an architect in Manchester, and to Harry, 23, pursuing a PhD in marine biology. They had built good lives for themselves, despite the shadow that hung over their past. He couldn't bear the thought of all that coming crashing down now.

Sandra dished up their meal before walking away and paused as she passed Robert's old room, now serving as a guest bedroom. Her hand rested on the doorknob, and for a moment, she could almost hear the sounds of her boys laughing and playing, blissfully unaware of how one summer day would change their lives forever.

"Sandra?" Daniel's voice called softly from down the hall. "Are you coming to eat?"

She turned, forcing a smile. "Yes, dear. Just reminiscing, I suppose."

SHAME ON THEM

Daniel nodded, understanding in his eyes. Later, as they settled into bed, he reached for his wife's hand, squeezing it gently. "We'll get through this, love. We always have."

As they lay in the darkness, both pretending to sleep, Sandra and Daniel Davidson silently prayed that their words would prove true. That the secret buried in the woods would remain hidden, protecting their sons from a past they had tried so hard to leave behind.

***

In Manchester, Harry Davidson's phone buzzed showing a text notification on his screen.

"Did you hear from Dad?"

Harry stared at the message. "No, what's happened?" Harry responded.

"We need to talk." Robert texted back.

Harry stared at the screen and typed a message. "Robert? What's going on?"

"Dad's rang, that detective has been round to the Malham's house."

Harry's heart raced and his palms became sweaty. "What? What for?"

"Don't know yet, but mum and dad are assuming the worst. So, stick with what we said and we'll be fine, okay?"

Harry looked at the message and didn't respond. He turned his phone upside down on his bedside table next to the framed photo of him and Robert. The young faces grinned wildly at the camera without a care in the world. The picture had been taken just weeks before that fateful day in the woods. Before their lives had changed forever.

Harry closed his eyes, but sleep remained elusive.

Across the city, in his riverside apartment near the artisan bars and restaurants, Rob leaned over his balcony smoking a cigarette.

"Are you coming to bed, babe? A familiar female figure walked up behind him and nuzzled her lips into his neck. "I've been waiting for you," she said, feeling the rounded cheeks of his buttocks through his dressing gown.

"No, I've got too many things on my mind," he said, without looking at her.

"I can help you relax a little if you like?" The woman continued to stroke him in places trying to provoke a reaction.

"I said, no!" He snapped. He flicked his cigarette end into the river below and stormed off towards the bathroom. Inside he let his robe slip to the floor whilst he took a steaming hot shower hoping it would delete the memories of the past.

As the night wore on, four households connected by tragedy and deceit tried to find some peace. But sleep, when it finally came, was fitful and filled with dreams of dark woods, hidden bodies, and a relentless escape from the harsh reality of what was to come before it crushed them completely.

21

Detective Sergeant Mitchell unlocked the car and sat in the driver's seat. She started the engine, and before she crunched the gearbox into reverse, she adjusted the rear view mirror.

"What the?" She put the car back into neutral and pulled on the handbrake, left the engine running, opened the door, and got out.

Her heart raced as she recognised the familiar silhouette lurking in the shadows. Dexter Stone. The name sent a chill down her spine, memories of her past flooding back in a rush of adrenaline.

The fact he was following her made her angry. This was the latest of too many visits from him in too short a time. How had he found her here, in this quiet Cumbrian town? She'd been so careful, changed her name, and moved across the country. Yet here he was, a ghost from her past, threatening to unravel everything she'd built.

Fiona's mind raced with possibilities. Had Dexter been tracking her all this time? The thought made her feel exposed, vulnerable. She'd come to Kirkby Lonsdale for a fresh start, to escape the shadows of her past in Scotland. But her shadows had followed her, embodied in the menacing figure of Dexter Stone.

She turned around and took a step forward, her police training kicking in despite the fear churning in her gut. But before she could reach him, Dexter Stone was nowhere to be seen. The sudden disappearance left her more unsettled than if he'd stayed.

Was she imagining things? Had the stress of the case, combined with the anxiety of starting a new job, caused her to conjure up shadows from her past?

She got back in the car, took some deep breaths and drove off. Her hands shook slightly on the steering wheel, her mind a whirlwind of conflicting thoughts.

Should she tell Josh about this? But how could she explain Dexter without revealing the darker parts of her past, the secrets she'd hoped to leave behind?

Fiona knew she would have to sort this one way or another, but she didn't currently have a solution.

The presence of Dexter Stone complicated everything. What did he want? Revenge? To drag her back into the life she'd fought so hard to escape? She'd have to be on her guard now, watching every shadow, questioning every stranger.

She shook her head a little to ease her mind from her previous life and concentrated on the case in hand instead, driving back towards Kirkby Lonsdale.

Fiona expertly manoeuvred her car into a tight parking spot on one of Kirkby Lonsdale's narrow side streets. After locking up, she followed Alex's vague directions towards Fully Baked. Turning left down a cramped and dimly lit alleyway, she caught a glimpse of the cosy cafe nestled in front of her.

There were only a few patrons scattered around the outdoor seating area. She thought it would have been busier on an afternoon in a tourist town. The scent of freshly brewed coffee and warm pastries beckoned to Fiona, inviting her inside.

SHAME ON THEM

As she approached the cafe, Fiona couldn't shake the feeling of being watched. She glanced over her shoulder, half expecting to see Dexter's imposing figure looming behind her. The alley suddenly seemed too narrow, too confining. She quickened her pace, relief washing over her as she reached the cafe's entrance.

"We close in thirty minutes so you'll have to be quick."

Fiona's gaze fell upon the rotund man standing before her, his round body adorned with a tan coloured apron bearing the logo of the café, a whimsical cupcake. He did not exude the charming warmth of the typical cafe owner one would find in Edinburgh.

His features were plain, lacking any distinct character or charm. She couldn't help but feel disappointed as she had hoped for a more pleasant encounter at this quaint little cafe.

As Fiona approached the counter, she showed her police ID lanyard. She could see a flash of surprise and recognition flicker across the owner's face. "Who are you?" she asked, maintaining a calm but authoritative tone.

"Dave Potter, what do you want with me?"

"I don't know if you've heard, but there have been a couple of incidents in the town over the past few days and I'm just looking to corroborate someone's story. Do you have any CCTV?"

"Ha, you'll be lucky. Couldn't keep up with the payments, it's been tough you know, the past few months. Customers moaning about the prices or the quality of the food. I'm doing the best I can." He shook his head and wiped a table.

"I'm sure it's difficult, I don't think many made it through the pandemic so you should be pleased with yourself."

"Is that what you call it?" Dave's face was lined with exhaustion, his eyes drooping with worry. The once bright logo on his shirt was now faded and frayed, his apron stained with flour and cocoa.

Fiona frowned a little, incredulous at Mr. Potter's attitude. "Anyway, can you verify something for me?" Fiona pulled out a picture of Jess that Alex had given her. "Did you see this woman here a couple of days ago? She was with a gentleman, about five eight, mousy brown hair." As Fiona pulled out the picture, Mr. Potter's face went from surprise to annoyance. His eyes narrowed and his lips pressed together in a tight line.

"So, what if I did?"

Fiona thought she was missing something. "Like I say, I just want to corroborate a story."

Dave Potter paused and placed his hands on his hips, recalling the encounter. "Oh yeah, I remember them. They came around two o'clock and boy, were they rude. The woman was quite stuck up; she even complained about our freshly baked bread. Can you believe it? I tried to explain that it was made just that day, but she still wasn't satisfied."

"Did that annoy you, Mr. Potter?"

"Don't be absurd, it's just part of the job dealing with difficult customers. There's nothing we can do about it these days but carry on." He quickly wiped down the next table, balancing a few dirty mugs in his other hand.

"And you didn't see anything or anyone acting suspiciously?"

"Of course not," Mr. Potter said, looking up. "You must be new to this town, I can hear a faint Scottish accent and I don't recognise you."

Fiona thought the cafe owner was starting to relax a little. "Pretty new, yeah," she said, not wanting to delve further with a stranger into her past or why she had moved. She moved on quickly. "So, there is nothing you want to tell me, maybe something you thought was unusual but thought nothing of it at the time?"

"No. I'll give you a call if I remember anything. Oh hang on, there was something which was weird, the stupid cow came back the next day with her husband. Why would you do that if you didn't like something the first time around?"

"Right, well, here's my card. If you remember anything else, please contact me."

Fiona couldn't shake off the feeling of unease as she quickly made her way out of the cafe. She looked over her shoulder and her eyes darted directly at the cafe owner who was staring right back at her. It gave Fiona Mitchell the chills.

Fiona got back into her car and immediately checked her rearview mirror. She scanned the streets too many times, to the point of obsession. Every tall, broad-shouldered man made her heart skip a beat, wondering if it was Dexter.

The town that had seemed so quaint and welcoming now felt full of potential threats, hiding places where her past could lurk, waiting to pounce.

Fiona fastened her seatbelt, put her foot down, and headed for the motorway.

22

After a two hour drive from Kirkby Lonsdale, Fiona Mitchell stepped foot into the foyer of Hambledon House in city centre Manchester. An imposing purpose built glass building housing the offices of Catalyst Consulting. The foyer's ceiling was right at the top of the building, at least fifteen stories high Fiona thought to herself.

With plenty of artificial plants and leather seating, it could be mistaken for a top class consultant's waiting room in the centre of London. *'Still,'* she thought, *'I'm sure Catalyst's clients are paying through the nose for a foyer like this.'*

She walked over to the reception desk, where an immaculately dressed woman with a dark sleep ponytail and manicured nails sat waiting for her to approach.

"Good morning, and welcome to Hambledon House, how may I help you today?"

"I'm here to visit the offices of Catalyst Consulting, could you tell me which floor please?"

"Who are you here to see specifically, madam?"

"Mm, well, I'm not sure you need to know that as it's private and you don't appear to be a part of Catalyst Consulting."

"That's where you're wrong, I'm sub-contracted by all the offices to manage their visitors, so if you tell me who you have an appointment with, I can telephone ahead and let you through the security gate," the receptionist said with a stern smile.

Fiona looked at her name badge. "In that case, Felicity Chapman, I'm here to see Bill Smith."

"And what time is your appointment with him today, Miss ..."

"Detective Sergeant, Fiona Mitchell, and I don't have an appointment," she said, showing the receptionist her ID.

"I'm very sorry I can't let you through then. Mr. Smith has left very firm instructions not to be disturbed today. He has something important to deal with."

"Well, Miss Chapman, I expect it's the same thing I'm here to speak to him about. So if you could let him know I'm here, that would be really helpful."

Without a further word, Felicity Chapman pressed her touchscreen and spoke through her headset.

"Yes, yes, says she has no appointment but needs to speak to Mr. Smith, it's urgent apparently. Mm hmm, mm hmm, okay I'll tell her to come up." Felicity pressed a button on the side of her ear piece to end the internal call. "Okay go on up please. Walk through that gate, to the lift on the right, and Catalyst Consulting are on the top floor."

"Of course they are," Fiona said, smiling. "Because their clients are paying penthouse prices," she muttered under her breath.

"I'm sorry, I didn't quite catch that."

"No, you weren't meant to," Fiona said, walking off.

Fiona stepped into the lift, her mind racing with the possibilities of what she might uncover during her meeting with Bill Smith.

The death of Dan Walsh had sent shockwaves through the community, and the pressure was on to find answers. As the lift ascended to the top floor, Fiona took a deep breath, steeling herself for the confrontation ahead.

The doors opened, revealing a sprawling, opulent office space. Sunlight streamed through the floor-to-ceiling windows, casting a warm glow over the expensive furniture and modern art pieces. Fiona stepped out, her eyes scanning the room for any sign of Bill Smith.

"Ah, Detective Mitchell," a smooth voice called out from across the room. "I've been expecting you. Bill Smith," he said, holding out his hand in advance.

Fiona turned to see Bill Smith striding towards her, a confident smirk on his face. He was short and impeccably dressed, his tailored suit and polished shoes exuding an air of wealth and power. As he approached, he reached for her hand, his grip firm and almost painful.

"How can I help?" He asked, his tone dripping with condescension. "I must say, I'm not surprised to see you here after what happened to poor Dan."

"How did you know?"

"Oh, his ex-partner, Julia, she telephoned me to let me know. Poor woman is devastated."

"Anything you can tell us would be helpful, Mr. Smith. I'd just like to ask you a few questions."

Bill's eyes narrowed. "And what questions would they be, exactly? Because as far as I'm concerned, we don't have anything to do with Dan's death."

Fiona met his gaze, her voice calm but firm. "I'm not saying you do, but I've heard rumours that Dan was experiencing some stressful situations at work before he died. I was hoping you could shed some light on those."

Bill scoffed, his posture stiffening. "Stressful situations? Please. Dan was one of our top consultants. He thrived under pressure. If anything, he was more stressed about his personal life than his work."

Fiona raised an eyebrow, her interest piqued. "His personal life? What do you mean by that?"

Bill waved his hand dismissively. "Oh, you know how it is. Relationship troubles, family drama, that sort of thing. But it never affected his work. He was a consummate professional."

Fiona nodded, her mind racing with the new information. "I see. And you never noticed any changes in his behaviour leading up to his death? No signs that he was struggling with anything?"

Bill's eyes flashed with anger, his voice rising. "Are you deaf, Detective? I just told you, Dan was fine. He was one of our best employees, and the clients loved him. There was nothing more to it, as far as I'm concerned."

Fiona felt her own frustration mounting, but she refused to let it show. "With all due respect, Mr. Smith, it's my job to investigate all possibilities. I'm not accusing Catalyst Consulting of anything, but I have to follow up on every lead, no matter how small."

Bill leaned forward, his face inches from hers. "Let me make something very clear, Detective Sergeant Mitchell. Catalyst Consulting is a respected, successful company. We have a reputation to uphold."

"I appreciate that, but we have Dan's death to look into. By all accounts, a valued employee of your firm. So surely you want to know what happened to him? That is ... unless you have anything to hide?" Fiona waited for a response but Bill Smith remained silent, so she continued. "Now, if you would cooperate without the attitude that would be greatly appreciated."

Bill moved to sit back in his leather chair and straightened his Oxford striped tie. He bit his bottom lip before speaking. "Of course, I apologise."

"Thank you. Now I believe Dan had uncovered some fraudulent figures within the company but you refused to investigate."

Bill fidgeted in his seat and bit the wicks of his thumb nail. "I ... I'm not sure what you mean. Who has told you that?"

"It's irrelevant, but we do have to look into it and make sure we're satisfied it has nothing to do with his death."

"What are you implying, Detective?"

"I'm not implying anything. I'm simply asking a question."

"It's true that he thought he had found some anomalies but I did go away and investigate, contrary to what you have been told. Marcus Blackwood, one of our directors, had incorrectly entered some figures on the system. I didn't pursue it further than that because Mr. Blackwood's wife had just died of cancer and he was grieving. I allowed him to come back to work shortly after the funeral because he said he needed to take his mind off it. In reality, I should have insisted he stay at home until he felt he was ready to return to the office."

"I see. So it was something that was easily fixable. You didn't have to report it to your regulatory body or any clients?"

"No, I didn't. There was no actual cash missing from the bank account, just a transposed figure that was rectified by the accounts department. I called Dan into a meeting and told him what had happened."

"And was Dan happy with the outcome? He wasn't angry in any way?"

"Not that I recall, no."

Without being asked, Fiona sat down and leaned back in her chair and crossed her legs whilst keeping her notebook open. "Okay, and there were no disputes between Dan and perhaps any other member of staff? Nothing that was brought to your attention?" Fiona thought she saw Bill hesitate and his eyes flit to the side.

"Erm, no, no, definitely not."

"You seem very sure of that," she said, looking up. "I'm only asking because it has been inferred that you were, I quote *'cutting corners.'*"

Bill Smith sat up in his seat. "How dare you. I would do no such thing. I have worked here for ten years and take my role very seriously. Now, I don't know who told you that, but as I said, there was nothing else that I recall, Detective," he said, abruptly.

"Hm," Fiona said, looking down briefly at her notebook. "Just one last question then, where were you on Thursday evening, say between the hours of 10pm Thursday night and 2am Friday morning?"

"I was at home, in bed!"

"Is there anyone who can verify that?" Fiona sat for what felt like minutes.

"I'd rather not say, it's private."

Fiona raised her eyebrows. "And I would rather you did. This is an investigation. I'm sure you don't want to be seen as withholding information given your position with the firm, and how seriously you take your role here," she said, smiling sternly.

"We had a few drinks after work, we took advantage of *'Thirsty Thursday.'* Dan said he couldn't make it as he was away."

"That doesn't tell me what I need to know, Mr. Smith. Who were you with?"

Bill Smith looked over Fiona's shoulder, making sure the door was firmly closed. "Look, do I have to? I'm a very private man."

"I appreciate that, but I will do my best to keep this between us unless it's needed in court."

Bill Smith gulped and looked up to the ceiling. "Needed in court?" He frowned. "I couldn't possibly say under oath what I'm about to tell you, it would destroy everything I have."

Fiona smiled inside, *'what a shame,'* she thought.

Bill Smith continued when Fiona didn't respond. "Myself and ... Felicity ... we erm ..."

Fiona interrupted. "That would be Felicity on reception downstairs?"

"Yes, yes, that's right," Bill said, almost in a whisper, whilst twisting his wedding ring.

Fiona's eyes fell to the platinum band on Bill Smith's finger. "Look, Mr. Smith, if it makes it any easier, I'm not here to judge. We all have secrets we would rather stay buried, but I do need to eliminate you from our enquiries."

Bill sighed and his demeanour softened a little. "Felicity and I shared a hotel room. My wife was at home with our six month old daughter, and things have been a little... strained to say the least."

Fiona nodded. "And you were with Felicity until when?"

"The next morning until around 8am. I told my wife I was staying at Duncan's house, he's a friend of mine. I've done a few favours for him in the past so he does the same for me. Felicity and I left the hotel separately and came straight to work on the Friday morning."

"Okay, that's all for now, I'll have to speak to Felicity to confirm your story, but it shouldn't take long."

"Look, Detective, I can tell her to come up now so you can tick it off your list. I'm sorry for being so cold with you when you arrived, it's just, things have been a little rough around here. Business isn't as good as it should be and I'm under pressure."

Fiona offered a compassionate smile. "Do you think Dan has been mixed up in that in any way?"

"No, not at all. I guarantee it. Dan was as good as you got and I'm genuinely sad this has happened to him. He was a great guy with an eye for detail, hence finding the transposed figures. Good with clients, everyone liked him."

"Okay, thank you," Fiona sighed. "If you can call Felicity up that would be helpful."

A few minutes later Felicity Chapman sat down in front of Fiona, a mahogany desk between them. She pulled her skirt down to reach her knees and folded her hands in her lap.

Bill had closed the blinds and switched the sign on the front of the glass door to '*Engaged*' so they wouldn't be disturbed.

Felicity looked at Fiona then burst into tears.

"Felicity? What is it?" Fiona frowned and spoke softly, dropping the harsh attitude she had earlier demonstrated with the receptionist.

"I'm sorry, I'm just upset that this has happened."

Fiona sighed. "You know then?"

Felicity nodded and pulled a handkerchief out of her black handbag. "Bill told me early this morning, I can't believe it. Who would do such a thing to Dan?"

"That's what I'm trying to find out. I need to ask you a couple of questions, is that okay?" Fiona said, gently.

Felicity nodded.

"Where were you on Thursday night, Felicity, between the hours of 10pm Thursday, and 2am Friday morning?"

Felicity's cheeks turned pink, the flush spread down her neck and covered the top part of her chest on show in the 'V' of her open neck blouse.

"It's okay, it won't go any further at this stage," Fiona confirmed.

"I spent the night with Mr. Smith, but I felt so bad. I was angry and feeling hurt after Dan said he wasn't coming for drinks. He was going on his friend's stag do but I would have much preferred him to come out with us."

"Why is that, Felicity? Were you and Dan close?"

Felicity nodded as tears fell down her mottled cheeks. "We had started seeing each other but only briefly. He was feeling lonely after Julia, and I had liked him for a while. Stupidly, I thought I could cheer him up."

"Go on," Fiona said, taking notes.

"Bill ... sorry, Mr. Smith had arranged some drinks after work for everyone. The department needed a bit of cheering up, they have been under a bit of pressure apparently. I was invited, you know, because I help out at the reception. I was so excited that Dan would be there." Felicity sniffled into her tissue then looked up before carrying on. "I liked him a lot. But then I found out he wasn't coming. So ... I had too many drinks, and went back with Mr. Smith." Felicity looked towards the desk.

"Felicity, how long were you with Mr. Smith?"

"All night, until around 7.30am the following morning when I left the hotel and came straight here. I used the work showers to freshen up before I started work. We were together all night," she said, shaking her head.

"Why not use the shower at the hotel?"

"I was so ashamed at what I had done, I just wanted to get out of there as quickly as possible."

"Okay, thank you, that's all for now. Can you go home and get some rest?"

"No, I'd rather keep working. I don't want to think about what's happened, this is just awful."

"Actually, just one more question if I may. Do you think Dan's ex, Julia, may have known that you liked him?"

"I don't know if Julia knew, I suppose it's possible. I mean, Dan was pretty cut up about the split, so he may have told her to make her jealous, but he didn't say anything to me."

"Thanks, Felicity, I'll leave you alone now." Fiona stood up and smiled at Felicity, then turned around and walked out of the room leaving Felicity to her grief.

With that, she turned and walked back towards the lift and felt someone watching her. The tiny hairs on the back of her neck stood on end and she turned around sharply. "Oh, Mr. Smith, it's you."

"Got everything you need?"

"For now. I'll be in touch if there is anything else." Fiona let out a long breath, her mind reeling with the new information she'd gleaned.

23

Fiona pushed the double swing doors open and walked into the department.

Josh stood facing the incident board, the end of a biro in his mouth.

Fiona walked over to her desk, removed her leather jacket and placed it over the back of her chair, then confidently walked over to the incident board and stood next to her partner. She watched him draw a black line connecting photographs and facts to try and make some sense of what had happened.

"How did you get on? Anything interesting?" Josh didn't need to turn around; he could sense his partner's presence.

"It was a little strange, to be honest."

"What was?"

"I'll come to Bill Smith at Crystal Consulting in a minute, but as for Dave Potter, he is one weird guy!"

"How come?"

When I asked him about Alex and Jess being at the cafe, his behaviour seemed strange. And when I showed him a photo of Jess, I could have sworn I saw a glimmer of fear in his eyes."

"Sure you're not imagining it? I know we are all keen to get this resolved. Don't let your mind play tricks on you."

"I'm not. I've seen enough suspicion over the years to know what's genuine and what's not. I think we should bring him in for questioning."

"On what basis?" Josh said whilst still concentrating on the board."

"I don't know, I'll think of something," Fiona sighed a little. As for Bill Smith, I don't think there's anything there to follow up on. Smith has an alibi for the whole evening and although I thought he may have had something to do with it after speaking to Julia, he was with the receptionist all night. Seems a bit of a mistake on her part. When I asked her where she was the night of Dan's murder, her story was the same as Bill's. She was with him all night in a hotel. She had gotten drunk after pining for Dan. Felicity Chapman had a thing for Dan and was disappointed when he said he wasn't going for drinks after work. I suppose if he had done, he might still be alive."

"You don't think the murder could be the result of a jealous love triangle?"

"What do you mean, Josh?"

"Julia finds out about Felicity liking Dan, Julia still loves Dan, regrets getting together with Mark, and kills Dan out of frustration?"

"I doubt it. Felicity didn't sound convinced that Dan had told Julia about him and Felicity."

"Mm. Okay well let's park that for now. Aside from the cafe owner being a bit weird, we don't have anything to go on after today's questioning?" Josh turned around.

Fiona put her hands on her hips. "Not at the moment, I still don't know if these murders are linked. There seems to be no crossover."

"They might be two completely random murders but close together time wise?" Josh replied.

"What did you say to me? No coincidences?" Fiona said.

"You're right," Josh said.

Suddenly, Graham barged through the double doors leaving them swinging on their own.

"Sir!"

"Yes, Graham?"

"Jess' phone is unlocked and I've printed out the call history. Other than James' name repeated often by text and phone call, there doesn't seem to be anything else of interest. But I'll let you figure that one out."

"Thanks, Graham," Josh said, taking the computer printout off his colleague.

"I've highlighted the entries and his number is on there."

Josh scanned the text and numbers. "I wonder what James' relationship was with Jess?"

"Don't know but he rang again about thirty minutes ago too. I ignored it obviously. I'll leave you to call him back," Graham said, walking out of the department.

"Right, time to make a call," Josh said, walking over to his desk and taking his mobile out of his pocket.

24

Josh dialled the number highlighted on the call log, putting the phone on speaker so Fiona could hear. After three rings, a man's voice answered, tense and brittle with barely contained emotion.

"Hello? Who is this?" The voice demanded.

"This is Detective Chief Inspector Josh Mills from Cumbria Police. Am I speaking to James Wilkinson?"

There was a sharp intake of breath on the other end of the line. "Yes, that's me. Is this about Jess?"

Josh exchanged a glance with Fiona before responding. "Yes, Mr. Wilkinson. We're investigating the circumstances surrounding Jessica Chepstow's death. Can you tell me about your relationship with her?"

The line went quiet for a moment, then James' voice came back, thick with emotion. "She was... we were... Look, you need to know something. It wasn't me. Whatever happened to Jess, I had nothing to do with it. It was that bastard, Alex, I'm sure of it!"

Josh's eyebrows shot up at the vehemence in James' voice. "Mr. Wilkinson, that's a serious accusation and we didn't tell you about Jess' death, so who informed you?"

"Him! He texted me and said *'I hope you're happy now she's gone.'* I've never read anything so heartless in all my life."

"Are you referring to Alex?"

"Of course I am, who else would I be talking about?"

Josh heard James sigh on the other end of the phone. "And can you explain why you think Alex Chepstow might be involved in his wife's death?"

James' words came in a rush, as if a dam had broken. "Because he's a controlling, jealous bastard! Jess was miserable with him. She was going to leave him, you know. We were in love. We were planning a future together."

Fiona leaned in closer to the phone, her interest piqued. "Mr. Wilkinson, how long had your relationship with Jess been going on?"

"Six months," James replied, his voice softening slightly. "Six wonderful months. Jess was finally happy. But Alex was furious. He had found a message from me that Jess forgot to delete. Alex assumed Jess was seeing me behind his back."

"Well, you were, weren't you?" Josh said.

"Yes, but that's not the point, Jess told me they had a blazing row just before they left for Kirkby Lonsdale. Apparently, Alex stormed out of the house and refused to go away with her. Jess rang me in tears. Alex is always checking her phone, he's so controlling and watching her every move, she felt like a prisoner in her own home!"

Josh's voice remained calm and professional. "And you're certain Alex knew about your relationship with his wife?"

"He must have!" James insisted, his voice rising again. "Why else would Jess be dead? She was supposed to meet me with him. We were going to tell Alex together. But she never showed up, and now... now she's gone."

The raw pain in James' voice was palpable, even through the phone. Josh pressed on, "Mr. Wilkinson, where were you on Friday afternoon and into the evening?"

"I was at home, waiting for Jess to turn up with Alex so we could tell him," my sister can verify that. She loved Jess," James replied, a note of desperation creeping into his voice. "I called and texted Jess dozens of times. I thought... I thought maybe Alex had stopped her from leaving. I never imagined... God, I should have gone to find her. I should have known something was wrong!"

Fiona interjected. "Did Jess ever mention feeling threatened by Alex? Did she fear for her safety?"

There was a pause, then James spoke, his voice lower now. "Not directly. But she was always on edge, always checking over her shoulder. She'd make excuses for why she couldn't meet, saying Alex was suspicious. I begged her to leave him sooner, but she was scared. She said Alex had a temper, that he'd never let her go."

Josh and Fiona exchanged significant looks. This was a new angle they hadn't considered before.

"Mr. Wilkinson," Josh said, "we'll need you to come down to the station at some point to make a formal statement. Can you do that?"

"Of course," James replied quickly. "Anything to help find out what happened to Jess. But please, you have to believe me. I loved her. I would never hurt her. It was Alex. It had to be Alex. He couldn't stand the thought of losing her, so he... he..." James' voice broke, unable to finish the sentence.

"We'll investigate all possibilities, Mr. Wilkinson," Josh assured him. "Please come to the station as soon as you can. And thank you for your cooperation."

As Josh ended the call, the office fell into a stunned silence.

"Well," Fiona said after a moment, "that certainly complicates things."

"Yeah, well I'm not ruling either of them out. The only alibi for the time of the murder is that he was at home. And, apparently, Alex was not too happy to hear from Jess about this previous relationship. He never mentioned that outside the hotel, did he?" Josh stood up from his desk and walked over to the board, he added James' name to it and drew a black line between him, Jess, and Alex. He stood there for a moment. "What motivation would James have to kill Jess? If he couldn't have her then no one else could? A strong possibility but if James is right about being at home there is no way the timings would fit. Fiona, ask Stewart to call James and arrange for him to make a formal statement." Without waiting for an answer he pressed on. "I'm not happy about these allegations. We need to bring Alex in again. And Sam, did you get anywhere with Jenny?"

"There's been no answer, let me try again now."

"She lives thirty five miles North of the town, and by all accounts she was surprised to see him in a police car," Josh said to Fiona.

"Very odd if you ask me that she would be there when Jess is murdered, and Alex is sat in a police car. Particularly because she has a job not far from her home."

"I agree." Josh looked over to Sam's desk when he heard him speak.

"Hi, Jenny, this is PC Sam McKay, my colleague Detective Sergeant Fiona Mitchell, spoke to you outside the Kings Hotel yesterday, I just need to ask you some more questions if that's okay?"

"Oh, hi, yes I remember, how can I help?"

"Can I ask, what were you doing in Kirkby Lonsdale? It's a bit of a coincidence you should bump into Alex, isn't it?"

"First of all can you tell me what happened please?" Jenny asked.

"Mrs. Jess Chepstow was found dead under suspicious circumstances so we are investigating."

"Good riddance." Jenny did not seem to shred one ounce of remorse.

Sam wrote this revelation down in his notebook.

"I was shopping, I needed to get my mum and dad a present, their birthdays are close together and it's their 70th's, there isn't a shop in Coniston that had what I wanted."

"Isn't it a bit of a long way to come from Coniston? And don't you work, Jenny? Alex mentioned to me that you work for The National Trust. Day off was it?"

"Not quite a day off, no. I felt a bit ropey in the morning so I called in sick but felt a bit brighter at lunchtime so, I decided to get some fresh air and cheer myself up with some shopping."

"And how did you get to Kirkby Lonsdale?" Asked Sam.

"By bus. I caught the number 505 from Coniston to Kendal, then the 567 from Kendal to Kirkby Lonsdale. I arrived around 2pm."

"Seems a bit extreme doesn't it? Two buses just to buy a couple of gifts? Was anybody with you? Do you have any witnesses, Jenny?"

"No, of course I don't. I don't need chaperoning when I go shopping, you know."

"And what is your history with Alex? How do you know each other?"

"We are best friends. I love him. Always have, I guess he just never felt the same way about me. I never stopped hoping he would give up on her and come and live with me instead. Jess didn't deserve him. He was far too good for that cow." Jenny said angrily.

Sam seemed surprised at Jenny's outburst. "Thanks for your time, Jenny. I will get on to the bus station right away and ask for the CCTV footage. Also, could you come in and give us a DNA sample? So we can eliminate you from our enquiries?"

Jenny hesitated for a few moments. "Erm, yes, yes, I suppose I can do that. I just hope that Alex may finally decide to live his life with someone who genuinely cares about him now that she's gone."

"Thanks for your time." Sam put the phone down and pondered what Jenny had told him.

"Any luck?" Josh shouted over.

"She's a bit of a feisty one, isn't she? She almost seemed pleased that Jess was dead. I think she's hoping Alex and her will be together now. Odd if you ask me, it's not the sort of thing you say when you have heard of the death of your best friend's wife. I've asked her to come in to give a DNA sample and I'll check CCTV with the buses."

"Good work," Fiona said. "Let us know if you find anything from the CCTV."

"On it," Sam said.

"I just have no idea at the moment, do you?" Josh asked.

"No, I don't." But Fiona's mind was also elsewhere.

"Fiona? Are you okay? You seem miles away."

"Yeah, I'm fine. Just fine." She hoped she had spoken with conviction because she certainly didn't believe the words that had come out of her own mouth.

25

The results of the post-mortems of Dan Walsh and Jess Norris were back. Mills and Fiona sat reading them. Pinned to the nearby noticeboard were the pictures from the crime scenes.

"The causes of death are pretty clear," Fiona said, her voice tight with tension. "Deep cuts to the stomach and chest on Dan Walsh, but it was a heart attack that eventually killed him, probably from the shock, poor sod. A deep cut to the neck on Jess Chepstow, severing the main artery. She would have bled out within minutes."

Josh nodded, his eyes fixed on the report. "The knife used in both instances was an 8-inch kitchen knife, non-serrated."

Fiona looked up, her brow furrowed. "I think we just got our first connection with the knife, don't you?"

"It's possible," Josh replied, his mind racing with possibilities. "But we can't jump to conclusions just yet. There are still a few things that don't add up."

The crime scene photos, pinned to the noticeboard, served as a grim reminder of the brutal nature of the murders. The silence in the room was heavy, broken only by the occasional rustling of papers and the soft hum of the fluorescent lights.

Josh stood up and walked over to the incident board, his eyes scanning the grizzly photos. "Look at this," he said, pointing to a picture of Jess' body on the bed. "The cut was made from behind, yet she was found flat on her back. And the blood splatters on the carpet and the wall, they're consistent with someone being cut while standing up."

Fiona joined him at the board, her eyes narrowing as she studied the photos. "So, either the killer threw her onto the bed after cutting her throat, or..."

"Or Jess was conscious for a few seconds after the attack," Josh finished, his voice grim. "Long enough to stagger back to the bed before she collapsed."

Fiona shuddered at the thought.

Josh shook his head, his mind spinning with possibilities. "Maybe the killer was disturbed with Jess, and had to change their plans. Unlike with Dan, where the killer disposed of his body in the bin before he left the scene."

"What do you mean?" Fiona asked, her curiosity piqued.

"Think about it," Josh said, his voice low and intense. "If the killer had planned to dispose of Jess' body, they would have had to move quickly. But if they got interrupted, they might have had to improvise."

Fiona nodded, her mind racing to keep up with Josh's train of thought. "So, you think the killer might have been forced to leave the body where it was?"

"It's possible," Josh replied, his eyes distant as he considered the implications. "But if that's the case, it means they're more than just a cold-blooded killer. They're adaptable, able to think on their feet."

Fiona shivered, the thought of such a cunning and ruthless killer on the loose sending a chill down her spine. "What about the knife?" she asked, trying to steer the conversation back to the facts at hand. "We must have enough information to trace it back to a specific manufacturer or retailer?"

Frustration was etched on Josh's face. "Let's get Stewart to investigate where the knife was bought. Honestly, I'd start in the hardware shop on the main street. Long shot but might as well."

Fiona sighed, the weight of the case pressing down on her. "So, where does that leave us? We have two victims, killed in similar ways, but no clear motive and no solid leads on the killer."

Josh turned to face her, his eyes blazing with determination. "It leaves us with a lot of work to do. We need to dig deeper, look for any connections between Jess and Dan that we might have missed."

Fiona nodded, her resolve strengthening in the face of Josh's conviction.

Josh considered the idea for a moment, then shook his head. "We can't make an appeal just yet. If the killer is as smart as we think they are, they'll be watching the news, waiting to see what we know. An appeal might spook them, make them more cautious."

"So, we keep it quiet for now," Fiona said, her voice low and conspiratorial. "Work the case from the inside, see what we can turn up."

"Exactly," Josh replied, a grim smile playing at the corners of his mouth. "And we don't stop until we catch this bastard, no matter how long it takes."

Fiona returned his smile, her eyes glinting with a fierce determination. "Damn right. We owe it to Jess and Dan, and to every other victim out there who hasn't gotten justice yet."

"There's something else," Josh frowned, tapping his pen against the desk. "Jess' room key - where is it?"

Fiona looked up from her notes, her brow furrowing. "You're right. We never did find it, did we? And we forgot to ask Alex about it."

"Exactly," Josh said, leaning back in his chair. "Let's think this through. If Alex still has the key, that could be significant. But if he doesn't..."

"Then someone else must have it," Fiona finished. "But who? And why?"

Josh stood up, pacing the room. "Okay, let's consider our options. If Alex doesn't have it, Jess could have lost it."

"Which seems unlikely," Fiona interjected. "She was found in her room, after all."

"Right," Josh nodded. "So, if she didn't lose it, and Alex doesn't have it, then who does?"

"The killer must have taken it," Fiona said, her eyes widening with realisation.

Josh snapped his fingers. "Exactly. But why? What purpose would that serve?"

Fiona tapped her chin thoughtfully. "Maybe to cover their tracks? To make it look like Jess let them in willingly?"

"Possible," Josh mused. "Or maybe they're planning to return to the scene. Though that seems risky." Josh's eyebrows shot up. "We need to speak to Alex about the room key."

"Should we bring him in for questioning again?" Fiona asked.

Josh shook his head. "Not yet. Let's call him first. We don't want to spook him if he is involved."

Fiona nodded, reaching for her phone. "I'll do it now. What exactly should I ask?"

"Keep it casual," Josh advised. "Just say we're following up on a few details. Ask if he remembers what happened to their room key. Don't let on that we think it might be important."

"Okay."

"One thing is really bugging me," said Josh. "If Alex and Jenny wanted Jess dead, would they do it? And would Jenny be stupid enough to be caught in the area trying to talk to Alex?"

"Let's see what the CCTV shows from the bus when we have it." Said Fiona. "But for now, all we have is her husband, best friend, and lover, as potential suspects. Other than that the trail has gone cold. Just like the investigation into Dan Walsh's murder too."

Josh sighed, running a hand through his hair. "And now we have this missing key to contend with. It could be nothing."

"But it could be everything," Fiona finished. "I'll get on to Alex now."

26

Pete Bowler let out a contented sigh as he envisioned his evening plans with Natalie.

After a long day at work, all he wanted was to get home and spend time with his girlfriend of twelve years. Struggling into clothes that were too tight for him and would leave a red ring around his belly, Pete and Natalie would chat about their take-out dinner and a bottle of wine, followed by cuddling on the sofa while watching the latest blockbuster on Netflix.

Even though it was a midweek night, they didn't care - it was their ritual after a busy weekend. The thought of being in each other's arms, surrounded by the comforting glow of the TV screen, made Pete's heart swell with warmth and happiness.

Natalie had waited anxiously for a proposal for twelve years. She had vivid images of the wedding of her dreams - a lavish celebration with a grand buffet filled with delectable delicacies, tables adorned with delicate peach flowers, and a voluminous meringue dress that would make her feel like a princess. It may have been considered outdated by some, but this was the wedding she had dreamed about since she was a little girl, playing dress up in her mother's old gowns. Every detail had been meticulously planned in her mind for years, which would make the moment when Pete finally proposed, even more exciting.

Pete's heart overflowed with love for his girlfriend, but he couldn't bear the thought of her looking back on their wedding photos and seeing a reflection of him far too overweight. Determined to change, he promised himself and her that he would work towards a healthier lifestyle. However, as guilt crept in for not being able to provide the extravagant wedding she desired, Pete found solace in fast food and crisps during the day, feeding his emotions while satisfying his cravings.

Every evening, as he drove home from work, Pete made sure to discreetly dispose of any evidence of his indulgence before facing Natalie, hoping to spare her from disappointment and maintain the facade of progress.

As Pete drove through the quiet, winding roads of Cumbria, his mind drifted to Natalie waiting for him at home. The thought of her smile and the warmth of their shared moments eased the long day's fatigue from his bones.

Despite the growing darkness outside, a flicker of anticipation lit up in Pete's eyes as he imagined their cosy evening together.

The headlights of his delivery van cut through the enveloping dusk, casting fleeting shadows on the familiar houses along his route. Pete had made a mental note of which parcels to drop off first, eager to finish his shift and reunite with Natalie. He couldn't wait to see her face light up when he walked through the door, bringing with him the promise of a peaceful night in their little haven.

Tapping his fingers on the steering wheel and checking for the next address, he found himself blinking quickly. He didn't think he was that tired, he had a good night's sleep last night regardless of the amount of alcohol he and Natalie had drank at the local. But he was used to it, and the beer made sure he was comatose all night.

Desperately trying to stay awake, the twenty nine year old delivery driver started to feel confused. He tried to remember the next delivery address. He was sure this was the house whose occupants had complained about the delay to their last delivery. He had to get the parcel there on time to avoid being penalised, but his mind then became blank, and his vision started to blur.

He pulled in at the next lay-by and before he could make any sense of what was happening, he tried to loosen the neck of the tee shirt that felt like it was strangling him.

Undoing his seat belt as he opened his door, he managed to stumble out of the van, and threw up all over the road. He got back into the driver's seat with effort. His eyes glanced from left to right trying to find his phone to call Natalie before losing consciousness.

Meanwhile, the car behind had slowed to a stop, and the driver watched Pete's every move. A sly grin forming on his face. The van couldn't have stopped in a more perfect place. A country road with no houses for at least a couple of miles, and with no street lights, the chances of being seen were slim.

He had been tailing Pete for days, meticulously studying his routine, waiting for the perfect moment to strike. He was of medium build, his features obscured by a nondescript baseball cap pulled low over his eyes. His hands, encased in dark leather gloves, gripped the steering wheel tightly as he observed Pete's distress with a cold, calculating gaze.

This wasn't a random act of malice. No, this was carefully planned retribution. The figure's mind flashed back to the moment that had set this plan in motion - a casual conversation overheard in a pub, Pete's loose lips spilling words that shouldn't have been said. The fool had no idea of the consequences his words would have, or the person he had inadvertently crossed.

After a couple of minutes, he got out of the car, his movements fluid and practised. He glanced up and down the deserted road, ensuring no unexpected witnesses were present. Satisfied with the isolation, he approached the van with measured steps, his rubber-soled shoes making no sound on the asphalt.

He reached Pete's side, observing the unconscious man with a mixture of contempt and satisfaction. This was almost too easy. He pressed his gloved fingers to Pete's pulse point, confirming that the drugs had done their job. The steady, slow rhythm beneath his fingertips brought a twisted smile to his lips.

From his pocket, he produced an empty silver strip of diazepam. He turned it over in his hands, admiring how the moonlight glinted off its surface. This little piece of evidence would be crucial in selling the story he was crafting.

With deliberate care, he placed it on the dashboard, positioning it just so - visible enough to be noticed, but not so obvious as to arouse suspicion. He took a moment to admire his handiwork, ensuring Pete's fingerprints were firmly imprinted on the empty packet of tablets.

He re-fastened the seatbelt around his victim and carefully positioned the water bottle in Pete's lap, allowing a small amount to spill onto his trousers for good measure.

The figure stepped back, surveying the scene with a critical eye.

Everything was in place - the unconscious man, the empty pill packet, the water bottle. To any investigating officer, it would look like he'd had enough of life and his job, taking an overdose to end it all.

But he wasn't quite finished. From another pocket, he produced a small notebook and pen. In a handwriting style deliberately different from his own, he scrawled a brief, cryptic message: "I'm sorry. I couldn't take it anymore." He tucked this final piece of manufactured evidence into Pete's jacket pocket, the coup de grâce in his elaborate setup.

As he prepared to leave, he paused for a moment, looking at Pete's slumped form. A flicker of something - perhaps regret, or maybe just cold satisfaction - passed across his face. But it was gone in an instant, replaced by the same impassive mask he'd worn throughout.

His final act of retribution was done, until someone else unwittingly took a chance and said something they may regret later. He allowed himself a small, grim smile at the thought.

People never learned, did they? Always talking when they should stay silent, never realising the power their words held.

With one last glance at the unconscious Pete, the figure retreated to his car. He slipped behind the wheel and started the engine, its soft purr barely disturbing the night's silence. As he drove away, leaving Pete to whatever fate awaited him, the figure's mind was already turning to who his next target might be. After all, in his line of work, there was always another loose end to tie up, another secret to bury.

The taillights of his car disappeared into the darkness, leaving behind no trace of his presence save for the carefully orchestrated scene in Pete's van. The night settled back into its quiet routine, hiding the dark deeds that had just transpired beneath its veil of shadows.

27

The call came in jolting Josh and Fiona's thoughts from Jess' postmortem results. A body found in a van near Arkholme—a suspected suicide.

As Josh and Fiona raced to the scene, the weight of uncertainty settled like a heavy shroud over their shoulders.

They drove along the B6254, a picturesque stretch of road that wound its way through the charming countryside of Cumbria. Surrounded by rolling hills and lush greenery, on a clear day it offered breathtaking views of the scenic landscape. But tonight, it felt as if the road was closing in on the detectives.

Up ahead, they could see the scene bathed in a glow of flashing emergency lights casting long shadows, which danced across the blocked off road.

The victim's van was parked in the lay-by on the left and Josh could make out Serena and her team working candidly at the scene.

Josh parked up a hundred yards or so back from the scene and got out of his car, Fiona followed.

Fiona had offered to drive but Josh preferred the comfort and smooth drive of his new hybrid Cupra as opposed to Fiona's battered Ford KA.

They both walked in silence to the scene unfolding in front of them. A screen had been erected around the driver's side of the van, blocking the gruesome sight from any rubberneckers driving past the incident.

"Josh, Fiona," Serena said with a nod. "Diving straight in, this doesn't add up," she murmured. Her voice was a whisper against the backdrop of murmured conversations and distant sirens and Josh asked her to repeat herself. "This," she said, pointing to the seatbelt. "Why would he still be strapped in his seat? You would have thought he wouldn't have the energy or inclination to fasten it after throwing up at the side of the road. He could have been sick of course whilst still being seated, but that would mean the pool of vomit would be nearer to the van with spatters."

Fiona winced at the thought, she'd never had a strong stomach despite what she had both experienced and witnessed in her past.

Josh's brow furrowed in thought, his mind racing to piece together the puzzle laid out before them. "Perhaps he didn't have time to unfasten it," he suggested, his voice tinged with uncertainty. "Maybe whatever he ingested took effect before he could react."

"But like I say, the vomit would be nearer," Serena responded.

As the words left his lips, doubts gnawed at the edges of his consciousness. Pete's death seemed too convenient, too neatly packaged—a sinister tableau designed to deceive and mislead. "Have you found a suicide note, Serena?"

"Yes, in his jacket pocket." Serena held up three evidence bags, each revealing separately the note, the empty packet of Diazepam, and the water bottle.

Josh raised his eyebrows quickly followed by him furrowing his deep dark brows together.

As they scoured the van for clues, Fiona's sharp eyes caught sight of something glinting beneath the pedals—a sleek, black smartphone, its screen cracked and smeared with fingerprints. "Here we are, his phone." She pulled on a thin pair of gloves and reached between the pedals to pick up the phone.

"Here, I'll bag it," Serena said.

Fiona nodded, "Sure, let me just see if there is an ICE contact," she said. She tapped the emergency icon and found details for Natalie Mathieson. "I have the details," she said, passing the phone to Serena so it could be bagged and logged.

"Okay, keep a note, we'll make contact." Josh continued around the van then peered inside the cabin to see if he could spot anything out of place.

"I bet you any money that's what killed him," Serena said, looking at the Diazepam packet. "I won't be able to confirm until ..."

"Until you've done toxicology. Yeah, I know, thanks. I bet this isn't suicide. Something just isn't right for me."

"Leave us to it, we'll report back as soon as we have something," Serena said whilst diligently working.

"Thanks," Fiona said. "Right, are you ready to deliver more bad news?" she asked Josh.

Josh sighed heavily and followed Fiona back to the car.

28

Natalie walked towards the front door whilst muttering under her breath, *'why didn't he take his key?'* She unlocked the front door. "Why didn't you take your key, you daft—" she stopped mid-sentence when she saw two strangers on her doorstep.

"Who might you be?"

"Natalie Mathieson?" Fiona asked.

"Yes, how can I help?"

Josh and Fiona introduced themselves and showed their ID. Natalie's face turned from a cheery, happy go lucky character, to one of fear. Her skin turned pale, and Fiona thought she might faint. Fiona reached forward to hold Natalie's arm and support her.

"Oh my God, it's Pete, isn't it? He was due home over an hour ago, we're meant to be eating Chinese and drinking wine around now."

Despite many years in the police force and having to do countless notifications, Josh was still surprised when he heard what came out of people's mouths out of shock. "Let's go inside, shall we?" he said, with a sympathetic smile on his face.

Josh followed Natalie and Fiona inside and watched Fiona steady the woman onto the sofa.

Fiona left the room and walked into the kitchen to make Natalie a strong cup of sweet tea. The age-old remedy for shock still worked to this day.

Natalie's emotions had overwhelmed her, Josh was worried how she would react when she heard what he had to say. He stood up and walked over to Natalie and sat down next to her, ready for the response. "Natalie, I'm so sorry."

The young woman wailed louder than a howling dog.

Fiona heard the sound from the kitchen and winced. *'Poor cow,'* she thought to herself. Shaking her head she poured the tea and added three heaped teaspoons of sugar to the mug.

The atmosphere in the room felt suffocating, it was thick with grief, sadness, and uncertainty.

"How did he ... you know?"

Josh knew what she meant and glanced up at Fiona as she walked back in the room.

"Was it a car accident? Did someone drive into him? You hear of that nowadays, don't you? Inconsiderate or drunk people not concentrating and either swerving, dangerously overtaking, or driving through a red light."

Josh couldn't defend the idiot drivers, she was right and it was becoming all too common. But that's not what happened here. "It wasn't like that, I'm afraid."

Natalie looked at him, confused. "What was it then? He didn't drive into a tree or something did he?"

"Why do you say that?"

"He's really bad at using his phone when he's driving. I've told him not to do it, but he rings me about five times a day to tell me that he loves me." She burst into tears again.

Fiona crouched down in front of Natalie with the mug of hot, sweet tea. "Here, drink this, it will help."

Natalie smiled at Fiona's kindness and took the mug off her.

Josh made a mental note to check Pete's phone records. It couldn't do any harm to see if he was on the phone to someone around the time of death, a conversation that maybe had caused him to kill himself. Nothing could be ruled out.

"Natalie, I know this is really hard, but I need to ask you some questions to help us find out what happened to him," Josh said sensitively.

As he spoke, Josh's mind raced, years of experience warring with the empathy he felt for the grieving woman before him. He'd done this countless times, delivered the worst news imaginable to unsuspecting loved ones, but it never got easier. Each time, he felt the weight of their grief, their shock, their disbelief. And each time, he had to push through, had to find a way to get the information he needed while still being compassionate.

Fiona glanced at Josh, and Natalie nodded slightly.

"Was there anyone who might have had a grudge against Pete?" Josh asked gently, his voice a soothing balm amidst Natalie's turmoil. His eyes searched hers, hoping to glean any insight that could lead them closer to the truth. "Maybe someone whose delivery was late or who had a disagreement with him?"

As he spoke, Josh's mind was already several steps ahead, considering the implications of each possible answer. He knew from experience that in cases like these, the first forty eight hours were crucial. Every detail, no matter how small or seemingly insignificant, could be the key to unravelling the mystery of Pete's death.

Natalie's brow furrowed in thought as she considered Josh's question, her mind racing through memories and possibilities. "No, nothing like that," she replied, her voice trembling with emotion. "But his boss at Excelerate Delivery would know more. Let me get you his details."

Josh wanted Natalie to feel as if she was being useful and it may direct her mind to some important detail that may help crack this case. As he watched her leave the room, he couldn't help but reflect on the delicate balance he had to maintain. Push too hard, and he risked shutting Natalie down completely. But if he didn't push hard enough, vital information might slip through the cracks.

As Natalie returned to the living room, a realisation seemed to dawn on her. Her eyes widened in disbelief, fear flickering behind their depths. "Wait," she said, her voice barely above a whisper. "You don't think... You're not suggesting that Pete was... murdered, are you?"

Josh felt a familiar tightening in his chest. This was always the hardest part - the moment when the reality of the situation truly hit home for the bereaved.

He exchanged a meaningful glance with Fiona, silently acknowledging the gravity of Natalie's words. Even though it was looking that way, he didn't want to mention it just yet.

"We're not jumping to conclusions, Natalie," he reassured her, his tone steady and reassuring. "We're just trying to gather all the facts. We don't know for sure how Pete died. Also, we found a very brief note and an empty packet of Diazepam was found. Was he prescribed Diazepam, do you know?"

"What? You don't think he took an overdose, do you? He's never been prescribed Diazepam in his life. Not that I know of anyway."

"We're really not sure, Natalie. As I say, we are not jumping to conclusions." As he spoke, Josh was acutely aware of the fine line he was walking. He needed to keep Natalie calm enough to continue answering questions, but he also couldn't lie to her. If Pete's death was indeed a murder, she would need to be prepared for the long and painful journey ahead.

But Natalie's emotions were already spiralling out of control, her worst fears threatening to consume her. Tears welled in her eyes. "I can't believe this is happening," she whispered, her voice choked with anguish. "I just can't."

Sensing her distress, Josh cast a sympathetic glance towards Fiona, silently communicating their shared concern for Natalie's well-being. He felt the familiar pull of empathy, the desire to comfort warring with his professional need to remain somewhat detached. It was a balance he'd struggled with throughout his career, and moments like these never got easier.

"Is there anyone we can call to come and sit with you?" He asked gently, his voice a beacon of comfort in the storm of her emotions. Even as he asked, Josh was mentally reviewing the next steps of the investigation. They'd need to search Pete's van, check his phone records, and interview his colleagues. But for now, Natalie's well-being had to be the priority.

Natalie nodded, her hands trembling as she reached for her phone, her lifeline in this moment of darkness. "My family, they are in Grassington," she murmured, her voice barely audible above the tumult of her emotions.

She took out her phone from her cardigan pocket with shaking hands.

Fiona watched her struggling to scroll and find a number. "Here, let me," she said, offering out her hand.

"My mum's number is in there, could you ring her for me please?"

Fiona took the phone off Natalie, then walked through to the kitchen, to make the call. Her voice was soft and soothing as she spoke to Natalie's mother. Moments later, she returned with the phone, a sympathetic expression etched upon her features. "Your mum wants to talk to you, Natalie," she said as she handed the phone back.

"Mum? Oh, mum, I can't believe it," Natalie sobbed, her words barely audible. Choked with tears and grief pouring out of her, she doubted she would ever be the same again.

Meanwhile, Josh discreetly made a call to the on-duty doctor, his expression grave as he relayed the urgency of the situation. He returned to find Natalie off the phone, her shoulders shaking with silent sobs, her anguish palpable in the air. "My mum and dad ... they ... they are on their way."

"The doctor is also on his way, I called him briefly to ask him to come and see you, I hope you don't mind?" asked Josh. Natalie simply shook her head showing no objection. She would take anything away right now to break the darkness and take her out of the nightmare that she was living.

"Natalie, we'll stay with you until your parents arrive, is that okay?"

"That would be lovely," Natalie said, soaking up the kindness of strangers who had just shattered her world. The young woman remembered her manners even in the midst of heartbreak and her world having been turned upside down. The gratitude evident in the tear-streaked lines of her face.

29

As Josh and Fiona walked out of Natalie Mathieson's home, the weight of her grief seemed to cling to them, a physical presence that hung heavy in the air. They climbed into the car in silence, both lost in their own thoughts, trying to make sense of the scene they had just witnessed.

"I can't imagine what she's going through," Fiona said at last, her voice soft and sombre. "To lose someone you love like that, someone who you think you will spend the rest of your life with, so suddenly and so senselessly."

Josh nodded, his eyes fixed on the road ahead. "It's the worst kind of pain. The kind that cuts you to the core, leaves you raw and bleeding."

Fiona glanced at him, a flicker of compassion passing between them.

"Do you think it was suicide?" Fiona asked, her voice hesitant. "The note, the empty pill packet, it seems to point that way."

Josh shook his head, his brow furrowed. "I don't know. Something doesn't feel right. The timing and the circumstances seem too convenient."

"But what's the alternative? Murder? Who would want to kill a delivery driver?"

"That's what we need to find out. There has to be a connection, something that links Pete to the other victims."

They lapsed into silence again, the only sounds were the hum of the engine and the distant wail of a siren. The streets of the town flashed by, a blur of neon and shadow, the night closing in around them.

When they arrived back at the station, the building was nearly deserted, the hallways echoing with their footsteps. They made their way to the incident room, the fluorescent lights flickering to life as they entered.

Josh and Fiona stood before the incident board, staring at the photos and notes that covered its surface. Dan Walsh, Jess Chepstow, and now Pete Bowler. Three lives cut short, three mysteries waiting to be unravelled.

"Okay, let's go over it again," Josh said, his voice low and focused. "What do we know about the victims? What connects them?"

Fiona stepped closer to the board, her finger tracing a line of red string. "Dan Walsh, a management consultant, who was found dead in a pub courtyard. Jess Chepstow, a corporate finance executive murdered in her hotel room. And Pete Bowler, a delivery driver found dead under suspicious circumstances."

"Three different people, from three different walks of life," Josh mused. "But there has to be a link. Something that made them targets."

"Could it be related to their jobs?" Fiona suggested. "Maybe they stumbled onto something they shouldn't have or saw something that put them in danger."

Josh considered the idea, his head tilted in thought. "It's possible. But we don't have any evidence of that yet. No witnesses, no clear indication of a shared connection."

"And then there's James," Fiona said, tapping Jess's photo. "He was convinced that Alex killed her. But even if that's true, it doesn't explain the other deaths."

"Exactly," Josh agreed. "If Alex is guilty of Jess's murder, what motive would he have for targeting Dan or Pete? As far as we know, he had no connection to either of them."

They stared at the board in frustration, the pieces of the puzzle refusing to fit together. The only tentative link they had between Dan and Jess was the murder weapon used in their deaths. Josh's stomach chose that moment to growl loudly, a sudden reminder of the late hour.

"We're not going to crack this on empty stomachs," he said with a wry smile. "Let's call it a night, come back fresh in the morning. Maybe a good night's sleep will give us a new perspective."

Fiona hesitated, clearly reluctant to leave the mystery unsolved. But she knew Josh was right. They were both exhausted, their minds clouded by fatigue and the emotional toll of the case.

"Okay," she agreed with a sigh. "But first thing tomorrow, we need to start digging deeper with anyone who might have information. There has to be a connection, and we're going to find it."

Josh nodded, his expression grim but determined. "Absolutely. We're not going to let this killer slip through the cracks. We owe it to the victims, to their families, to find the truth."

With a final glance at the board, they gathered their things and headed for the door. The incident room fell silent behind them, the photos of the victims staring out into the empty space, their eyes pleading for justice.

"Get some rest," Josh said as they reached their cars. "Tomorrow, we hit the ground running. We're going to find this killer, no matter what it takes."

Fiona met his gaze, her eyes blazing with determination. "Damn right we are. For Natalie, for all the victims. We won't let them down."

30

Alex sat alone at the kitchen table, the only sounds in the room was the quiet hum of the refrigerator and the soft patter of rain against the windowpane. In front of him sat a steaming cup of strong, dark coffee, its bitter aroma hung in the air. He took a slow, deliberate sip, the warmth of the liquid offering a brief respite from the cold reality that surrounded him.

It had been four days since he had discovered Jess' lifeless body, her pale face etched into his memory like a haunting refrain. In the wake of her death, Alex found himself retreating into a numb, detached state, his emotions locked away behind a wall of stoicism.

He couldn't allow himself to feel the weight of his grief, not when there were practical matters to attend to, not when there were still unanswered questions lingering in the air.

When he had gone to break the news to Jess' parents, he had done so alone, refusing the assistance of the police. He couldn't bear the thought of them witnessing his composed facade, couldn't bear the scrutiny of their questioning eyes.

It was easier this way, he told himself, easier to appear strong for their sake, to shield them from the full extent of his anguish.

As he sat lost in thought, memories of his relationship with Jess flickered through his mind like old film reels. They had started out with such promise, Jess bridging the gap between their disparate worlds with effortless grace. But beneath the veneer of affection lay a chasm of unspoken truths, a divide that widened with each passing day.

His parents, too, had seen the strain that Jess had placed on their son, the suffocating weight of her presence pressing down upon him like a leaden blanket. They had never spoken openly of their concerns, choosing instead to suffer in silence, to preserve the illusion of normality for Alex's sake.

But now, as Alex sat in the quiet solitude of his kitchen, the reality of their situation loomed large. Trapped in a cycle of financial hardship because of Jess wanting to impress her corporate colleagues and living beyond their means, dreams of a better life slipping further from his grasp with each passing day. And Jess, with her careless words and thoughtless actions, had only served to exacerbate their struggles, her presence had been a constant reminder of everything they could never have.

Lost in his thoughts, Alex absentmindedly reached for the local newspaper that lay forgotten on the table, his eyes scanning the pages without really seeing them. It was only when a familiar face caught his eye that he snapped to attention, his heart pounding in his chest.

There, staring back at him from the pages of The Cumbrian Metro, was Dan Walsh's face, his features frozen in a look of determination. Alex's mind raced as he tried to place where he had seen the man before, a sense of unease settling over him like a heavy shroud.

As he stared at the photograph, Alex felt a sudden, overwhelming urge to see Jess' face. He needed to ground himself, to remind himself of what he had lost. With trembling hands, he reached for his wallet, fumbling with the worn leather as he searched for the familiar photograph he always kept tucked away.

He opened the small pocket where the photo was, and his heart sank. The space in his heart was empty, devoid of the comforting presence of Jess. His tears dripped onto the table as he stroked her smile on the worn photo and his breath caught in his throat, a cold sweat breaking out on his forehead.

He tried to rationalise Jess' death, but he battled with his inner torment. His connection with Jess was gone once and for all.

Ignoring the feeling of emptiness, anger, and guilt, his focus returned to the present. He made a mental note to return the room key to The Kings Hotel later that day, a small act of kindness in the midst of chaos.

But as he reached for his jacket, a sinking feeling settled in the pit of his stomach remembering that he had leant his key to Jess.

The missing key sent Alex's mind into overdrive. He began to connect dots that he wasn't even sure existed.

Alex's hands shook as he ran them through his hair, his breathing becoming shallow and rapid. He felt as if the walls were closing in on him, as if every certainty in his life was crumbling away. The composed facade he had so carefully maintained since Jess' death was beginning to crack, revealing the turmoil that lay beneath.

With a sense of resignation, Alex picked up the phone and dialled the station, his voice hollow as he spoke to DCI Josh Mills.

He needed answers, and he needed them now. But as his finger hovered over the keypad, he hesitated. Who could he trust?

The rain continued to patter against the window, a constant reminder of the world outside. But for Alex, trapped in his spiral of fear and uncertainty, that world had never felt more distant or more threatening.

Whatever was happening, whatever forces were at play, he knew one thing for certain: nothing would ever be the same again.

31

"DCI Mills, who am I speaking to?"

"It's me, Alex."

"Alex, can you just hold on one moment please?" Josh didn't wait for an answer. He covered his phone with his hand and looked across to Fiona. "Fiona," he whispered. "I have Alex on the phone, did you get through to him yesterday?"

Fiona shook her head, "no answer, and it wouldn't let me leave a message."

Josh shrugged his shoulders. He took his other hand away. "Alex, what can I do for you?" Josh asked.

"I've seen that face before, you know," Alex said, sitting on the side of his bed and biting his fingernails.

"Which face?" Josh sounded confused.

"You know, the one in the paper, the guy who got murdered."

"Dan Walsh?" A note of scepticism evident in his tone.

"Yes, that's the one," Alex could feel the adrenaline pumping through his veins. "I couldn't sleep last night, kept tossing and turning, and then it just hit me."

Josh leaned forward in his chair, his interest piqued. "Go on, Alex. Tell me exactly what you remember."

Alex took a deep breath, his words tumbling out in a rush. "It was at that café, Fully Baked. This guy – Dan Walsh – he was at the table next to us the day we arrived. We went for coffee and cake before we checked into the hotel. I remember him because he struck up a conversation."

"What did you talk about?" Josh prompted, grabbing a pen to jot down notes.

"At first, just small talk. The weather, how bad the coffee was and how stale the cakes were. But then he mentioned he was in town for a stag do. Said he was looking forward to it because..." Alex paused, his voice catching slightly. "Because he'd just split up with his girlfriend."

Josh's eyebrows shot up. "That's quite personal information to share with strangers, isn't it?"

"I know, I thought so too," Alex agreed. "But he seemed... I don't know, relieved to be talking about it? Like he needed to get it off his chest."

"Did he mention the girlfriend's name?" Josh asked, his mind racing with possibilities.

Alex furrowed his brow, trying to remember. "I don't think so. No, I'm pretty sure he didn't. But he seemed really upset about the whole matter."

Josh made a note of this, his pen scratching quickly across the paper. "Anything else you remember about him? What he was wearing, who he was with?"

Alex closed his eyes, trying to visualise the scene. "He was alone when we talked. Wearing a blue shirt, I think. And he had this nervous energy about him. Like he was excited but also a bit on edge."

"On edge, how?" Josh pressed.

"Just fidgety, you know? Kept looking at his phone, glancing around the café. At the time, I thought maybe he was meeting someone and they were late."

Josh nodded, even though Alex couldn't see him. "This is all very helpful, Alex. Can you remember anything else? Anything at all, no matter how small it might seem?"

Alex was quiet for a moment, thinking. "There was one other thing. When he was leaving, he got a phone call. I remember because his ringtone was really loud, some instrumental version of a love song. He looked at the screen and his whole demeanour changed."

"Changed how?"

"He went pale, like he'd seen a ghost. He answered it, but he walked out of the café quickly. I couldn't hear what he was saying, but he looked scared."

Josh felt a thrill of excitement. This could be the break they needed. "Alex, this is great information, but could you also come down to the station to make a formal statement? We need to ask you a few questions too."

"A few questions? Why?"

"We just want to clarify some details with you, that's all. It would really help."

Alex sighed silently and rolled his eyes. This was the last thing he needed. "Well, I suppose if it will help, then of course I will."

"Great, let's say 3pm, give you a chance to get here."

"Okay," Alex said without further words.

"Fiona?" Josh shouted at his Detective Sergeant who was standing in front of the incident board.

"Yes?" She said without turning around.

Josh walked up to her. "I have Alex coming in at 3pm, he recognised Dan Walsh in the paper."

"Really? From where?'"

"That cafe of all places."

"Interesting. It will give us a chance to ask him about the row with Jess too."

"Yes, that's what I thought."

Josh felt the dopamine hit the more he thought about the snippets of information being fed back to him. "We may get the breakthrough we need, you know."

"I hope so," Fiona said. "Because we certainly need it."

32

Detective Chief Inspector Josh Mills and Detective Assistant Fiona Mitchell sat across from Alex Chepstow in the dimly lit interview room. Alex shifted uncomfortably in his seat, his eyes darting between the two detectives, a mixture of grief and apprehension etched onto his face.

Josh leaned forward, his elbows resting on the table, his gaze locked onto Alex. "Alex, thank you for coming in today. We know this is a difficult time for you, but we have some questions that we need to ask."

Alex nodded, his hands clasped tightly in front of him. "Of course. Anything to help find out what happened to Jess."

Fiona flipped open a file, her eyes scanning the pages. "Alex, can you tell us about your relationship with your wife? How were things between you in the days leading up to her death?"

Alex's brow furrowed, a flicker of emotion crossing his face. "Things were complicated. We had our ups and downs, like any couple. But we loved each other. We were trying to work through our issues."

Josh's eyebrows raised slightly, his tone even. "We've heard from a source that you and Jess had a pretty heated argument before you left for Kirkby Lonsdale. Can you tell us about that?"

Alex's eyes widened, his posture stiffening. "An argument? Who told you that?"

Fiona leaned in, her voice calm but firm. "We're not at liberty to disclose our sources. But we need to know what happened between you and your wife. It could be crucial to our investigation."

Alex sighed heavily, his shoulders slumping. "Yes, we had an argument. Jess had been distant lately, spending more and more time away from home. I confronted her about it, and things got heated. I said some things I regret."

Josh's gaze never wavered, his voice low. "What kinds of things, Alex."

Alex's eyes closed briefly, his voice barely above a whisper. "I accused her of cheating on me. I told her I knew she was seeing someone else. She denied it, but I didn't believe her. I was angry, hurt. I stormed out of the house, told her I wasn't going to Kirkby Lonsdale with her."

Fiona's pen scratched across her notepad, her eyes flicking up to meet Alex's. "What happened then?"

Alex shook his head, his voice hoarse. "I drove around for hours, trying to clear my head. I ended up at a pub in Leeds and had a couple of drinks. I didn't want to face Jess, not after what I'd said."

Josh's expression remained impassive, his tone even. "And what time did you eventually return home, if at all?"

"Hey? Of course I returned home, it was just empty threats."

"So, you returned home, and we know that you went to Kirkby Lonsdale."

"That's right, we went to Kirkby Lonsdale the next day," Alex gulped down the emotion that was sitting in his throat like a big ball of steel.

"And had you made up by the time you went away?"

"Yes, almost. We looked forward to a few days away in the end," Alex said, looking beyond Josh and Fiona.

"But then you found another text message from James didn't you?" Fiona said, looking down at the scribbled notes in her file.

"So that's who told you we had an argument, it was him!" Alex's hands were clenched under the desk.

"Does that make you annoyed, Alex? The fact that James told us that?"

"It's none of his business, it's because of him that she's dead!"

Josh and Fiona looked at each other.

"Why would you say that, Alex?" Josh questioned.

Alex shook his head. "None of this would have happened. If she hadn't been in touch with him again, we wouldn't have gone away to Kirkby Lonsdale to try and save our marriage, and she might ... she might still be alive," Alex said, taking short, emphatic breaths. His voice trailed off, his eyes glistening with unshed tears.

Fiona offered him a tissue, her voice softer now. "We understand how difficult this must be for you, Alex. But we need to ask: did you have anything to do with your wife's death?"

Alex's head snapped up, his eyes blazing with sudden anger. "No! God, no. I loved Jess. I would never hurt her. Never. How could you even think that?"

Josh's expression remained neutral, his voice level. "We have to consider all possibilities, Alex. Your wife was found dead under suspicious circumstances. You admit to having a heated argument with her shortly before her death. You can understand why we need to ask these questions."

Alex's shoulders slumped, his anger dissipating as quickly as it had appeared. "I know. I know. It's just... I can't believe this is happening.

Jess is gone, and I don't know why. I don't know who could have done this to her."

Fiona's eyes narrowed slightly, her tone probing. "Were you always suspicious about James and Jess?"

Alex's jaw clenched, his hands gripping the edge of the table. "He was Jess' ex-fiancé, of course I was suspicious. She was speaking to him, they were texting each other. I thought at one point she was going to leave me!" Alex broke down and let his tears fall to the floor. "The whole thing made me angry!" Alex gritted his teeth with rage.

"That's quite a temper you have, Alex."

"Stop it! Just shut up will you? I would never hurt her. Look ... I knew that Jess had been seeing James. I found the text messages, she owned up to the affair. We had an argument but after we had both cooled down, I told Jess how much I loved her. Jess broke down and said how much she loved me too and how she was sorry for all the hurt she'd caused me. She said she would speak to James and call the whole thing off with him. Jess and me, we had decided to stick together, to give things another chance. That's what makes this whole thing even more heartbreaking. She was my wife, I loved her!"

"Tell me, Alex, I want to know your whereabouts again. Because the way I see it is the timings are close and you were in the vicinity." Josh stared at Alex without blinking and tapped the pen on his notebook.

"I already told you, I was in the bar then I went upstairs and found her. It wasn't me!" Alex threw his head down onto his arms which were folded on the desk in front of him. But then he looked up suddenly. "That's another thing, did you ever find another room key?"

"No we didn't, why?" Josh didn't mention that he knew one was missing. He wanted to see what Alex had to say about it without any prompting.

"It's missing," Alex said.

"Missing?" Fiona questioned.

"Yeah, missing. It's weird. Jess had lost hers somewhere in between checking into the bedroom, and leaving the brewery. She went to get her room key out of her bag for when she got back to the hotel. But it wasn't where she left it, so I leant her mine."

Josh looked at Fiona then briefly terminated the interview. "We'll be back shortly, Alex," Josh said.

Both detectives stepped outside the room. "Fiona, check with Serena again about potential DNA from Alex that could implicate him. We know she was his wife, but if there is any DNA anywhere that could be suspicious, this could be the angle we are looking for. Alex wasn't found with blood on him so it's unlikely he was involved but we need to check."

"I think that's odd in itself. I mean, if you found your loved one unresponsive, wouldn't you shake her, check she's okay, have blood on your hands, literally?"

"I agree. But if his hands were clean, did he hide the knife and where? Did he wash his hands and where? From what I recall there was no blood in the sink, none on the door handle."

"I'll check with Serena," Fiona said, walking off to make the call.

33

"Alex, when you went up to the room to look for Jess, how did you get in?" Josh asked when they resumed the interview.

"The door was slightly open, almost like she had opened it to leave but then she mustn't have made it," Alex said, shaking his head.

"And you don't have anything else you can give us?"

Alex shook his head. "No, nothing. I just want to know what happened to her."

"What about Jenny? How do you think she knew that Jess had died when she saw you in the police car outside the hotel?"

"I don't know, I have no idea. She must have wondered what the fuss was about, asked someone, then when she saw me, put two and two together."

"Seems a bit of a coincidence though, doesn't it? Jenny appears very fond of you."

"Ignore her. I've known her for years but there was never any intention of it being anything other than friendship at best. She keeps pestering me and won't leave me alone."

Josh and Fiona didn't spot anything in Alex's behaviour to suggest he was lying.

"Okay, Alex, I think that's enough for now. We're going to release you for the time being, but we will be in touch if we need anything else."

"I'm heartbroken, you know, despite her going behind my back, I truly loved her. She was my everything."

Josh's expression remained impassive, his voice level. "We appreciate your cooperation, Alex. We'll be in touch if we have any further questions."

Alex nodded, his shoulders slumping in defeat. "I understand. I just want to know what happened to my wife. I want justice for her."

As the detectives watched Alex leave the room, Fiona turned to Josh, her brow furrowed. "What do you think? Do you believe him?"

Josh's expression was pensive, his eyes distant. "I do, I'm not sure he's emotionally capable of killing her."

Fiona nodded, her own expression troubled. "And we don't have any hard evidence tying him to the crime. Just a lot of circumstantial details and James' hearsay."

Josh's jaw clenched, his voice low. "That's why we need to keep digging."

"I agree."

"I'm starting to think this missing room key is going to lead us to the killer you know."

"I think you're right. But how it connects to Dan and Pete I have no idea," Fiona said.

As the two detectives gathered their files and prepared to leave the room, a sense of unease hung heavily in the air.

34

When Josh and Fiona sat at their desks, they decided on the next course of action. "We need to go back to Fully Baked and speak to the owner, what's his name again?" Josh said.

"Dave Potter. He wasn't very cooperative last time, I know I had a bad feeling about him."

"Okay, I think before that though, do you want to call the delivery company that Pete worked for? Maybe they can shed some light on whether there were any grudges against Pete."

"Will do," Fiona said. She walked back to her desk and dialled the number for Excelerate Delivery.

"Oh, hi, who am I speaking to?" Fiona said, looking up.

"This is Amelda Green, how can I help?"

"Could I speak to Pete Bowler's manager please?"

"What is it regarding?"

"My name is Detective Sergeant Fiona Mitchell, I would like a private word with him."

"No problem, I'll put you straight through," Amelda said.

'That was easier than Catalyst Consulting,' Fiona thought to herself.

"This is Jeffrey Sawhurst, can I help? I'm assuming this is to do with Pete Bowler. Such terrible, terrible news. I just can't believe it."

"Have you heard then?"

"Yes, a terrible tragedy for a lovely family. His mum contacted me and told me what happened. Can I help in any way?"

"I just have a few questions if that's okay?"

"Sure, go ahead, anything I can do to help," Jeffrey said with sadness in his voice.

"I was wondering, was there anyone who had a grudge against Pete? Maybe a customer who had made complaints about delayed delivery, or perhaps a colleague?"

"There was the odd complaint but nothing serious that was taken anything further. I mean, you get them all don't you these days," he said stroking his wiry beard. "The customer who whines about you delivering five minutes late, the ones who thank you regardless of the delay, the old dears down the road who shout at you for not closing the gate. But no, nothing serious."

"Mm," Fiona said, curiously. "And did Pete have any regular deliveries that he made?"

"There were just three on his list that he delivered to twice a week." Jeffrey said. "Let me just check the files, I won't keep you a moment." Jeffrey stood up and walked over to a filing cabinet.

Fiona could hear a metal draw on runners being opened and waited patiently. She heard Jeffrey come back to the phone and sit in his chair.

"Now, Pete did the regular runs to the Dog & Grain ..."

Fiona raised her eyebrows. "Yes, where else?"

"Hang on a moment. Ah yes, the brewery and ..." Jeffrey flicked over pages in the white ring binder.

Fiona impatiently tapped the end of the pen on her desk and sighed silently. She counted to ten in her head.

"Oh yes, here we are. A cafe called Fully Baked."

"Wait, did you just say Fully Baked?"

"I did, yes, why?"

"Thank you, Jeffrey, you've been very helpful. I'll call you again if I need you." And without waiting for a response, Fiona pressed the red call icon on her phone, pushed her chair back, and walked into Josh's office.

"Josh, you won't believe this."

"Please tell me something that will push us forward with this."

"One of Pete Bowler's regular deliveries was Fully Baked."

Josh looked up from the papers on his desk, his eyes widened, and his mouth opened a little. "Was it now? I think we need to get our coats, don't you?"

Josh grabbed his coat off the back off his chair, a brown tweed effect jacket which he placed over his black turtleneck. He instinctively patted his chest to check he was wearing his lanyard, then waited by the door for Fiona.

Fiona did the same. Put her jacket on, checked for her ID and followed Josh.

They both left the building and climbed in Josh's black Cupra. As Josh spun out of the car park, Fiona held the handle above her passenger door to stabilise herself.

"Steady, Josh, talk about in a hurry."

"We need to get there sharpish, we don't want him to disappear. I want to catch him before he closes, because right now, that cafe is the only thing that connects all three victims. A weak connection maybe, but still, a connection." Josh looked both ways before turning out of the T-Junction heading for Kirkby Lonsdale.

"I agree, but you can go easy on the speed, we have plenty of time."

Josh's adrenaline rushed through his veins, and for the first time in days, he felt like they had a lead.

"I think we need to threaten him with arrest if he doesn't cooperate. He might be more helpful. He's a person of interest as far as I'm concerned. Dave Potter saw both victims shortly before they were killed, and now we know that Pete Bowler made deliveries to him," Fiona said.

"Yeah, best leave the questioning to me so he doesn't get complacent with you. Let me give him the heebie jeebies, hopefully he'll start talking."

"Right. Let's see what he has to say for himself."

Josh reversed into a parking space at the end of the ginnel that led to the popular cafe and didn't bother waiting for Fiona. He started to stride up the pathway and checked his watch for the time. Ten to five, that should do it, he thought. There won't be anyone there to distract or discourage him.

Fiona eventually caught up with her partner as he stepped inside the empty cafe.

"Dave Potter?" Josh asked.

"Yes," he said, leaning to the side and spotting Fiona behind. "Don't know why you're asking, she knows who I am," he said, his hands fumbling slightly with the cake tray he was holding.

Josh noticed the slight tremor in Dave's fingers, a tell-tale sign of nervousness. He filed this observation away for later consideration.

"Josh Mills," he quickly flashed his ID before letting the lanyard rest against his chest.

"Not the police again, I told her yesterday everything I know about what happened," he said, briefly nodding in Fiona's direction. As he spoke, Dave's eyes darted between Josh and Fiona, never quite settling on either of them.

"And what exactly did happen?"

"I told her, I remember that couple but that's about it." Dave's shoulders tensed visibly as he spoke, his posture becoming more rigid. "God knows why they came back again; they did nothing but complain about the coffee and cake the first time around."

"And what about this gentleman?" Josh pulled out a photograph of Dan Walsh.

Dave Potter glanced at it briefly before continuing to reorganise the cakes and wipe down the glass display plates. His movements became more hurried, almost frantic, as if he were trying to keep his hands busy.

"Don't know him, never seen him."

"Take another look, carefully." Josh continued to hold up the photograph.

Dave Potter stuck his neck forward to get a closer look, curled his top lip, and said, "Nope, never met him." As he spoke, Josh noticed a bead of sweat forming on Dave's forehead, despite the cool temperature in the cafe.

"We beg to differ, Mr. Potter," Fiona offered.

"Differ all you like, still haven't seen him," the irritation was clear in Dave Potter's voice. His right eye twitched slightly, an involuntary movement that hadn't been present before.

"You see, the gentleman who you saw with his wife, remembers seeing this man in this cafe. He had a conversation with him."

"I mustn't have served him, that's all. It must have been Joanna," he could feel himself flustering. Dave's hands, which had been busily rearranging cakes, suddenly stilled. He gripped the edge of the counter, his knuckles whitening with the force of his grip.

"Who is Joanna?" Josh asked, trying to keep calm.

"She is my part-timer, works here the odd day when I need her."

"Why didn't you mention her yesterday?" Fiona enquired.

"You didn't ask." Dave's response came too quickly, his words tumbling out in a rush. He licked his lips nervously; a gesture Josh had often seen in suspects who were trying to buy time to think.

"Mr. Potter, if you continue to be difficult, this may be better continued down at the station with you as a person of interest. I'm happy to take you there now," Josh said, his head turning in the direction of the door. "And perhaps you can give us Joanna's contact details so we can ask her what she remembers."

Dave Potter wiped his forehead with the back of his hand, smearing the sweat that had accumulated there. His breathing had become more rapid, his chest rising and falling visibly under his apron.

"Let me see that photograph again."

Josh looked at Fiona briefly and raised his eyebrows. He held up Dan's photograph.

"Oh! Oh, him, yes I think I remember him." As Dave spoke, his eyes widened slightly, a flicker of recognition passing across his face before he could mask it.

"Do you read the local paper, Mr. Potter?"

"Yes, of course I do. I have to keep up with the local news so I can join in conversation with the blasted customers." Dave's voice had taken on a defensive tone. He crossed his arms over his chest, as if trying to create a physical barrier between himself and the detectives.

Josh noticed the harshness and frustration in his voice. "So, it didn't occur to you to come forward when you must have read the request for information about Dan Walsh?"

"In the news, was he?"

"Look, Mr. Potter, I've said we can do this here, or you can come down to the station."

"Okay I saw it. Okay?" Dave's voice rose in pitch, his face flushing a deep red that spread from his neck to his cheeks. "But I know what you police are like. Have one thing pinned on you and you're immediately under suspicion. I was in a car crash twenty years ago, ruined mine and my wife's life, hers especially. Do you think I'm proud of that? Hey? Do you?"

As Dave's emotional outburst continued, Josh observed the man's body language closely. Dave's hands were now gesticulating wildly, his whole body seemed to vibrate with tension. His eyes, which had been avoiding direct contact earlier, now bore into Josh with an intensity that spoke of desperation.

Fiona noticed Dave Potter getting redder and redder in the neck. "Calm down, Mr. Potter, it's just a few questions."

"My wife's in a wheelchair and I still blame myself for the accident," the cafe owner said, tears forming in his eyes. His shoulders slumped, the fight seeming to drain out of him in an instant. "If I'd admitted seeing that man too, you would have arrested me straight off. Like I say, I know what you lot are like."

"No, we wouldn't, not without evidence." Josh turned around at hearing the door opening.

"I'm sorry, we're closed. Go somewhere else," Dave snapped.

The customers tutted at his rudeness, frowned, then turned around and walked away.

"I'm sorry, I got confused and I messed up, okay? Doesn't mean I'm guilty. Now if there is nothing else, I must finish up here and get home to my wife, the carer finishes in an hour, so I have to be there."

"Just one last question, what were your whereabouts last Thursday from 10pm, to Friday at 2am? On Friday from 4pm to 7pm, and Monday 3pm to 7pm?" Fiona had her notebook to hand again.

"I was here or at home. All of those times cross between me working here at the cafe, and looking after my wife, Alison. My whole life is consumed by her and this place, I don't have time for anything else."

"Can anyone verify that apart from the customers here? What about your wife?"

"You'll be lucky, can't get a word out of her these days, it's the trauma. Muted her for life."

Josh offered a sympathetic smile. "Okay, if we need anything else we'll let you know."

Fiona and Josh walked out of the cafe.

"That's convenient, his wife not being able to talk. I think we should still visit her anyway and see if there is any facial movement when we ask her questions," Fiona said.

"Make sure we get permission off Potter first though. We don't want IPCC breathing down our necks for being unreasonable and unsympathetic. I wouldn't put it past him to make a complaint about us, Fiona."

Josh and Fiona got back in Josh's car, grateful for the cover as it had started to rain heavily in the town. The droplets of rain falling on the streets giving the tourists an excuse to pile into the brewery.

"What do you think?" Josh asked, rubbing his chin.

"He's hiding something, but I don't know what. He was so worked up and he had guilt written over his face. But we have no evidence to arrest him, he was just being arsey."

"True. And what motive would he have had?"

"At this moment in time? I don't know, I think it's time for us to do some more digging."

"I've heard that about you, you don't let things go. Rob Mackie, head of CID, rang me before you transferred, said you were like a dog with a bone in an investigation. I like that."

"It's the first time you've smiled at me since I've arrived."

"Yeah, sorry about that, we've been busy and—"

"What? Fiona asked at Josh's hesitation."

"Bloody hell, I've got my Nana's hundredth birthday party and that file is still sitting on my desk." Josh looked out of the window thoughtfully.

Fiona could sense the urgency and empathy in his voice. "Why don't we go back to the station, I'll crack on with more digging and you can look at the cold file. When is your Nana's birthday?"

"Weekend."

"Surely we'll have this wrapped up by then?"

"If we do, it will be the quickest resolved murder case I've ever known, you'll get a gold star against your name, and my wife will be happy if I'm going with her to Prestatyn.

"Prestatyn? I have not heard of that place for years. What's in Prestatyn?"

"My Nana's care home," he said, looking at her and raising his eyebrows.

"Oh, sorry to hear that."

"Don't worry, she's doing well for her age. Gets sick, the family thinks it's the end, then she bounces back. Even at the age of one hundred."

"Resilient then?" Fiona said?

"Yeah, you could say that. Right, let's get back." Josh went to push the ignition button when his phone vibrated in the holder on the dashboard. "Josh Mills?"

"Sir, it's me, PC Whippet."

"Hi, Stewart, what have you got for me?"

"CCTV, sir, and juicy stuff too. I gathered the CCTV from as many cameras as I could following Pete Bowler's route. Nothing really of interest."

"Why are you ringing me then?"

"Because the CCTV came in from the Dog & Grain and the Main Street from the town."

"And... don't keep me waiting, I can tell you're about to drop a bombshell."

"Pete Bowler not only made a delivery to the pub, but he was also seen delivering to that café, Fully Baked."

"Yeah, we know, thanks Stewart. I guess it does confirm what Pete Bowler's boss said though."

"Yeah, but boss, he delivered to Fully Baked just one hour before his body was found."

"Did he now?" Josh ran his hand through his hair and Fiona's eyes widened. "See you shortly Stewart, we need to go and make an arrest I think."

"Sir?"

"Yes, Stewart?"

"I haven't finished yet. This is the best bit. I spoke to the hardware shop on the main street. They recognise the knife as a brand which they sell."

"Go on," Josh said.

"The owner of the shop told me he sold a knife identical to the one in the picture to Dave Potter, from Fully Baked, just two weeks ago. He hasn't sold another one since."

"Right, that does it. Dave Potter's coming in for questioning. Thanks, Stewart, we need to go."

Josh and Fiona were about to open their car doors when they heard a man shouting.

"Stop, Stop!"

Josh saw two hands land on the front of his car bonnet. He opened the driver's side electric window all the way. "Mr. Potter?"

"I forgot to give you this, I—I er ... I found it on the floor the other day." Dave Potter handed him a room key.

Josh looked at Fiona and nodded briefly at her.

Fiona got out of the car and walked around to where Dave Potter was standing on the driver's side of the car. She walked up to him. "Dave Potter, you are under arrest on suspicion of murder. You do not have to say anything, but it may harm your defence if you do not mention, when questioned, something which you later rely on in court. Anything you do say may be given in evidence." Fiona pulled Dave Potter's arms behind his back and handcuffed him.

"Hey? Why? I thought I was helping by giving you that room key back. Let go of me! This is ludicrous!" He said, whilst struggling. "I've not done anything!"

"We have just received new information we would like to ask you about," Fiona said.

"What new information? Tell me?"

A few minutes later, Josh having made a call to control, a marked police car arrived to take Dave Potter to the station.

"What do you think, Josh?" Fiona said as she watched Dave Potter being led away.

"Something definitely is not right about him. We just need to find out what."

35

Dave Potter sat in a chair, alongside his solicitor, facing Josh and Fiona in interview room two on a cold and wet evening. He wiped his snivelling, bulbous nose on his sleeve then placed his arm back in his lap and locked hands.

Josh sat staring at the sorry state of a man who was now under suspicion. Now all Josh and Fiona had to do was ask the right questions, prove he was involved somehow, and charge him.

"Can you tell me where you were between the hours of 10pm on Thursday evening and 2am on Friday?" Josh asked.

Dave Potter looked down into his lap and without warning started to cry.

Josh looked at Fiona and frowned.

"Mr. Potter, did you hear me?"

Potter's solicitor, Mr. Nunn, whispered something incomprehensible in Dave's ear.

The room went silent, Josh clasped his hands together and placed them on the desk in front of him. He was a patient man when it came to interviewing suspects. Most of the guilty ones cracked eventually, unable to take the pressure or be weighed down by the guilt any longer. It appeared that Dave Potter fell into that category.

SHAME ON THEM

"Please, please have mercy on me," Potter wailed.

"What do you mean, Dave? Do you mind if we call you, Dave?" Fiona asked softly.

Dave Potter looked up at the voice, his eyes red, his soul void.

"Dave," Josh said, leaning forward. "Would you care to tell us what you know?"

Mr. Nunn leaned into his client again.

"Oh, shut up," Dave Potter said, looking at his solicitor. "You've never been in my position, I can't take this anymore!" He shouted. "I killed them. I killed them all, okay?"

Fiona glanced at Josh trying to remain emotionless and impassive to the confession.

"We still have to prove you did it, Dave. So why don't you tell us what happened? You must have had a good reason."

"We need it verifying for the tape, Dave. We have a case to build to send to the CPS, we need the details to prove you committed the murders."

Dave Potter looked up and spoke matter of factly. Every ounce of emotion had gone. "On Thursday, 19th October I was at the Dog & Grain pub, murdering that idiot, Dan. Friday, 20th October, I killed that stuck up bitch, and three days later I murdered the fat slob of a delivery driver."

Josh wanted to reach over the table and punch him for the name calling alone. Defamatory, unkind verbs didn't feature in Josh's vocabulary.

"They all deserved it too, they had to die, ruined my life they did."

"I think you did that, Dave, to be honest," Fiona chimed in.

"Why did you do it, Dave?" Josh asked. He had a hungry need to find out why someone would do such a thing.

"Why? Are you serious? Have you not seen their reviews on Trip Advisor? The first one, that wide eyed boy, who thought he was God's gift, came in grumpy as hell. I told him we were busy, but he ignored me. Gave him the best food and service and he still complained and put it on TripAdvisor. He had what was coming to him." Dave Potter tutted then went silent.

"That seems a bit harsh, Dave. Murdering someone because they left you a bad review?" Fiona said.

"It wan't just that. He had it all that lad. Fancy clothes, nice aftershave, one of those posh watches, I was jealous I suppose. He had a nice life, I didn't and it frustrated the hell out of me. What makes him different to me? Why should he have it all when I'm struggling? It's just not fair."

"People lives are not all they are cracked up to be, Dave. Things go on that we don't see. Just because he looked well dressed, doesn't mean he was happy," Josh replied.

"Yeah, well, after I'd done him, it was easy after that. It was too bloody for my liking but then I was on a roll and felt like I didn't want to stop getting my own back. Nasty people deserve bad things as far as I'm concerned." Dave sniffed and shrugged his shoulders dismissively.

Next, Josh looked down at the open file in front of him. The attractive Jess Chepstow was staring back at him, the photograph taken on her wedding day, which was probably the best day of her life with hopes and dreams for the future for her and Alex. He wondered when it went wrong for them. By all accounts it was when Jess got promoted, but that's rarely a reason for a relationship to drift apart. It normally goes much deeper.

"What about Jess Chepstow? What did she do to harm you? Just a normal woman enjoying a few days away with her husband - then you come along and ruin Mr. Chepstow's life. I don't think he will be the same again."

"Shame. He'll just have to learn to live with the grief like I have."

"But why?"

Dave Potter shrugged his shoulders. "Same, I suppose. She was stuck up and nothing satisfied her. Her attitude was disgusting. She walked in like she owned the place. Said the cake was dry and the coffee was bitter. I was surprised they came back to be honest. Stiff upper lip she had; I knew as soon as I saw her she would be trouble. Another one star review. Stupid cow, she should have thought about what she wrote first. Reviews like that destroy lives you know. They destroy lives!" Dave tried to lurch himself across the table without much success. He just ended up looking like a bumbling idiot.

Dave sat down again and composed himself.

Josh sighed at what was to come.

"Let's move on to Pete Bowler, a long-standing delivery driver by all accounts and one that you had probably built a relationship with. The delivery company told us that Pete had delivered to you since you first opened the cafe."

"That's right." Dave looked to the side and ran his tongue around his teeth.

Josh thought he spotted a hint of guilt in Dave about Pete. Maybe he had touched a nerve, so he continued. "Knew him well did you? Know his girlfriend? Meet him for the odd drink? Shared stories and woes?"

"Don't you even go there—" Dave stood up again, scraping his chair back, which fell to the floor as he leaned over the table. "Pete was a friend," he hissed in Josh's face.

Mills remained calm. "Is that so? Why kill him then?"

Dave Potter fell silent for a few moments and Josh wondered what he was thinking.

"Fatso," he laughed, referring to Pete's bulging beer belly. "I felt sorry for him. But that didn't stop him slagging off the quality of my cooking. So, do you know what I did? I gave him a free ham sandwich and cake so he could fill his fat face. I laced a bottle of water and take out tea with my wife's diazepam. Gave him enough to kill him. He took a bite out of the sandwich before he left and still complained even though it was free. All of 'em. All three of 'em left shitty reviews. That will affect my trade that will."

"Too late to think about that now, Mr. Potter," Fiona said. "You won't have a trade anymore."

Dave Potter shrugged his shoulders. "Not bothered."

"And what about your wife, do you not think she needs you?"

"Nah, better off with one of them nurses."

Josh thought he could see remorse behind Mr. Potter's eyes and had a glimmer of sympathy for the situation with his wife.

"So, what are you saying, Mr. Potter? Why did you kill them?"

In reality, Josh knew why. But it still both puzzled him and worried him that someone would take to murder because of keyboard warriors' scathing reviews.

"Why did it matter, Dave? The reviews?" Fiona asked.

"Listen, I am up to my fuckin' neck in debt. I work my arse off day in, day out, to make ends meet. I get home, exhausted, and Alison needs looking after. I just snapped, I couldn't take it any longer. I felt my blood boil, I couldn't take it anymore."

Josh cringed at the swearing. No matter how many swear words he heard from suspects, he would never get used to it. Swearing in Josh's world was unpalatable and unnecessary.

"Still, it seems a bit extreme," said Fiona, yet she knew how easily someone could snap and pull a knife. She had first-hand experience of it in her druggie days and it wasn't pretty.

Dave Potter went silent. He sat looking down at his feet as if all his revenge had expired. He was suddenly exhausted and just wanted to sleep. It had been days of adrenalin fuelled killing that had satisfied his soul, and now he just wanted to sleep.

Josh noticed the murderer slowly blinking, his shoulders rising and falling with every breath. He knew when suspects got tired, and that it was the perfect time to interrogate. Their unconscious mind taking over and enabling DCI Josh Mills to get to the root of the problem.

He decided on a different tact this time. He knew there was something deeper going on and he wanted to find out what.

"Do you have a family, Dave? Parents? Siblings?"

Dave Potter slowly looked up, fire raging in his eyes. He shifted uncomfortably in his chair and pumped his fists in his lap trying to keep control of his temper.

The question had hung heavily in the air and made Dave's mind race back to the horrific memories he had long tried to bury. A childhood filled with remorse, pain, and neglect.

Suddenly, it was as if a dam had broken. Dave's words came pouring out in a torrent of long-suppressed emotion.

"Family?" he spat, his voice dripping with venom. "You want to know about my family? Let me tell you about my so-called mother." Dave's eyes took on a distant, yet evil look, as if he were seeing something far beyond the confines of the interview room. "She was a monster. A drunk who cared more about her next bottle than her own child. I can still smell the stench of cheap vodka on her breath when she screamed at me for existing."

Josh and Fiona exchanged a glance, realising they were about to hear the dark origins of the man before them.

"I was five the first time she locked me in the cupboard under the stairs," Dave continued, his voice eerily calm. "Said I was making too much noise as she was trying to watch the TV, whilst swigging from a vodka bottle. Left me there for two days. No food, no water, just darkness and spiders."

Fiona felt a chill run down her spine, imagining the terror of a small child in that situation.

Dave's fists clenched and unclenched as he spoke. "When I was eight, I spilt a glass of milk. She held my hand on the hot stove burner as punishment. Said I needed to learn to be more careful. On my ninth birthday, she watched whilst our next-door neighbour abused me, dirty cow. Oh, and when I was ten, she tried to shove her hand down my pants. Want to know anymore? I've got a whole catalogue of horrid, dirty, nasty events that would have you both turning in your graves."

Josh's face remained impassive, but inwardly he recoiled at the cruelty Dave described.

"And what about your dad, Dave, did he not do anything about your mother's cruelty?" Josh said, acknowledging what Mr. Potter had been through as a child.

"My father?" Dave let out a bitter laugh. "Never knew him. Probably for the best. The parade of men my mother brought home was bad enough. Some ignored me. The others..." He trailed off, shaking his head. "I learned to be quiet," Dave said softly, "to make myself invisible. But it was never enough. Nothing was ever enough for her."

His voice took on a harder edge. "When I was twelve, I tried to run away. Made it three towns over before the police caught me. When they brought me back, she beat me so bad I missed two weeks of school. Told the teachers I had pneumonia."

Dave's eyes refocused on Josh and Fiona, burning with a mixture of pain and rage. "You want to know why I did what I did? Because every complaint, every criticism, every negative word... it was her voice I heard. Her disappointment. Her disgust. And I couldn't take it anymore.

I should have killed her long ago when I had the chance."

"Killed who, Dave?"

"That woman who gave birth to me. I was born to the wrong woman I was. She didn't care about me, she was a monster in my eyes."

Josh remained unruffled, his gaze steady as he leaned forward slightly. He knew he had hit a nerve with Dave Potter.

"I hated her," Dave confessed, his voice barely above a whisper. "I wished she was dead every single day. And do you know what? I'm glad she died before I could lay my hands on her. Snuffed it she did before I had the chance to do anything about it." Dave's shoulders slumped, as if the weight of his confession had physically drained him. "I never had a chance, did I? Never knew what it was like to be loved, to feel safe. All I knew was fear, anger, and pain. And now..." He gestured vaguely at the room around him. "Now I've become the very thing I hated most."

The bitterness in Dave's tone was palpable, his words were laced with rage, regret, and anger from a childhood lost, no love in his life, and an emotionally distant mother. He had spent a lifetime carrying the weight of his childhood trauma, nursing his wounds in silence as the years slipped by. But now, as an adult responsible for his emotions and behaviour, he had chosen to seek the opportunity for revenge against the ones that reminded him of his mother.

Josh could see how Dave's traumatic upbringing had warped his perception of the world. Every criticism, no matter how small, had become a devastating attack in Dave's mind.

The negative reviews that most business owners would brush off or use constructively had, for Dave, reopened old wounds and triggered a lifetime of pent-up rage.

Fiona gulped hard. It always fascinated her how some adult children loathed their parents so much they would do anything to be rid of them. Meanwhile, women like herself longed to even have a mother and not to have been rejected at birth. She thought fleetingly of where her birth mother was.

Josh listened intently and could see the pain etched into the lines of the man's face, the torment that had twisted his soul and turned him into a monster. But beneath the anger and the hatred, Josh sensed something else – a profound sense of loss, a longing for the love and acceptance that had been denied to him.

And as he sat opposite the broken man, he wondered how many more lives would be destroyed by the scars of the past.

Dave Potter's childhood experiences had clearly shaped his entire worldview. His mother's constant criticism and abuse had created a man hypersensitive to any perceived slight or negative feedback.

The cafe, which should have been a source of pride and accomplishment, had instead become a constant reminder of his inadequacies. Every complaint, every negative review, had been like a knife twisting in old wounds, until finally, the pressure had become too much to bear.

DCI Josh Mills parked Dave Potter's outburst and words in his mind, satisfied with the motivation he had been given as to why the terrible murders had been committed. Now it was about the finer detail.

"Let's get to the finer details of how you killed them, Dave." Josh looked down at the open file briefly to remind himself of what he needed to cover. "How did you kill Dan Walsh?"

"He was the easiest. I was walking home from the cafe and saw him walking towards the pub with his mates. I hung back, then followed them into the bar. Dropped a couple of pills into his drink when he wasn't looking. As soon as he went to the loo and started throwing up, I knew I had him. I saw him head towards the back door when his mates left, so I walked out of the front door, then made my way to the courtyard at the back of the pub. It was so dark around there, no one could have seen me. I saw him crawling on the floor looking for his phone. He was a dribbling mess compared to how he acted in my cafe. He looked pathetic. When he stood up, I made my move." Dave made a fist and pretended to stab himself in the stomach and chest.

"And how did you get hold of the key for Jess Chepstow's hotel room?" Mills asked, keen to finally tie up the loose ends. "We know you had the key, you brought it out to us. After checking with the hotel, it was confirmed as Jess Chepstow's bedroom door key. Her prints were all over it, as were yours.

"I took it. I took it out of her bag. She went to the toilet after complaining about the food. Except she wasn't just complaining, she was shouting so everyone else could hear. Two customers who came in for something to eat left again because they heard her say the food and service were shocking. Then her boyfriend or whatever you want to call him, came to the counter to pay. As he walked out of the cafe without waiting for her, I went to clean the table, saw the bag on the floor with the key on top, and took my chances. When I closed for the day, I walked to the hotel and entered through the side door pretending to use the toilets near the reception desk. I left it for five minutes, came out, saw her husband go to the bar, then walked up to her room."

"Stroke of luck that, wasn't it?" Fiona enquired.

"What was?"

"The fact that her husband had gone to the bar, giving you a chance to get her on her own."

"He was desperate to get away from her, I could tell. I don't think I meant to kill her though."

"Care to explain? A moment ago you said you wanted your revenge. And you took her room key, that screams clear intention to me, otherwise you wouldn't have taken her key."

"I suppose I just wanted to talk to her, I knocked on the door at first then lifted the key to unlock the door. But then she opened the door and I saw the look of shock on her face. She was about to scream, so I didn't have any choice. I pushed her on to the bed to try and make her listen, but she was having none of it. She was a right struggler, she was."

"That's strange, Dave, because you had the knife on you, didn't you? No one walks around with an 8-inch kitchen knife in their inside pocket."

Dave Potter shrugged his shoulders. "I don't have anything to say to that, the knife was there and that's it."

"Having a knife and stealing her room key are both intentional, as is spiking people's drinks." Fiona said.

Potter wiped the dribble from the end of his nose with the back of his hand then sat back in his chair. "Tried to kick me in the gonads she did, I lost my rag with her. She deserved it anyway. Good riddance."

Josh noticed Dave Potter was becoming flippant and arrogant with his attitude. "And Pete?"

"The guy was an idiot, pretending to be my friend for all those years then calling me behind my back. He'd left a review on Trip Advisor a few weeks before, didn't think I'd notice because he used a different ID to his social media. I knew all right, knew it was him. Then he had the audacity to still come to MY cafe for MY bacon rolls and MY coffee. The two-faced liar. He was an easy one. I nicked some of my wife's diazepam, stuck it in his tea and bottle of water, then followed him on his deliveries. A stroke of luck it was when he pulled into that lay-by. Finished him off with my hand over his nose and mouth." Dave gave a sly grin, wickedness evident in his dark, dangerous eyes.

Mills realised they were dealing with a nasty character, and he was pleased that Dave was in the interview room now rather than on the streets.

He was already thinking ahead that some normality could be brought to the tourist town again before word got round it wasn't a safe place to be.

Fiona was now trying to keep her distaste at bay, anybody who used a knife and drugs in her view was sick. Sick in the head. Most police are quite clinical about murders, knives, victims, and the methods used to bring other people's lives to an end. But for Fiona, the very thought of knives and people doing hurtful things because they didn't agree with something, made her shiver as she thought back to her past when she was stabbed twice on two separate occasions.

For Josh, it wasn't the extent of the viciousness of the attacks that sickened him, even though he still couldn't fathom why murderers would go to varying degrees of butchering their victims.

It was the motive for Josh, and having questioned Dave Potter, it was clear he had carried a heavy weight from his childhood. He knew he would never recover fully from his ordeal. Sure, he may get support inside prison, but he would never recover and would never be released. Josh would make sure of that.

Josh sat staring at the murderer opposite him whilst Fiona continued finalising the formalities and asked PC Stewart Whippet to take him to the cells to await the first hearing.

He thought about ordinary, everyday people, out living their lives, going about their work, and ending up murdered for purely saying what they wanted to say. But Josh knew from experience that when you can't take any more you just snap without thinking of the consequences.

Dave Potter had nothing to lose. No family, a wife who couldn't talk, or move without assistance, and no love in his life. Large amounts of debt and a failing cafe were not something to work for in his view.

Dave Potter was led away in his handcuffs whilst he mouthed his final words to the DCI and his assistant. He turned his head over the shoulder as he was about to be led out of the interview room. "Shame on them! Shame on them all! They'd still be alive if they hadn't bad-mouthed me! I wouldn't have killed anyone if they had kept quiet!"

PC Whippet momentarily battled with the murderer and hustled him sharply out of the room and down the cold, stark, soulless corridor back to the custody desk to be officially charged.

"I doubt that very much," Josh muttered.

"What do you mean?"

"If he hadn't murdered those poor people, he would have found another way to vent his pent-up anger and take it out on someone else. It wouldn't have been long."

"Tough case, that one," Fiona said.

"They all are in their own way. The sudden end of life, the lives of the murderer and the victim destroyed forever, and another guilt laden individual behind bars. "I'll never understand. Life is precious but people treat it with such disrespect."

All Fiona could do was agree as she walked back to her desk to finish the paperwork before sending the file to the CPS.

Josh walked back into the department followed by Fiona, and gathered his team around to give them the news about Dave Potter being charged with the three murders.

"Good result, Sir," Sam said.

"Thanks, Sam. And I just want to congratulate everyone on their hard work at getting this resolved quickly. I know there were things left that you didn't have a chance to question and investigate further, like Jenny's statement and the CCTV, but sometimes if you're lucky, the murderer appears before you without having to delve deeper."

"If it's okay with you, Sir, I'd like to be involved in the next one."

"I'm hoping there won't be another one. But we'd all be without jobs if there wasn't. Consider it done, Sam."

The young constable smiled at Josh Mills. "Thanks," he said.

Josh went around the department and shook everybody's hand as a sign of appreciation, as he did every time on a job well done. Then, grabbing his jacket, he walked out of the department and towards his car. He had somewhere to be.

36

Alison had been moved to a care home after her husband had been charged with murder. She sat in her wheelchair in front of the floor to ceiling window. Her eyes fixated on the beauty of the garden outside. The grass had just had its last cut of the year apparently, a small detail which her carer had whispered in her ear as she tried to make conversation.

Alison might not be able to speak fully, but in her head, she has a conversation with whoever is talking to her. It makes her happy and keeps her going. Her eyes flitted from side to side as the last colour of the begonias and other blooms drifted in the breeze.

The late summer sun came and went behind clouds casting shadows on the patio and the scene in front of her was a picture of tranquillity, in contrast to the heartbreaking turmoil that had plagued most of her life.

She had loved Dave when she married him, it had been the happiest day of her life, and his. Their wedding photos had sat on the polished mantelpiece of their modest home but there were no family portraits. The couple had tried and failed to have children, a heavy weight that had burdened Alison for years.

After ten years of marriage, Dave started to change. They had both decided on a change of career seeing that children weren't an option anymore. The cafe in the town was up for sale and they made a cheeky offer thinking it would never be theirs. But the offer was accepted, and they started to create hopes and dreams of what life would be like when they had a chain of restaurants all across the world.

Their dreams were brought to an abrupt end late one night when Dave was driving Alison home after a celebratory dinner. It was the first anniversary of them opening the cafe and life and business were going well. As Dave looked at Alison momentarily to capture a snapshot of her laugh at one of his silly jokes, a car came at speed through a red light from the left-hand side and ploughed into their Renault Clio. Their car spun, their bodies shook, and their heads bounced off the headrests. The car landed upside down after turning and it took three hours to clear the scene.

Dave, remarkably, was not seriously injured. Alison on the other hand had taken the brunt of the accident. Her new dress, soaked in blood and almost torn from her body from the impact, didn't need much cutting in the trauma department at the hospital in Carlisle.

Placed on a life support machine for ten days, it was touch and go for Alison. Dave insisted on being by her side despite having concussion and a broken arm. He would sit at the side of her bed, his head resting against her arm, crying, and begging for forgiveness even though technically, it wasn't his fault.

For years, Alison had been confined to a wheelchair, her voice silenced by the trauma of the devastating car accident. The memories of that fateful night still haunted her, the screeching of tyres, the blinding headlights, the sickening crunch of metal as the drunk driver careered into their car. And then the agonising pain, the overwhelming darkness that swallowed her whole, so she never truly saw the light again.

But now, as she sat in her wheelchair, bathed in the soft glow of the afternoon sun, a smile graced her lips. For the first time in what felt like an eternity, Alison felt a glimmer of happiness, a spark of hope flickering within her.

It wasn't just the sunshine or the peaceful garden that lifted her spirits. No, it was something far more profound, far more miraculous. Alison had found her voice again. It had started with a whisper, then a murmur which barely escaped her lips. When she was told by the dashing DCI Josh Mills and the caring, empathetic Detective Sergeant, Fiona Mitchell, that her husband was unlikely to see light again, the faintest of smiles crossed her lips. Her eyebrows raised slightly, and her heart relaxed to a steady, rhythmic beat.

Dave had claimed to love her since the day they met. She was under no illusion that he did to begin with. But that night, everything changed and she had been left broken and feeling alone. No matter how much attention he paid her, the sensitive way in which he dressed her, bathed her skin, and washed her hair, it made her cringe.

She loathed him.

She despised his attitude, and she heard every word that left his mouth even though he thought she couldn't register them. The incessant swearing, the emotional abuse, and the harsh reality of living with a bully of a man had almost been the death of her.

Now, she had been set free. Alison felt for Dave's victims and felt guilty that she was enjoying her newfound freedom because her husband had chosen to bring their lives to an end. But you couldn't have everything, could you?

And as she looked out at the garden, her heart swelled with gratitude for the new life that lay before her.

For the first time in years, Alison felt hopeful. Hopeful for the future, hopeful for the possibility of happiness, and hopeful that maybe one day, she would find someone who truly loved her for who she was.

And as she whispered *'thank you,'* whilst looking out onto the garden, she knew that she would never be silenced again. In fact, she very much looked forward to her husband's trial.

37

As Josh strode towards his car, the weight of the recent case slowly lifting from his shoulders, he couldn't help but feel a pang of disappointment.

The conclusion of the investigation had brought a sense of closure, but it also meant he hadn't had the chance to delve further into the cold case that had been gnawing at him for years.

The unsolved mystery of the young child's body, discovered ten long years ago, haunted his thoughts like a persistent shadow, a reminder of unfinished business and unresolved pain.

He couldn't bear the idea of another day passing without progress, and the guilt weighed heavily on him as he considered the anguish of the grieving parents, still waiting for justice.

As he drove through the winding streets of Kirkby Lonsdale, Josh's mind was consumed by the familiar details of the cold case. The quaint buildings and cobblestone paths blurred past him, their familiarity only adding to his frustration.

His grip on the steering wheel tightened as he replayed all the evidence in his mind for what felt like the hundredth time. The crisp night air filled the car, carrying with it a faint scent of woodsmoke from nearby chimneys.

But Josh's thoughts were too consumed by the mystery at hand to appreciate any beauty or charm in the small town.

For an hour, he had been poring over the clues, desperately trying to find a link. But each time he thought he was getting closer to the truth, his mind couldn't help but wander to Archie.

Each passing landmark, each familiar corner, seemed to whisper secrets of the past, urging him to uncover the truth buried beneath layers of time and silence.

Josh blinked. Maybe he was making things up in his head. Maybe he wanted the two young boys to be victims of The Midnight Hunter so the reckless, heartless, murderer would be given more life sentences. Not that he would ever be set free anyway. But Josh wanted him to suffer. Badly. Deep down he also knew that that itch would never be satisfied, no matter that the murderer was locked up in prison for life, or how many times he would be beaten and abused by cell mates.

Josh sighed and instead he focused on the present, determined to celebrate his Nana's milestone birthday with joy and gratitude.

Arriving home, Josh found his wife waiting for him, a warm smile lighting up her face as she greeted him.

"Hello, my love," she said, grabbing hold of him.

"You look tempting, do we have time?"

Caroline's dress wasn't her best, but she always felt good in it, and it was fine for Nana's 100th.

"No, we don't, we'll be late. It's at least a two-hour drive, if we leave now, we'll make it in time."

Josh followed his wife through to the kitchen. "Do I have five minutes? I need deodorant and a clean shirt, maybe some cold water over my face."

"No more than five, hurry," she said, slapping his behind playfully. "Oh, I made a cake by the way."

"You're the best," he shouted back down the stairs.

Caroline smiled to herself, he may be busy all the time but boy did she love him with all of her heart, no matter what had happened.

The soft glow of the evening sun bathed their cottage in a golden hue, casting long shadows across the hallway as they prepared to embark on their journey to Prestatyn.

Josh locked the door behind them and rushed to the passenger side of the car and opened the door for his wife, trying to take the cake off her whilst she climbed in.

"Ah, I'll keep that, thank you, knowing your luck it would end up on the floor."

"Why do women do that?"

"Make men feel inferior and be able to juggle five million things at once?" She asked. "It's in their nature apparently, a nurturing thing," she said, raising her voice as he closed the door on her.

Their conversation drifted effortlessly from the recent case to his wife's work caring for children with disabilities, her compassion evident in every word she spoke. Josh listened intently, his heart swelling with pride and admiration for her unwavering dedication and empathy.

"It touches my heart working with those children, you know. And when I read about people like Dave Potter's wife, I think, what chance has she got?"

"Don't worry," he said, reaching over and touching her left knee. "She is doing well, and she is now able to speak a few words."

"Really? I have heard that can happen as people recover."

"I'm just wondering if she stayed mute all those years because she blamed her husband for the accident. I know he blamed himself even though he was found not to have contributed to the crash."

Caroline raised her eyebrows. "I wouldn't be surprised if she just couldn't bring herself to speak to him after what had happened."

Josh looked over briefly at Caroline. "Would you speak to me if something like that happened?"

"You don't know until it does. All I can say right now is you are the love of my life, and I will always be by your side." Caroline looked sideways at Josh. "Hey, is that a tear I see?"

"What?" he said, wiping the droplet from the corner of his eye.

"No, just tired and emotional after the case I think."

Caroline's brow furrowed with concern. "Josh, love, there's more to it than that, isn't there? You've been carrying something heavy these past few days."

Josh sighed, his shoulders slumping slightly. "It's the Tommy case," he admitted, his voice barely above a whisper. "Ten years, Caroline. Ten years that poor family has been waiting for answers."

"Oh, Josh," Caroline reached out, squeezing his arm gently. "You're doing everything you can."

"But what if it's not enough?" Josh's voice cracked with emotion. "What if I'm missing something crucial?"

Caroline watched her husband's profile, noticing the tension in his jaw. "Is it something specific that's bothering you?"

Josh nodded, his grip tightening on the steering wheel. "It's Colin Malham. There's something... off about him. I can't put my finger on it, but every time I see him, I get this unsettling feeling."

"Colin?" Caroline's interest was piqued. "Tommy's father? What about him?"

"It's... it's his height," Josh said, feeling slightly foolish. "He's unusually tall. I mean, I'm six foot one, and he towers over me. He must be at least six foot four, maybe more."

Caroline's breath caught in her throat. "Tall, you say?" Her voice trembled slightly.

Josh glanced at her, noting the sudden change in her demeanour. "Caroline? What is it?"

She hesitated, her fingers twisting in her lap. "It's probably nothing, but the day Archie died, I saw someone. A walker, passing by the back of our property. He was unusually tall too."

Josh's detective instincts flared to life. "A tall walker? Caroline, why haven't you mentioned this before?"

"I... I didn't think it was important," she said, her eyes glistening with unshed tears. "It was just a random person walking by. But now that you mention Colin's height..."

"Tell me everything you remember," Josh urged, his mind racing with possibilities.

Caroline closed her eyes, recalling the memory. "It was late afternoon. I was in the garden, and Archie was playing near the pond. I turned away to go back in the house to make a cup of tea, just for a moment, and that's when I saw him. A man, walking along the path behind our property. He was so tall, Josh. His head was above the fence line."

Josh's heart pounded in his chest. Could it be possible? Could Colin Malham have been there the day Archie died?

"Caroline," he said, his voice tight with tension, "this could be important. Very important."

As the implications of this new information sank in, Josh felt a surge of conflicting emotions. On one hand, this could be the breakthrough he'd been waiting for in both Tommy's case and Archie's death. On the other, they were on their way to his Nana's hundredth birthday celebration.

"Josh?" Caroline's voice cut through his thoughts. "What are you thinking?"

He took a deep breath, making a decision that tore at his heart. "We need to cut our visit short," he said, his voice filled with determination and regret. "I'm sorry, love, but I need to follow up on something."

Caroline nodded, understanding the gravity of the situation. "Of course. Nana will understand."

As they continued their journey, now with a new sense of urgency, Josh's mind raced with possibilities.

38

Josh's fingers drummed an erratic rhythm on the steering wheel as he navigated the familiar streets of Kirkby Lonsdale. The conversation with Caroline about the tall walker replayed in his mind, each detail seeming more significant with each passing moment.

He pulled into the station parking lot, his mind already racing ahead to the next steps. As he strode through the department, he caught sight of Fiona hunched over her desk, pouring over case files.

"Fiona," he called, his voice tight with urgency. "Got a minute?"

She looked up, instantly alert at his tone. "What's up?"

Josh perched on the edge of her desk, lowering his voice. "I need your perspective on something. Caroline mentioned seeing an unusually tall man the day Archie..." He paused, swallowing hard. "The day Archie died."

Fiona's eyes widened. "Go on," she prompted gently.

"She described him as *'unusually tall.'* But Caroline's only about five seven. I'm trying to gauge what that might mean from her perspective."

Fiona leaned back, considering what Josh had just said. "So how can I help?"

"You're around Caroline's height. So what would you consider as *'unusually tall'*?"

"We might be talking six foot four, or more."

Josh nodded, "that fits with what I know of Colin Malham's height."

"Colin Malham?" Fiona's brow furrowed. "Tommy's father? You think there might be a connection?"

"I don't know," Josh admitted, running a hand through his hair. "But I can't shake this feeling. I need to talk to the Malham's again."

Fiona nodded, already reaching for her jacket. "Want me to come with you?"

Josh shook his head. "Not this time. I need to approach this carefully in case I am wrong."

"And if you're right?" Fiona asked, her voice barely above a whisper.

Josh met her gaze, his eyes hard with determination. "Then we might finally have answers."

"I think I should come with you, Josh. I also think you need to speak to Helen, this could have implications and you won't be allowed to get involved if Colin is connected with Archie's death."

"Mm, I know. I want justice but I must do the right thing. I will go and see her."

Josh stood up from his chair and walked out of the department towards Helen Musgrove's office.

He arrived at her door, took a deep breath, and knocked.

"Come in," the dulcet tones of the Chief Inspector could be heard.

Josh walked in and smiled.

Helen looked up. "Josh, it's good to see you. I hear congratulations are in order and Dave Potter has been charged."

"Yes, it was a good result, especially so quickly too. It demonstrates the competency and closeness of the team."

"I agree, but you don't need me to tell you that. You know I commend your work and that of your team. You have some strong people in there. Which reminds me, how is Fiona getting on?"

"Good. I'm impressed. She did well on the recent case, I like her."

"I sense a *'but'*."

"Not really. I think she has something on her mind but it's too early to tell and I wouldn't expect her to reveal anything to me so soon." Josh gave the Chief Inspector a flattering smile.

"You have a way of getting through to people, Josh. I'm sure you'll help her out if needed."

Josh scratched the back of his neck.

"What can I do for you anyway? Surely you haven't come in here for my glorification of a job well done. You're better than that."

"Haha, no I haven't. I've come to discuss, let's say, a delicate matter," Josh said.

"Oh?"

"Yes. It was Fiona who recommended I speak to you, actually."

"Very well, what is it?" Helen put her pen down and sat back in her chair, waiting for Josh to elaborate.

"The Tommy Malham case."

"Ah, yes, how are you getting on with that?"

"I've been to see his parents again to see if there was anything we missed at the time?"

"And did we?"

"Not as far as I can tell. But something linked to that is bothering me. It's to do with Archie," Josh said, with a solemn smile.

Helen leant forward. "What is it?"

"I left the Malham's house the other day wondering why I kept thinking something was odd about Colin Malham."

"And what is that? Do you know? It doesn't take you long to figure things out when you have all the pieces."

"Caroline mentioned to me in the car the other day that an *'unusually tall'* walker was at the back of the house the day Archie died."

"And ...?"

"Colin Malham is unusually tall, six foot four tall, at least."

Helen bit her bottom lip and raised her eyebrows. "That doesn't mean anything."

"No, it doesn't."

"But you have a hunch, don't you? I know where your hunches lead to, Josh."

"I need to look into it. But I'm sure it's linked to Archie."

"What do you suggest?"

"I act as if nothing has happened and I'm still investigating Tommy's death, which I am of course. But I don't want him to become suspicious or that I'm looking into Archie's death again."

"Mm hmm. Go on."

"I go and see the Malham's alone again, make amends with them. Mrs. Malham was upset the last time I saw her and Colin. Go round, apologise, and take it from there."

Helen sat back again and thought about Josh's suggestion. He was a damn good detective, she knew that. But this situation was different. It was personal. "Okay. Do that. But the minute you suspect he is the least bit involved with Archie, you let me know. Do you hear? I don't want your record or that of the department tarnished because you lost your temper."

"I understand." Josh stood up and went to walk out of the door.

"One more thing, Josh."

He turned around and looked back at his friend and superior. "Yes?"

"Be careful."

Josh smiled and closed the door behind him.

39

The drive to the Malham's house seemed both interminable and far too short. As Josh pulled up outside, he took a deep breath, steeling himself for what might come.

He was about to exit his car when movement caught his eye. An elderly woman was shuffling along the pavement, a heavy-looking shopping bag in her gnarled hand. As she passed the Malham's house she paused, her rheumy eyes fixing on Josh.

Instinct made him step out of the car. "Good afternoon, can I help you with that bag?"

The woman squinted at him. "Aren't you that detective? The one asking questions about the young lad?"

Josh's heart skipped a beat. "Yes, I am. I'm DCI Josh Mills, pleased to meet you," he said offering out his hand.

"Mavis Carter, lived here almost thirty five years, I know a fair thing or two about this place, and the people in it, mind."

"I'm sure you do. It must be good living in a place where you know so many people. I expect there are a few helpful souls around here that would help you out if needed."

"Help? I don't need help."

Josh's cheeks flushed pink.

"I'm just pulling your leg young man, I might be getting older, but I still have my sense of humour," she said, letting out a short chuckle.

Josh smiled. "Do you remember Tommy Malham and the story well?"

A sad expression played across her weathered features. "I remember seeing it on the news. Such a shame what happened. Those older boys should have known better."

"Older boys?" Josh fought to keep his voice casual. "What older boys would those be, Ms Carter?"

"Please, my dear, call me Mavis." The woman waved a dismissive hand. "Oh, it was all so long ago. My memory's not what it used to be." She peered at him hopefully. "I don't suppose you'd help an old lady home. These bags are awfully heavy."

Josh glanced at the Malham's house, then back at Mavis Carter. His gut told him she knew more than she was letting on. "Of course, I'd be happy to help. Maybe we could have a cup of tea and chat a bit more about what you remember?"

The woman's face lit up. "Oh, that would be lovely. I made a delicious fruit cake three days ago and have no one to share it with, I think you'll enjoy it," she said, tapping Josh's hand lightly.

As Josh took the heavy bag from her frail hand, his mind raced. What did this woman know? And how would it tie into the web of secrets he was only just beginning to unravel?

With one last look at the Malham's house, Josh followed the elderly woman down the street. The interview with Colin could wait.

40

Josh stood on the doorstep of Mavis Carter's house, his heart pounding with anticipation. It was a two storey, double fronted house that was neat and had a tidy front garden with pansies bordering the path leading to the front door. Josh assumed Mavis had a gardener looking at how slowly she was shuffling up the path.

Josh looked up at the house then stepped inside. The living room was cosy, filled with the warm scent of a comfortable home, and the soft ticking of an antique clock. Josh settled into a plush armchair, his eyes scanning the room for any clues that might jump out at him.

The woman, her silver hair pulled back in a neat bun, sat across from him, her eyes sharp and curious.

"So, you're looking into what happened to little Tommy Malham?" She asked, her voice soft and tinged with sadness.

Josh nodded, leaning forward. "I'm hoping to find some answers, to finally bring closure to his family."

Mavis sighed, her gaze distant. "It was such a tragedy. I remember it like it was yesterday." She paused, lost in thought for a moment before continuing. "I was a schoolteacher back then, you know. Taught at the local school for over thirty years."

Josh's heart skipped a beat. A schoolteacher. She would have known the children in the area, maybe even taught some of them. "I don't suppose you would have known Tommy though, he would have only been in nursery," Josh said, trying to keep his voice steady.

The woman nodded. "I didn't really know him from nursery although I did see him from time to time if I needed to borrow something from the nursery teachers. I suppose I got to know his family more, you know, with them living across the street. I'm surprised they have never moved to be honest."

"I don't suppose they would, they are probably trying to hang on to the memories for as long as possible."

"Oh, yes. He was such a bright little boy. Always had a smile on his face." She hesitated, her brow furrowing. "And those older boys, the ones who used to look after him sometimes, they adored him."

Josh's pulse quickened. "Older boys?"

"Yes, I'm sure I have a photo of them somewhere." The woman pushed herself up from her chair, shuffling towards a bookshelf in the corner. She pulled out a dusty box, rummaging through it until she found what she was looking for. "Ah, here it is."

She handed Josh a faded photograph, and he felt his breath catch in his throat. There, staring back at him, were the faces of Robert and Harry, the same boys he had seen in the photo on the Malham's shelf. The same boys who had occasionally looked after Tommy.

"I remember them," the woman said, her voice distant. "They were a few years older than Tommy."

Josh's mind raced, trying to piece together this new information. He had known that Robert and Harry had spent time with Tommy, but something about the way the woman spoke made him wonder if there was more to the story.

As Mavis walked to the kitchen to finish preparing the tea, she called out over her shoulder, "You know, I always wondered about those boys. I'm surprised they weren't hurt the day Tommy died."

Josh froze, his heart hammering in his chest. "What do you mean?" He asked, quizzically.

The woman returned, setting a steaming cup of tea in front of him. "Well, I saw them that day. Running towards the woods with little Tommy between them. It was odd, really. I wondered where they were heading. I knew they looked after him sometimes, but I never saw them out on the street or in the woods with him."

Josh's mind reeled, trying to process this revelation.

Robert and Harry had been with Tommy the day he died. They had been running towards the woods. Why had no one mentioned this before?

"Did you tell the police about this? Back when they were investigating?" Josh asked, his voice urgent.

The woman nodded, sipping her tea. "Oh, yes. I told one of the officers who came to my door. A nice young man, he was. Seemed very interested in what I had to say."

Josh took a bite of the fruit cake, crumbs dropped onto his plate as he held it up nearer his chin. "This is delicious, Mavis, you have a real talent," he said, making a mental note to follow up the notes taken from the conversation with Mavis all those years ago.

"Been baking all my life, I miss having people around to taste what I make."

Josh felt a pang of sympathy in his heart. How sad it must be growing old and feeling lonely. He knew his Nana felt lonely in the care home even though she was surrounded by other residents and carers. "Do you have any family, Mavis? Anyone who visits you?"

"Not now, they all moved away. They come occasionally but they are all so busy with their own lives, I can't expect them to be here every day." Mavis looked nonchalantly out of the window whilst Josh considered whether he would have any more children with Caroline.

He couldn't imagine not having anyone to call on if something went wrong when they were older. "I think I will get going now, I have a few more things to do. The cake and tea were delicious, thank you."

"You are most welcome, I've enjoyed your company."

"Would you mind if I took that photograph?"

"As long as you promise to return it, perhaps you can come for more cake and tea."

"That would be lovely, Mavis, it's been a pleasure talking to you."

As he thanked the woman for her time and made his way back to his car, Josh's thoughts were a whirlwind of questions and possibilities. Robert and Harry had been with Tommy that day. They had been running towards the woods. But why? What had happened out there?

He knew he needed to tread carefully, to not jump to conclusions. But he also knew that this was the first real lead he had uncovered in his investigation. The first glimmer of hope that he might finally be able to unravel the truth behind Tommy's death.

Josh sat in his car, thinking. A pen between his teeth and his head resting on his hand leaning against the door panel, his mind whirred. What really happened that day? Murder? Foul play? Or simply a tragic accident.

After taking a few moments to compose himself, with a deep breath and heavy heart, he got out of his car again, and walked up the driveway to knock on the Malham's door, photograph in hand.

41

Josh made his way to the front door, he took a deep breath, trying to calm his nerves.

Christine opened the door, her eyes widening in surprise as she saw Josh standing there. "Detective? Is everything all right? I'm surprised to see you here after the way I spoke to you last time."

Josh forced a smile, stepping inside. "Don't worry, you are entitled after what you have been through. Your emotions and memories are always with you when you lose someone precious. And remember, it's Josh to you."

Christine nodded, leading him into the living room where Colin sat, his face etched with worry. Josh's gaze swept over the man, taking in his height, his build. The nagging suspicion that had been growing in his mind since his last visit intensified.

"I'm sorry to bother you both again. I just have a few more questions, if that's okay."

Colin nodded without speaking.

Josh noticed his long legs stretched out and crossed over each in front of him.

Josh sat down, leaning forward. "I spoke with an elderly woman today, a former schoolteacher. She mentioned seeing Robert and Harry with Tommy the day he died. Running towards the woods."

Christine gasped, her hand flying to her mouth. "What? That can't be right. They would have told us, surely."

Colin shook his head, his eyes narrowing. "No, that's not possible. We would have known if they were with him that day."

Josh studied their faces, looking for any hint of deception. But all he saw was shock and confusion. "The schoolteacher seemed quite certain. She even mentioned telling the police about it during the initial investigation."

Christine's brow furrowed, her voice trembling slightly. "But why wouldn't the police have followed up on that? Surely they would have questioned Robert and Harry, or at least told us about it."

Josh leaned back, considering her words. "I can't comment on that now until I find out more, I'm afraid. But I assure you, I will be looking into it thoroughly."

Colin's jaw clenched, his eyes flashing with anger. "This is ridiculous. Those boys were like brothers to Tommy. They would never have hurt him or kept something like this from us. We've lived next to them for years, become good neighbours, even better friends. That dithering, interfering old woman must have got it wrong."

Josh held up his hands, trying to diffuse the tension. "I understand your frustration, Mr. Malham. But I must follow every lead, no matter how unlikely it may seem."

Christine closed her eyes, her face pinched with concentration. "It was so long ago, Josh. I'm surprised Mavis remembers anything. All I know is that Robert and Harry would never do any harm to our Tommy, they loved him, didn't they, Colin?"

Josh looked up at Mr. Malham, noticing he seemed a little distant.

"Colin? Is that right? They loved Tommy enough to never hurt him?" Josh asked.

"Yes, yes, that's right," Colin said, a tinge of impatience in his voice.

Josh desperately wanted to question Colin Malham about the day Archie died. He had an urge to follow his instinct and challenge him right here, right now.

Instead, he took a deep breath and stood up, having made more notes in his book. "Thank you both for your time. I know this isn't easy, dredging up the past like this. But I promise you, I will do everything in my power to find out the truth about what happened to Tommy."

As he stood to leave, his gaze fell on Colin once more. The man was tall, at least six foot four. The same height as the figure Caroline had seen walking near the woods. Josh's heart raced, his suspicions growing stronger with each passing moment.

But he couldn't confront him, not yet. He needed more evidence, more proof. And he couldn't ignore the pain and grief etched on Christine's face. They were still mourning the loss of their son, still grappling with the reopening of old wounds.

Josh made his way to the door, his mind torn between his duty as a detective and his compassion as a human being. He paused, turning back to face them. "I'm sorry for your loss, truly. I can't imagine how difficult this must be for you."

Christine's eyes met his, a flicker of gratitude shining through the tears. "Thank you, Josh. We just want answers, closure. For Tommy's sake."

Josh nodded, his throat tight. "I understand. I'll do everything I can, I promise you that."

Josh took the short walk between the Malham's and the Davidson's to see if he could uncover the truth. He wouldn't rest no matter how painful or devastating it might be.

He walked along the gravel driveway past the metallic blue BMW 3 series, and the Anthracite Audi A3. He stepped up to the front door that was set back from the front of the house, an archway providing shelter from the elements.

Josh knocked three times, then stood waiting with his hands hanging down and crossed in front of him.

Someone answered.

Josh lifted his ID and showed his photo. "Mr. Davidson?"

"Yes?"

"Do you have a moment?"

42

Josh stepped inside the Davidson's house, the pieces of the puzzle slowly falling into place but there was still more to uncover.

"Come through," Daniel said, directing Josh to the living room.

Sandra had been reading a magazine whilst crocheting, her glasses were hanging off the end of her nose when she looked up. When she saw Josh, her face was etched with worry and fatigue. "Detective? What brings you here?"

Josh offered a sympathetic smile. "I'm sorry to bother you both, but I have some new information about Tommy Malham's case, and I was hoping to ask you and your husband a few questions."

Sandra hesitated for a moment, her eyes darting behind her before she nodded. "Of course. Please, come and sit down," she said, glancing fleetingly at her husband.

Daniel and Sandra sat together on the plush sofa in front of the living room bay window. Josh couldn't help but notice the tension in the air but ignored it to focus on the questions.

"I spoke with an elderly woman today, a former schoolteacher. She gave me some new information about the day Tommy died."

"You mean Mrs. Carter? That old, interfering ..."

"Daniel! She is not! That woman served the local school for years," Sandra said, issuing a warning glance at her husband.

Daniel ignored her.

"Anyway, regardless of your personal feelings against Mrs. Carter, she has given me some information that I must follow up on."

"Go on then, Detective, it must have something to do with us if you are here."

"Shh, Sandra, let him speak." Daniel reached across for his wife's hand and held it a little too tightly.

Josh studied the couple carefully as he asked the next question. "Mrs. Carter mentioned seeing your sons running with Tommy towards the woods the day he died."

The atmosphere in the room changed in an instant. Sandra and Daniel sat bolt upright on the sofa, clasping hands, and squeezing each other tightly. They showed no facial expression.

Sandra looked at her husband then gasped, her hand flying to her mouth. Daniel's eyes widened, his face turning a deep shade of red. "That's impossible. Our boys would never have kept something like that from us."

Josh studied their faces, looking for any hint of deception. "I understand this is difficult to hear. But I need to know the truth. What happened that day? What were your sons doing with Tommy in the woods?"

"They weren't! They were with me all day!" Daniel said.

"That's very studious for you to remember such detail from so long ago, Mr. Davidson."

"Of course I remember, it was a horrible day for everyone. Poor Tommy, we were all out looking for him."

"What do you mean for everyone?" Josh enquired.

"Look, stop focusing on semantics, and do your job instead!" Daniel's face turned red with rage.

Sandra's eyes suddenly filled with tears, her shoulders shaking with silent sobs. Daniel reached out to comfort her, but she pulled away, her voice trembling. "I can't do this anymore, Daniel. I can't keep living with this secret."

Daniel's face contorted with anger, his voice rising. "What are you talking about, Sandra? Shut up! You don't know what you're saying!"

But Sandra ignored him, turning to face Josh with a look of utter despair. "It was an accident. A tragic, horrible accident." She gazed towards the floor, shaking her head in disbelief.

Josh's heart raced; his pen poised over his notebook. Seconds of silence followed. "What do you mean Mrs. Davidson, what exactly happened?"

Sandra looked at Daniel, he shook his head at her and loosened his grip on her hand.

Sandra took a deep, shuddering breath. "Our boys, Robert and Harry, were playing with Tommy and went to the woods. They told me that Tommy's cat had gone missing, and they wanted to help find her. They were so sweet, they cared for Tommy deeply, he was like a brother to them." She paused, her eyes distant and red rimmed.

"Carry on," Josh said, gently.

They came running through the front door, Robert and Harry that is. Something had happened, I could tell by their faces. It was so awful." Sandra pulled a tissue from her cardigan pocket and blew her nose.

Daniel stood up, his fists clenched. "Sandra, stop it! You're going to ruin everything. Think of the boys!"

Sandra looked up at her husband and blinked slowly, her face pleading for forgiveness for what she was about to say.

Daniel simply shook his head and walked to the other end of the room, gazing out of the patio doors which led on to their manicured back garden.

"I knew something had happened," she said, in a daze, as if she couldn't stop the words from flowing. "The boys, they ... they had blood on their tee-shirts and dirty knees. Not much, but enough to know there had been an accident." Sandra continued, her voice growing stronger with each word. "Robert and Harry had panicked. They didn't know what to do. They tried to wake Tommy up, but he wasn't moving. They thought he was dead." Sandra's words couldn't come out quick enough. The result of hiding a secret for years, unable to speak about for fear of destroying everything she had.

Josh's mind raced, trying to process the information. "What did they do then?"

Sandra's face crumpled, tears streaming down her cheeks. "They came to us, told us what happened. We were so scared, so worried about what would happen to our boys. We didn't know what to do."

Daniel's face was ashen, his voice barely above a whisper as he turned around. "We made a decision. A terrible, awful decision to try and protect them."

Josh was shocked by Daniel's sudden input.

"I went with the boys to see where Tommy was. When we got there, I felt for a pulse but there was nothing. I didn't know what to do. The boys told me it was a tragic accident, but I was terrified the police wouldn't see it like that. Robert was doing his GCSEs, Harry had got a place at the private school. I wanted everything the world could offer for my sons."

Josh looked at Daniel, willing him to go on.

"I moved Tommy's body nearer the old stone building. I covered it as best I could. Of course, I knew he would be found. But I thought it would give us some time to get back home and remove every trace of him."

Josh felt a wave of nausea wash over him, his hand shaking as he wrote down the details. "You covered it up. You let Tommy's parents grieve for hours whilst the police looked for their son?"

Sandra nodded, her face a mask of shame and regret. "We thought we were protecting our boys. But we were wrong. We were so wrong."

Daniel sat down again next to his wife, he slumped back in his chair, his head in his hands. "It's been eating us alive, all these years. The guilt, the fear of being found out. We couldn't take it anymore."

Josh blinked slowly, dumbfounded at what he'd just heard. A ten-year secret disclosed in minutes. "Excuse me a moment, will you please?"

Daniel ignored him and looked at his wife, their foreheads meeting in the middle and tears pouring from their eyes.

43

Fiona arrived at the Davidsons with assistance after Josh had put in an urgent call to the station.

"Are you okay?" Fiona asked, when Josh opened the Davidson's front door.

"Not really."

"I can tell, you look angry. Let me deal with this."

Josh nodded at her once and silently followed Fiona into the living room. He noticed that Sandra and Daniel were sitting in the same position. "Sandra, Daniel, this is my Detective Sergeant, Fiona Mitchell. Given what you have told me, I have no alternative but for you to be arrested and questioned further."

Sandra and Daniel said nothing. They simply stood up and waited for Fiona to explain the formalities.

"Sandra and Daniel Davidson, I am arresting you both on suspicion for perverting the course of justice and concealing a body. You have the right to remain silent. Anything you say, can, and will be used against you in a court of law."

Whilst Fiona was talking, Josh's mind was already racing ahead. He needed to find Robert and Harry to bring them in for questioning.

He needed to uncover the full truth of what had happened that day in the woods.

Josh and Fiona stepped outside and watched Stewart and Ben escort Sandra and Daniel to the waiting cars.

"That was a surprise, was it not?"

"Just a little," Josh responded.

"How was that uncovered so quickly? Was there anything you weren't telling me, Josh?"

"No, not at all. I am surprised as you are. Thanks to Caroline leading me back to Colin Malham, I met an old schoolteacher today, Mavis Carter. She gave me some information I wasn't expecting."

"Oh? What was that?"

Josh watched Sandra and Daniel being driven away. "She told me that she saw the Davidson's boys running with Tommy towards the woods the day he died."

"How was that missed?"

Josh blew out a frustrated breath. "I don't know, I need to follow it up when I get back to the station."

"It might be something or nothing, I'm sure you won't jump to conclusions."

"Of course I won't. The whole department was under pressure at the time. It's sad but true that sometimes things are missed. It's just unfortunate that if it had been followed up, the Malham's might have had closure before now."

"And Colin? Were your instincts right?"

"I still need to deal with that," he said to Fiona, walking back to his car.

As Josh and Fiona drove back to the station, his heart heavy with the weight of the revelation, Josh couldn't help but feel a sense of relief.

Finally, after all these years, the truth was coming to light. Finally, Tommy's family would have the closure they so desperately needed.

Josh also had something else to deal with that would bring him even closer to home.

44

Josh's heart was heavy with the weight of revelation and confession, but he couldn't help but feel a sense of relief. After all these years, the truth was coming to light. Finally, Tommy's family would have the closure they so desperately needed.

As he walked into the station, he was met with a flurry of activity. He looked around with a smile on his face, feeling grateful for the best team there was.

Josh saw Fiona sitting down at her desk, photographs and post it notes spread about which would form part of the final puzzle as to why and how the death of Tommy Malham happened.

"Fiona, can I have a word, somewhere private, please."

Fiona frowned and followed Josh towards his office.

"Sit down for a moment."

"What is it, sounds serious."

Josh's face was grim.

"Before you start, just to give you an update, Greater Manchester Police have arrested Robert and Harry. They are both co-operating and will be with us shortly."

"Good, that's good. One less thing to worry about. But what's worrying you?"

"I'm convinced now that we need to investigate Colin Malham further about Archie. It's sensitive and it's complicated," he said, leaning forward on his desk on his forearms, his hands clasped together. "As you know, I have had a strong suspicion that Colin Malham was involved in Archie's death somehow since my conversation with Caroline." Josh let out a sigh, closed his eyes, and shook his head in disbelief.

"You don't think The Midnight Hunter is involved now?"

"No, not since the revelation about Tommy's death. I think I was trying to blame him for Tommy and Archie's deaths. I want closure but I also knew in my heart that he had nothing to do with them. I dunno. Maybe I was looking for him to be responsible for more deaths so he would get punished further."

"Josh, you know they never feel guilty, these serial killers. They are too psychologically disturbed to feel any form of emotion. It would only be you destroying yourself if you pursued that line of enquiry."

"I know. I knew when I first went to the Malhams a couple of days ago that something was bothering me about Colin, but I didn't know what. It wasn't until Caroline mentioned this tall unknown walker that thoughts started swirling around in my head."

"So, from what you were saying this morning about his height, you definitely now think he was the walker at the back of your house the day Archie died?"

"Colin told me the other day that he was working away from home, and he watched Archie's story on the news. Who was I to disbelieve him? There was nothing to say that it was suspicious. But now ..." Josh looked up, opened his mouth, and exhaled. "If I'm right, this is going to change lives forever. Caroline will feel guilty for not mentioning it before. Christine's life will be destroyed, Colin may be behind bars, I..."

"Hang on, just a moment. You don't know he did anything. He might simply have been out for a walk. Do you think you're a bit ahead of yourself at the moment?"

Josh looked at his colleague but didn't say a word.

"Look, Josh. I know how important this is to you. And I'm pretty sure that finally solving the case of Tommy has opened up old wounds for you. But ..."

"Fiona, why would he lie then? Why would he say he was working away from home but he was really out walking? Look, I was going to dig further earlier on when I saw Colin Malham, but then bumped into Mavis Carter and the events of the day took an unexpected twist."

"Well, now that the Davidsons are being dealt with, let's go back to the Malham's, and question him at his house. We need to see him anyway to tell him and Christine about the Davidsons. I can ask discreetly where he was the day Archie died."

"Okay, but there are no coincidences, Fiona, you know that. If I'm right, you will have to do the questioning, I'm too close and connected to the case and Helen would see me out of the door if I went near him."

"Agreed. Let's go."

Josh and Fiona drove back to the Malham's leaving Josh feeling that his life was about to be changed forever.

45

The car hummed along the road as Josh and Fiona sat in silence, both lost in their thoughts. The weight of the recent revelations hung heavy in the air, the truth about Tommy's death was still fresh in their minds. Josh's grip tightened on the steering wheel, his knuckles turning white as he navigated the familiar streets.

"Do we need to discuss anything else before we get there?" Fiona asked.

"No, I think we know what we're doing and what we're going to ask. You do most of the talking, but I'll tell them about the Davidsons. I feel as if I have a duty to do it."

"Okay, no problem," Fiona said, looking at Josh with concern. "Can I ask you something before we get there, I just want to know one thing."

"Sure, what's that?"

"Did you ever have any evidence that The Midnight Hunter murdered your son?"

The question hung in the air, a painful reminder of the past. Josh took a deep breath, his voice barely above a whisper. "No, none. Like I said, it was probably just a deep desire to make his life harder. I want him to be punished forever after what he did to those kids. I was trying my best to link him to Tommy and Archie. But looking back, the only thing I had to go on was that The Midnight Hunter knew I was investigating Tommy Malham's death, and then of course, Archie died too."

Fiona nodded, her eyes filled with sympathy. "And when he was in jail, he taunted you, didn't he? Saying it was a shame your son had died, and that he had done it."

"How did you know?"

"Because I've seen it before. A high-profile detective, working his way through the ranks is on the hunt for a murderer. The accused then taunts the detective with threats or promises relating to their own family. These evil people are not stupid. They do their research, they dream up a fantasy in their heads and continue their psychological pursuit of hurt and revenge even when behind bars."

Josh kept his eyes firmly on the road ahead.

The honesty and revelation hit Josh square in the face, he felt his heart go heavy and his eyes sting.

"Look, Josh, I want complete closure for you as much as you and Caroline do. The question is, did Colin Malham have some involvement?"

They pulled up to the Malham's house, Josh's heart raced, dreading the conversation to come. "You know, just before we go in, I think he was involved somehow because I was investigating his son's death at the time. I don't know, maybe he became obsessed, didn't like the lack of progress, wanted answers, revenge, who knows. But let's go and find out."

Fiona and Josh stepped out of the car and walked up the familiar path leading to the Malham's front door. It felt all too familiar.

Josh knocked on the door, his hand trembling slightly. Christine answered and she glanced at Josh and Fiona, her face etched with worry.

"Detective? What's going on? It's not long since we saw you earlier."

Josh took a deep breath, his voice steady. "Christine, I'm afraid I have some difficult news. Could we come in please?"

Christine silently stepped back to allow Josh and Fiona to enter, she closed the door quietly behind them. They waited for Christine to lead the way into the familiar living room where Colin was standing in front of the fireplace.

"Hello, Josh."

"Hello, again."

"We see you have Fiona with you, it must be serious with the two of you here," Colin said.

"We have come with some news about Tommy."

Colin sat down next to his wife on the sofa in front of the living room window and reached for her hands. They held onto each other tightly.

"You know what happened, don't you?" Colin said.

Josh gave a faint smile. "I'm afraid so. Sandra and Daniel Davidson have been arrested on suspicion for perverting the course of justice and concealing a body. Robert and Harry are being questioned about Tommy's death."

Christine's face crumpled, her hand flying to her mouth as a sob escaped her lips. "No, no, this can't be happening." She leaned into her husband's arm and sobbed into his sleeve.

"I don't understand, Josh. What do you mean?" Colin asked.

"I can't say too much at this stage, I'm sorry. But Tommy's death appears to be a tragic accident, which the Davidson's knew about."

"What do you mean they knew? Does that mean they were involved somehow? They knew what had happened. What? Tell me!" Colin stood up sharply, making Christine sit upright.

"Colin, please, I know this is hard, but please sit back down."

After a moment's silence, Colin took a step back and took his place next to his wife again.

Christine reached out for his hand.

"What this does mean, is that currently we are not looking for anyone else connected with your son's death. When we have finished questioning the Davidson's, the file will be prepared for the CPS to see what, if any charges will be brought."

Christine Malham wailed, her eyes red from sobbing so hard. "The lies, the deceit... how will we ever recover from this?"

Colin appeared behind her, his face a mask of disbelief. "I don't understand. Why would they never say anything?" Colin rubbed his brow, wanting more answers than Josh and Fiona would give.

Josh's gaze met Colin's, his voice gentle but firm. "We don't know, Colin, but please, try not to jump to any conclusions."

Colin sat back. "What happens now?"

"Wait to hear from us, I know it's hard, but let us do our job and we will update you when we know more." Josh blinked slowly knowing what was coming next.

"Thank you for letting us know," Christine said, in a steady voice, all her upset and torment having been released.

Josh looked at Fiona and nodded.

Fiona coughed a little. "There is one other matter we need to clear up, Mr. Malham."

"What's that? Anything that will help, please, just ask."

"I need to ask you a couple of questions about a specific day."

"The day Tommy went missing?" Colin questioned.

"Sadly, no. I'm talking about the day another little boy died, Archie Mills."

Christine looked at her husband. "Colin, what are they talking about?" She said, trying to sound surprised.

Colin patted his wife's hand, "leave this to me, love," he said gently. "Go on."

"Where were you on that day, can you tell me?" Fiona asked.

"I already told Detective Mills here, I was working away from home. A terrible day it was for you, Josh. I remember seeing it on the news."

Josh bit the inside of his bottom lip and didn't say anything. He wanted to reach out and grab Colin by the throat and pin him against the wall demanding the truth.

"And you are sure about that, you couldn't have got the day wrong or mixed up with something else?"

Colin's eyes widened, his voice defensive. "I told you, I was away with work, watching the news in the hotel room."

"Which hotel were you staying in, do you recall?"

Colin gulped down the lump in his throat and pierced his lips together.

Josh noticed a light swing of Colin's foot, a sure sign of fabrication in Josh's experience.

"Erm, I'm pretty sure it was The Black Dog in Carlisle. Shall I go and check, I keep comprehensive records of my travel for my business." Colin went to stand, but quickly sat down again when Fiona spoke.

"No, it's fine, let us phone the hotel, they will be able to confirm your stay there."

Colin took a deep breath in and lifted his head slightly.

Josh nodded to Fiona, a silent signal to make the call to the hotel.

Christine's eyes darted between them, distress etched on her face.

Fiona stood up and turned around to leave the room to make a phone call.

"Colin! Please, just tell them." Christine's wailing started to surface again.

"Stop!" The whole room froze in time. "Please, you don't have to ring the hotel." Colin's resolve crumbled, tears streaming down his face. "It was an accident, I swear. I never meant for anything to happen, I didn't touch him, I promise." Colin collapsed onto the sofa and looked at his wife with tear filled eyes.

Josh didn't need to hear anymore. He took a deep breath in, stood up, then left the room before he did anything he might later regret. He stepped outside and called for PCs Whippet and McKay to take Colin Malham to the station.

Thirty minutes later, Josh stood in the hallway and watched Colin being led out of his own home. He managed to contain his anger, frustration, and grief, but only because he held his hands tightly behind his back as Colin was being led away.

After Colin left with Stewart and Ben, Josh walked back into the living room where Fiona was waiting with Christine.

Christine Malham stood up when she saw Josh walk in and collapsed to the floor, her body shaking with sobs. Josh knelt beside her, his hand on her shoulder. "I'm so sorry, Christine. I can't imagine how difficult this must be for you."

Christine looked up at him, her eyes red and swollen. "I don't know how to process this. My son, my husband, it's all too much. I should have said something."

Josh helped her to her feet, his voice gentle. "What do you mean? You should have said something?"

"I knew Colin had gone for a walk the day little Archie died. I mithered him about it, wanted to know where he was. Colin told me eventually what had happened, but promised me he had done no harm. I'm so sorry."

As they walked out of the house, leaving Christine's sister to support her, Josh's mind was a whirlwind of emotions. Relief, anger, sadness, all swirling together in a dizzying mix. He had finally uncovered the truth about Archie's death, but at what cost?

Fiona placed a hand on his arm, her voice soft. "You did the right thing, Josh. I know it doesn't feel like it right now, but you've brought closure to Archie's case, and to Tommy's. You've given their families the answers they so desperately needed."

Josh nodded, his throat tight. "But what about Christine? How does she move on from this?"

Fiona sighed, her eyes filled with sympathy. "It won't be easy, but she's strong. She'll find a way to heal, to rebuild her life, and at some point, she will have to deal with the guilt for not saying something at the time. It's a shame that there is nothing to charge her with though. If Colin didn't touch Archie, and it was a tragic accident, we can't exactly charge her with perverting the course of justice, can we?"

As they drove back to the station, Josh couldn't help but feel a sense of bittersweet satisfaction.

But the cost had been high, the toll on the families involved immeasurable. Lives had been shattered, trust broken, hearts left in pieces.

46

The drive back to the station was a blur, the weight of Colin Malham's confession that he was out walking the day Archie died, and not working away as originally confessed, hung heavy in the air.

Josh's mind raced with the implications, the realisation that his son's death couldn't have been at the hands of someone he knew. Beside him, Fiona sat in silence, her own thoughts a tangled web of emotions.

As they walked into the station, Josh felt a sense of numbness wash over him. He barely registered the sympathetic looks from his colleagues, the hushed whispers that followed him down the hallway. He walked straight to his office, Fiona followed closely behind. Josh collapsed into his chair and rested his head in his hands.

A knock on the door startled him from his thoughts, and he looked up to see Chief Inspector Helen Musgrove standing in the doorway. Her face was etched with concern, her voice soft but firm.

"Josh, I just heard about Colin Malham. I know this must be incredibly difficult for you, but you know you can't have any part in questioning him."

Josh nodded, his throat tight. "I know, Helen. I understand."

Helen stepped into the office and closed the door, her eyes filled with sympathy. "You need to let the team do their work. I promise, I'll keep you updated as soon as we have more information."

Josh took a deep breath, his voice barely above a whisper. "Thank you, Helen. I appreciate it. Oh, that reminds me, we may have a potential problem when it comes to Tommy Malham."

"Oh? Tell me more."

"Mavis Carter, the lady who led me to the Davidsons, told me that she mentioned important information to the policeman who knocked on her door when Tommy first went missing."

"Why is that a problem?"

"Because the information was what led me to the Davidsons. If we had known sooner, this whole case had the potential to be wrapped up years ago."

Helen hesitated for a moment, her gaze flickering between Josh and Fiona. "Hmm, okay. Presumably the policeman wrote it down in his book?" Helen questioned.

"I don't know, I need to do some investigating."

"Okay, but remember information and statements create mountains of paperwork on a live case, we both know that's when things can go wrong."

"I know. What do you want me to do when or if I find out who it was?" Josh asked.

"Come and speak to me when you know, and we'll discuss."

"Will do."

"There's something else, Josh," Helen said. "Robert and Harry Davidson are about to be questioned. I thought perhaps you two might like to observe, take your mind off what's happening with Colin."

SHAME ON THEM

Fiona glanced at Josh, her brow furrowed. "What do you think, Josh? It might be good to focus on something else for a bit."

Josh nodded, his mind already racing with the possibilities. "Yeah, let's do it. But maybe we should split up, cover more ground. I'll take Robert, you take Harry."

Fiona agreed, and they made their way to the observation rooms, each steeling themselves for what was to come.

As Josh watched Robert through the one-way glass, he couldn't help but feel a sense of dread wash over him. The young man looked terrified, his face pale and his hands shaking. But as the questioning began, a story began to emerge, a tale of tragedy and secrecy that had haunted the Davidson family for years.

"It was a hot summer's day," Robert began, his voice trembling. "Harry and I decided to go see Tommy, take him to play in the woods. We wanted to help him look for his cat. We saw his mum through the patio doors, in the kitchen. We shouted to her, telling her where we were going. We assumed she heard us."

The interviewer leaned forward, his voice calm but insistent. "And what happened next, Robert?"

Robert's eyes filled with tears, his voice cracking. "It was an accident. We were playing, pushing each other around. But then Tommy fell, hit his head on a rock. He wasn't moving, wasn't responding. We just panicked and didn't know what to do."

Josh's heart raced as he listened to Robert's words, the pieces of the puzzle falling into place. The decision to hide the body, the fear of consequences, the family's choice to keep the secret buried. It was a story of unimaginable grief and guilt, a burden that had weighed on the Davidsons for far too long.

"What happened then?"

Robert bit the wicks of his nails, his thumb started to bleed. He slowly looked up from the floor and glanced at his solicitor who nodded.

"Me and Harry, we ran home. Our hearts were racing, we tripped and fell so many times just to get back home. We arrived with bloodied knees and we both had Tommy's blood on his tee-shirt, you know, from where he tried to save him. Me and Harry, we ... we stood in the doorway and mum and dad just looked horrified. They looked at us and asked what had happened. Then they said not to worry, they'd take care of it."

"What do you think they meant by that, Robert?"

"I dunno, I mean, I was only fifteen. I had no idea. They asked us to show them where Tommy was, and then they said go home and put your clothes in the washing machine. Me and Harry just stood staring at little Tommy." Robert broke down again, he put his head on the desk and sobbed into his arms.

Detective Todd, who had travelled from Carlisle, waited for a few moments for Robert to compose himself. "I know this is hard, Robert, but can you continue?"

Robert sat up again and wiped his eyes with his sleeve. "Well, me and Harry, we just stared at mum and dad then mum screamed at us *'Go home, go home right now.'* I've never seen or heard her so upset and angry, me and Harry ran home."

"And nobody saw you?"

"I don't think so."

Detective Todd sighed and looked at Robert with empathy in his eyes. The poor, poor man, having to live with this. "Okay, Robert. You're doing great. What happened after you got home?"

"We put our clothes in the washing machine like mum asked, then mum and dad arrived home. We didn't ask them anything. Mum went straight upstairs and slammed the bedroom door, I remember that. She never does anything like that, so it sort of stuck with me. Then dad sat us both down and said we must not mention a word of what happened to anybody. I told him that we had shouted through to Tommy's mum to tell her where we were going. Dad looked horrified."

"And what did he do, Robert?"

"He said, don't worry about that for now, he will sort it out. Then we never spoke of that day as a family again."

Detective Todd brought the interview to a close and Robert was led away to the custody suite until it was known what he would be charged with.

As Robert's interview ended, Josh heard a knock on the door. He turned to see Fiona, her face ashen.

"A tragic accident, a secret that destroyed them all," she said, her voice hushed. That's what Harry said.

"Same with Robert." Josh's mind was reeling. "They shouted to Christine, telling her where they were going. But she must not have heard them. One split second if she had heard them and things could have turned out very differently."

Fiona sighed, her eyes filled with sadness. "They should have come forward from the beginning. The truth would have been painful, but at least it would have been out in the open. Instead, they let it fester, let it poison everything."

As they left the observation rooms, Josh bumped into Detective Todd. "What do you think they will be charged with, Bill?"

"I don't know, I'm not sure there is enough for involuntary manslaughter, definitely not enough for manslaughter. Perhaps perverting the course of justice at best? Same for Harry. As for the parents, I imagine they will be charged with concealment of a body too. We will have to wait to hear."

"Thanks, Bill, I appreciate it."

"No problem," Bill said. "Oh, and Josh," he said, noticing Josh was about to walk away.

"Yes?"

"Sorry to hear about Archie and this Colin character, if you need to talk you know where I am." Bill patted Josh on the shoulder and walked off.

As Josh and Fiona walked down the corridor, Josh looked up and his blood ran cold. He caught a glimpse of Colin Malham being led to an interview room, flanked by two officers. He felt a surge of anger wash over him, a desire to confront the man who had taken his son from him.

But then he felt a hand on his arm, and he turned to see Helen, her face stern but compassionate.

"Josh, go home," she said, her voice gentle but firm. "Be with your wife, support each other through this. Let us handle Colin."

Josh hesitated for a moment, his gaze lingering on the interview room door. But then he nodded, the fight draining out of him.

"You're right," he said, his voice heavy with exhaustion. "Caroline needs me. I need to be there for her."

He turned to Fiona, his eyes pleading. "Can you cover for me, just for a bit? If anything else happens, call me."

Fiona nodded, her hand squeezing his arm. "Of course, Josh. Take all the time you need. I've got this."

With a final nod to Helen, Josh made his way out of the station, his heart heavy with the weight of the day's revelations. As he drove home, he tried to imagine how he would break the news to Caroline, how he would explain the unimaginable.

47

The interview room was cold and sterile, the fluorescent lights casting harsh shadows on Colin Malham's face. He sat hunched over the table, his hands clasped tightly in front of him, his eyes fixed on the floor.

Chief Inspector Helen Musgrove had known Josh Mills for years and had watched him rise through the ranks of the department. She had seen the toll that his son's death had taken on him, the way it had consumed him, driven him to the brink of obsession.

And now, to learn that the man responsible for Archie's death was the father of a dead son himself, it was almost too much to bear.

With a deep breath, Helen entered the room, her face a mask of professionalism. She sat down across from Colin, her eyes searching his face for any sign of remorse, any hint of the truth.

"Mr. Malham," she began, her voice steady. "I think it's time we had a talk."

Colin looked up, his eyes red and swollen. "I never meant for any of this to happen," he whispered, his voice cracking. "I just wanted justice for my boy."

Helen leaned forward, her elbows on the table. "Tell me about Tommy, Colin. Tell me why you started following DCI Mills."

Colin took a shaky breath, his gaze distant. "After Tommy died, it felt like the whole world had stopped. Like nothing would ever be right again. And then, to watch the investigation go nowhere, to see the police fail time and time again, I couldn't stand it."

He paused, his hands clenching and unclenching on the table. "I started reading about other cases, other detectives who had solved the impossible. And that's when I found him. DCI Josh Mills, the golden boy of the department. The man who could do no wrong."

Helen nodded, her pen poised over her notebook. "And so you began to follow him, to watch his every move?"

Colin's face crumpled, tears spilling down his cheeks. "I didn't know what else to do. I was so angry, so frustrated. I just wanted someone to pay attention, to care about my son the way they cared about all the others."

He took a deep, shuddering breath, his voice barely above a whisper. "I found out where he lived and started watching the house. I saw his wife, his son. They looked so happy, so perfect. And all I could think was, why does he get to have this, when I've lost everything?"

Helen's heart clenched at the raw pain in Colin's voice, but she forced herself to remain impassive. "And then, one day, you saw an opportunity. A chance to confront DCI Mills, to make him understand your pain?"

Colin nodded, his eyes haunted. "It was a warm summer's day, hot and bright. I watched from the shadows as his wife played with their son in the garden. And then when she went inside, I couldn't help myself. I had to talk to him, to make him see me."

He paused, his voice trembling. "Archie was so small, so trusting. He didn't even question why a stranger was talking to him. I talked to him for a bit, about nothing really. And then…"

Colin's voice broke, his shoulders shaking with sobs. "He wandered towards the pond as he came closer to me. And I was so caught up in my own pain, my own anger, I didn't even notice the danger until it was too late."

Helen's heart sank as she listened to Colin's story, the pieces of the puzzle falling into place. "And what happened then?"

Colin's face was a mask of anguish. "When Archie fell into the pond, I just panicked, I ran. I didn't know what to do. I was so scared, so afraid of what would happen if they found out I was there. So, I ran, and I never looked back."

He took a deep, shuddering breath, his voice barely above a whisper. "For ten years, I've carried this secret. For ten years, I've lived with the guilt, the knowledge that I could have saved him, that I could have done something."

Helen sat back in her chair, her mind reeling with the implications of Colin's confession. There was no malice in his actions, no intent to harm. Just a broken man, consumed by his own grief and anger, making a terrible mistake.

She glanced at the one-way glass, knowing that Fiona was watching from the other side. With a heavy sigh, she stood up, her hand on the door handle.

"I'll be back in a moment, Mr. Malham."

As she stepped into the observation room, Fiona turned to her with a questioning look. "What do you think, Ma'am? Is there a case here?"

Helen shook her head, her eyes troubled. "I don't know, Fiona. From what he's told us, it sounds like a tragic accident. A moment of carelessness, of distraction. I'm not sure there's anything to charge him with."

Fiona nodded, her face pensive. "But the fact that he hid it for so long, that he let Josh and Caroline suffer, never knowing the truth."

Helen sighed, her hand rubbing her forehead. "I know. It's a terrible thing to carry that kind of secret. But in the end, he's just a man who made a mistake. A man who's been consumed by his own guilt and grief for far too long."

Helen paused, her eyes fixed on Colin's hunched figure through the glass. "In a way, I almost feel sorry for him. To lose a child, it's the worst pain imaginable. And to know that you could have prevented another family from suffering that same pain, I can't imagine the weight of that burden."

Fiona nodded, her own eyes filled with sadness. "And now, with the Davidsons, it's like he's reliving it all over again. The grief, the anger, the helplessness."

Helen took a deep breath, her mind made up. "We'll need to talk to the CPS, of course. But from where I'm standing, I don't think there's a case here. Just a broken man, in need of help and support."

She turned to Fiona, her face serious. "But that doesn't mean we're done here. Colin may not be facing charges, but he still has a long road ahead of him. He needs to confront his own guilt, his own grief. He needs to find a way to make amends."

Fiona nodded, her hand on her superior's arm. "He will get the help he needs, but not from me. I don't want anything to do with the man. For him to inflict years of paid, grief, torment, on another couple because of what he went through, is barbaric in my view. He hurt Josh and Caroline badly. I won't be helping him." Fiona stormed out of the observation room and slammed the door.

Helen sighed deeply. She knew this was going to be difficult. To tell Josh and Caroline there was no case to answer to was going to be one of the worst situations of her career. This case had been a roller coaster of emotions, a journey through the darkest corners of the human heart.

But in the end, it was a reminder of why she did this job, why she fought so hard for justice and truth.

After the interview, Helen telephoned Josh to give him an update. "Josh, are you okay to talk?"

"I've just pulled onto the driveway, have you spoken to him?"

"I have, Josh. It's not good news I'm afraid."

As Helen relayed the interview to Josh and concluded there weren't any charges to press, she ended the call leaving Josh to cry quietly before summoning the courage to tell his wife.

48

Josh saw her waiting for him at the kitchen window. A smile on her face and a tea towel in hand, he would need all his strength to tell her what had happened, that finally she would know what happened to their son.

He stepped out of the car, his legs feeling like lead as he walked towards her. She met him halfway, her arms wrapping around him in a fierce embrace. "Hello my love, have you resolved what you needed to?"

"Let's go inside, I have something to tell you."

Caroline wiped her hands on the tea towel, threw it onto the kitchen worktop, and followed her husband into the snug. "Josh what is it, you sound so serious."

Josh sat down on the comfortable sofa, Caroline took her place next to him. "Josh," she whispered, her voice thick with emotion. "Something isn't right, tell me."

Josh turned to face his wife, he took her hands in his and looked into her eyes.

"Caroline, listen to me. What I'm going to say isn't easy."

"Josh!"

Josh looked to the floor and back at his wife. "The walker you saw the day that our Archie died, we found him."

"What do you mean you found him? I don't understand. Why would you be looking for him anyway?"

"Because I went to see Tommy Malham's parents. I had been asked to look at the case again, to see if I could resolve it, bring some closure."

"That poor boy, and his parents. We know what they went through."

Josh smiled at the warmth and compassion in his wife's heart. "Yes, we do. But there is more to it than that. You see, when I went to see Mr. and Mrs. Malham, there was something about Colin that I felt was odd. Then, when you mentioned the unusually tall walker that day, I spoke to Fiona. She's the same height as you and she said unusually tall would be anything six foot four and over."

"I don't understand what you are saying, Josh, and you are scaring me so please tell me what's going on."

"Colin Malham, he's six foot four." Josh gulped down the heavy emotion in his throat, the reality of what he was about to tell his wife weighed down heavily on his shoulders.

"But what does that mean? That Colin Malham was walking along the back of the house the day Archie died?"

"It's so much more than that, Caroline." Josh's eyes started to water as he looked at his wife, wondering how she would handle the news.

"He saw Archie fall in the pond, Caroline. He had this ridiculous obsession with me for investigating the death of his child and had it in his head that I wasn't doing enough. He was jealous, vindictive. He found out where I lived and came to confront me. But as he walked along the back of the house he saw Archie in the garden."

"I was in the kitchen," Caroline said softly. "I was in the kitchen, and I never knew. I should have stayed with him, Josh, I should have stayed with him!" Caroline burst into tears.

Josh pulled her into his chest whilst she thumped his sides in anger. "I should have been there in the garden, I only left him for two minutes," she sobbed. "I shouldn't have put that stupid kettle on and started to cook dinner, but I thought he would be safe."

"Shh, Caroline, you weren't to know." Josh held on to his wife tightly, desperately wanting to feel the beat of her heart. "If Colin Malham hadn't been so obsessed, then Archie would still be alive today. It wasn't your fault, I promise you."

But Caroline Mills wasn't listening. She was crying heavily into her husband's chest soaking his shirt whilst he held her close, wanting to squeeze all the hurt, pain and grief out of every ounce of her being.

After a couple of moments, she sat away from Josh. "Will he ... will he be charged?"

Josh closed his eyes slowly and shook his head. "Doubtful. There is nothing really to charge him with. He claimed he didn't touch Archie. He spoke to him and because Archie was concentrating on what he was saying and walking towards him, he fell into the pond."

"Oh, Josh, what are we going to do?" Caroline cried out.

"Get through this together, that's what we'll do."

"I don't know if I can, I should have been there." She leaned back into him and he stroked her hair. They both slumped back into the deep sofa, closed their eyes, and wished they could have wound back time.

Caroline cried herself to sleep and Josh gently lifted her legs onto the sofa and placed a blanket over her. He knelt down beside her, stroked her forehead and held on to her hand.

Whilst looking at his dear, dear wife, Josh hoped the revelations would bring closure for them both. Or, would they reopen unhealed wounds? Only time would tell.

49

Fiona had made a good impression on the team she thought. The three murders in the tourist town of Kirkby Lonsdale were brutal and unnecessary. And it was obvious that the revelations and confessions about Tommy and Archie would split old wounds wide open, leaving devastation.

But Fiona had grown resilient to cope with a harsh, dark world. Yet, the solved cases had made her question whether people make too much of something and then take their rage out on someone else because of unrealistic expectations.

Fiona was sure that just because the three victims were honest about the cafe, they didn't expect to die as a result. It made her question her values, beliefs, and integrity. But most of all, it strengthened her already unquestionable doubt that she was doing the right thing being in the police.

Pouring herself a coffee from the cafetière, she sat down at her worn and weathered oak kitchen table. She had recently *'tarted'* it up with some half price faux-leather chairs to give it a lift. Some new place mats, a rug for the kitchen-diner, and a new light fitting, boosted her spirits and helped her settle when she had made the move from Edinburgh to Cumbria.

Fiona's house was a modest two bedroom mid-terrace. It was reasonably secure given that it was on a main road, so anyone would see a burglar climbing through the front living room window.

At the back was a cobbled alley between the backs of the row of houses. She hadn't met many of the neighbours yet, but from the banter she had heard on bin day, everyone seemed to get along and know each other.

So, what were the chances of someone managing to break in at the back of her house. With Mrs. Burton's three CCTV cameras fixed to the side of her house, which stood side on to Fiona's at the back, Fiona felt secure.

She opened her laptop, did a quick scroll on social media then headed for the news. She wanted to see what was being reported after Josh and his team had done everything they could to make sure Dave Potter was locked away for a very long time.

Fiona had told Josh that she didn't watch the news. But she was a secret scroller. Invariably checking the headlines on her app in the morning, then briefly watching the news channel at night, it kept her up to date with the misgivings of journalists.

"Hey, what's up Kitty?" She said, speaking to her tabby house cat who purred and moved seamlessly between her legs whilst she sat at the table.

Fiona reached down to give her trusty companion a scratch and a tickle, but it didn't pacify the fur laden feline.

"Shh, I have no work today, I'm all yours." Fiona stroked the cat with one hand and topped up her coffee from the cafetière with the other.

It was pitch black outside, she vowed she would get her dad to fix some outside lights next time he visited, it would give him something to do.

She felt secure enough with all the doors locked but it didn't stop her being afraid of the dark. With all the kitchen lights on, she turned up the volume on the TV to provide some false comfort that she wasn't alone.

Fiona shuddered slightly at hearing the details of the case on the news. Fabricated in places, but mostly true, about how Dave Potter had been accused of slashing and poisoning his victims to death because he was angry about their reviews.

The sound coming from the front of the house was silent yet audible and loud enough to make Fiona stand up and go and investigate. She stroked Kitty and moved her to one side, the cat was keen to follow its owner everywhere, but Fiona had an inkling.

She opened the creaking kitchen door, silently swearing to herself for making such a noise. Any intruder would hear her.

Had she locked the front door when she came in? She thought she had.

When she had first moved in, the windows were less than secure, and you could push them open with one finger. The window fitter had put in a screw next to the handle to help avoid the window having a mind of its own, but it wasn't perfect.

The door was secure enough, a key was still needed to get in and out but as a police officer, she knew it wasn't completely safe.

Moving from the kitchen to the hall to the living room, she found the living room door clicking slightly against the breeze that was coming in from where the windows should have been closed and screwed shut.

'Another thing to add to the list,' she thought. *'When I get that new carpet fitted, the living room door gets replaced.'*

Her heartbeat slowed a little at the sight of the empty living room. She checked the front door again and it was locked. She breathed a sigh of relief, blinked slowly, and took a deep breath in then out again.

She changed her thoughts and smiled to herself feeling grateful for joining a good team and Josh Mills seemed like the perfect boss and partner.

If only everything else was perfect in her little world.

Her adoptive parents who she had always treated as her real mum and dad, were far away, and she had yet to make friends in the new area. But worse than that, her history just wouldn't leave her dark mind.

The thoughts of personal retribution, the feelings of darkness that would sometimes sweep over her without notice, and the fear of meeting Dexter Stone face to face and alone, the pimp that got away, filled her with dread.

Shaking the thoughts away from her head, she stepped back into the kitchen. "Here Kitty, where have you gone," she said, opening the door.

As she closed the door behind her, and turned around, she felt like her heart had stopped. Her mouth went dry, and she crumbled inside. Her worst fears had come to life.

Kitty was sitting on Dexter Stone's knee who had taken his place at the kitchen table. He was stroking the precious tabby cat and she was purring away as if the stranger was her new best friend.

Fiona's heart cried for her cat and the thought of what Dexter could and might do to her. She suddenly felt guilty for bringing Kitty into her life and putting her at risk.

And deep inside her soul, she cried for herself.

Afterword

Hello and welcome to my very first crime novel, or in modern day terms 'police procedural.' I've kept this book particularly short as I get used to writing in this genre and if my readers have enjoyed it, I will go on to write longer stories next time.

I don't claim to get police procedures right, as it's difficult to keep up with police compliance and policies. I have vowed if I make enough money from my little books, I will hire an ex-detective as an editor

I know and appreciate that some readers like the nitty gritty of DNA and police procedure, but for me it's more about the story, the motivation of the killer(s), and the victims characters.

I live in Lancashire with my husband Mike, my dog, Daisy, and Frodo the cat (it's a she, don't ask!) Mike and I first visited Kirkby Lonsdale years ago and fell in love with the place instantly.

I wrote my very first book when I started self-publishing over five years ago and that too was set in the town.

I love the quirkiness of the old buildings, the narrow streets (Salt Pie Lane springs to mind,) and we have had a couple of great holidays there. We regularly visit for days out under the premise it's to unwind and have a picnic when the weather suits. But really, it's for me to do some quiet research on the side to see what my next book will bring.

I have kept distances, buildings, and streets as realistic as possible. You will have noticed that I have changed the names of some establishments but I'm sure you will recognise them for where they really are.

There will be some pedants amongst you that may pick up on detail, and that's okay. But what I would ask is that you do that privately to my email address. I am always learning and always happy to hear from my readers.

I hope you have enjoyed the story, if you loved or just liked the book, an Amazon review would be appreciated and of course you can get in touch personally here with any thoughts, and comments you have, or just to say hello:

It's normal for a writer to offer a link to their next book or email list. But in truth, whilst I have an idea for the next book, I haven't started it, and my regular newsletters have not been drafted.

Watch out for my next book if you enjoyed this one. The working title is 'I'm Not Dead,' but as always with authors, that may change.

Annie x

Printed in Great Britain
by Amazon